Shot Rock

OTHER BOOKS BY MICHAEL TREGEBOV

The Briss (2006)
The Shiva (2012)

Shot Rock

Michael Tregebov

NEW STAR BOOKS

2019

NEW STAR BOOKS LTD.
107 – 3477 Commercial Street, Vancouver,
BC V5N 4E8 CANADA
1574 Gulf Road, No. 1517, Point Roberts, WA 98281 USA
www.NewStarBooks.com   info@NewStarBooks.com

The publisher acknowledges the financial support of the Canada
Council for the Arts and the British Columbia Arts Council.

Cataloguing information for this book is available from Library
and Archives Canada, www.collectionscanada.gc.ca.

Cover and interior design by Robin Mitchell Cranfield
Printed and bound in Canada by Imprimerie Gauvin, Gatineau, QC

Published September 2019

To my parents, Benny and Sara Tregebov, who loved curling, and children, even their own, and absolutely.

Mit ein eige ois vishen,
Und mit die andere ois pishen.

This story is a story.

ONE

The craving for curling is like the craving for love. After a long spring and summer without the former and the last few months without the latter, an enthusiastic Blackie Timmerman stood in front of the Queen Victoria Curling Club looking up at the sputtering neon blue crown above the QV's crest and its motto: "Winnipeg's Friendliest Rink." Blackie had his broom tucked under one arm, his curling sweater in a Dominion Stores paper bag under the other. His curling boots dangled by their knotted laces over one wrist.

He dropped his broom and bag and scratched an itch on his head, but got no relief: his hair was as coarse as lichen and he got no scratching purchase through his gloves. He pulled them off with his teeth, tasted leather, had a good scratch and lit a cigarette.

In Manitoba, curling season arrived in late October, not soon enough for Blackie. It was already below zero most nights, and the urge to curl excited him to the point of sleeplessness. To make matters worse, when he did find a few sweet minutes of unconsciousness, the fact that Deirdre, his wife, had left him shocked him awake and buggered up the night completely.

She had left him the day after their holiday in August.

– You're really leaving?

– Can't stay.

– What do you mean can't stay?

– I've had a revelation. My life is going to shine.

At that moment Deirdre had looked about ten years younger

1

to Blackie; she was really stirring him up. He wondered if she'd met somebody, but he knew she hadn't.

She hardly hesitated before leaving. Nothing held her back. She'd suddenly acquired a knack for summing things up. His unassuming Deirdre, not his first love but certainly his longest, was getting on with it. These were supposed to be their cream and easy years, people said. Blackie thought that all their years had been their cream and easy years.

– What about all this, the house?

With her eyes he thought she was saying 'it's just a house.'

What was worse for him was what if she thought she hadn't been loved. That would have to be his fault.

And her leaving came just as he thought he had everything he had wished for in life. Goes to show.

Blackie had never been an unhappy man so his crappy bedtimes were new to him. He'd get up and stand in front of the picture window in the front room and stare through the smudged glass. 'Windows don't clean themselves,' Deirdre had written in a note one day after departing. He couldn't help thinking that there was some other idiot looking out his window, too. Most times he'd go down to the refrigerator to get a cold glass of milk.

He had the house on Inkster to himself since Deirdre and then Tino, his only son, had moved out and into the *shmutz* to be closer to university. If Deirdre had asked he would have moved out and let her keep the house, but once she'd made up her mind she'd run so fast to her sister's it was as if there was nothing at home that reminded her of their earlier happiness; maybe she'd never realized how unhappy she was until she made the deci-sion to leave. How had she kept her dissatisfaction in that long? Blackie wondered. Where had she buried all her criticisms of late? Where had she gotten the idea she was unhappy to begin with? Consciousness raising and yoga with her sister Edith?

Untroubled conventional Blackie was ill-prepared for this change. The emptiness Deirdre left behind had acquired

2

contours for him, albeit blurred because he didn't completely believe she had left for good. When he was away at work or at the rink she came over to vacuum and do a load of laundry and then dry and fold. She called it 'checking in' and left him notes with instructions about how to do things. Like he was lazy or an idiot. The fact that he looked forward to those notes confirmed he *was* an idiot.

He could have done a load himself, but whenever he went down to the basement with a basket of dirty laundry he found himself staring at the washing machine as if it was a UFO that had just landed. So he just left the basket on the porcelain lid and buggered off.

There was the shame he felt knowing that all the guys knew Deirdre had left and that made him smoke his cigarette down to the filter, sucking courage out of it. He stubbed out his smoke, picked up his broom and paper bag and boots and yanked open the door to the QV. Once inside he felt safer and happier than he'd been for months.

Christ but he loved the rink! Just the smell of it. The sight of the lunch counter and his friends sitting around a table not far away? Just being inside made him feel safer and happier than he'd felt in months. Through the huge windows that inclined down to the rink lay six sheets of ice gleaming under banks of fluorescent overheads. Since it was the start of the season, the ends had been freshly painted. Red and blue circles glowed up from under the ice, and the rubber hacks were wet, black, and snappy. He couldn't wait to get down there.

At the counter of the rink snack bar, Blackie ordered a hot dog and coffee with cream from Rita. 'I can't cook, but I can pay,' Blackie had said to Deirdre when she'd asked him what he'd do for meals.

Rita turned to him.

– You want a jumbo, Blackie?

– A jumbo'll do me.

– The works?

– Oh, boy!

Hands red from the knuckles to her fingertips, Rita let drop a block of lard on the griddle. When it melted in its froth, she dropped a jumbo wiener on it. From the stainless steel space-age warmer she extracted a bun, split it open, and spread relish and fried onions and chilli gravy on it. Rita was so generous with the works that Blackie didn't think there would be any room for the wiener.

– Okay like this? Rita said, wrapping the hot dog in a paper napkin.

– Beautiful.

– And your coffee.

– Thank you.

The first bite felt like biting into a balloon but it tasted scrumptious. It would be nice to have some soup once in a while, or fried chicken, or a slice of liver and onions, or a piece of goldeye, Blackie thought, taking another bite, the green and yellow works oozing out on his knuckles. Or hearing a word from Deirdre instead of having to read those stupid notes, even though they gave him hope she'd come back one day.

Blackie looked around to see if Tino was there but couldn't see him. Tino, who was no longer a junior curler, had moved up to curl for Bunny Rabinowitz, along with that nice *shagitz* kid, Michael MacGiligary, who wasn't there either.

Tino was still a crap curler because he didn't take it seriously enough. But that Michael MacGiligary kid could really hit the button, even when he was a junior. Tall, blond, no pimples — a real Jewess slayer, Duddy Joffe called him — with a pale complexion and blue eyes. They were the same age — 17 — but they looked odd together: the pallid *shagitz* who looked like the young Glenn Gould, very graceful on and off the ice, his hair trim for the times, and Tino, who was olive skinned and had thick black curls down to his shoulders. Tino always looked like his head was covered in

4

dollops of black shampoo that hadn't been rinsed out. On his first day of school Deirdre had to use half a tube of Brylcream before she could pack him off, but Tino was too excited about school and the prospect of other kids to play with to care that there was enough grease in his hair to fry a chicken. In the end they gave him brush cuts until he saw The Beatles on Ed Sullivan. Blackie loved that kid with all his might, but he didn't like it that Tino and Michael were always talking between and during ends, even when their skip was throwing his rocks. Blackie thought that was disrespectful and he wished he knew what it was that they had so much to talk about. Most of what he knew about Michael MacGiligary came from Tino. They had met at the rink in juniors and having both skipped a grade they were the youngest kids taking physics at university.

Blackie wasn't surprised not to see Tino yet. It wasn't league play, so there'd be a lot of horsing around tonight. Between university and BBYO, the kid was busy. Blackie liked that Tino was in B'nai B'rith Youth and that he was busy.

The rink cafeteria was packed and Blackie liked that too. He was always worried that membership would fall off and the QV would fold and fall by the wayside. It was like a thumbtack in his brain. And the revival of the rumour that Max Foxman, the QV president, was going to sell the club had been spoiling his digestion lately. The rumour was probably just that; they were always threatening to close the Queen Victoria.

– Did you hear they want to sell the QV? Blackie asked Oz.

– Never believe anything until it's officially denied, said Oz.

About forty guys were there early, with time to kill like Blackie, and more coming in as excited about being back at the rink as he was. They were changing into their curling boots and sweaters right in the cafeteria because there was no locker room and no showers, not like at the richer clubs. But you didn't need a changing room for curling. The most you changed was from your shoes into curling boots and then you put on your sweater. Christ, it was

5

winter anyway outside. And showers? Why would you go outside in 30 below weather with a wet head?

– How's the action Blackie? Duddy Joffe asked from a table near the counter.

It was the first time Blackie had seen Duddy since he got out of the penitentiary and he had to wonder if Duddy could still curl as good after two years away from it.

Duddy put his pinky in his ear and gave it a vigorous shake. He cocked his tweed Depression cap to get better access to the itch. Then he adjusted his black turtleneck dickie in order to pat, not scratch, the *semper* itchy mole on his neck, which looked as if a smidgen of tar had been flung there and stuck. Duddy was hot in his leather jacket, cap and black dickie but he blamed it on Rita keeping the radiators turned up high enough to cook something on.

Blackie left the counter, his coffee cup in one hand, and what was left of his hot dog in the other, the works running down his fingers. He licked each finger as he walked over and sat down with his friends and teammates: besides Duddy and Suddy Joffe, there was Oz and Chickie, who had subbed for Duddy while Duddy was in jail. Blackie felt better just being with his pals. How the world lit up! He forgot how sad and embarrassed he was about Deirdre's leaving him, which had put paid to his One God, One Wife policy.

– How're you? he asked Duddy.

– Getting better all the time.

– Look. Max Foxman wants to say something, said Oz.

Blackie looked at the club president over by the dais: Max Foxman, big and handsome, with rugged looks under moist skin, one of the South End bigshots who ran things and who, as Oz always said, was admired by many people, especially himself. It meant that much to him to be Max Foxman.

Next to Max was his clique of noisy superior people. There was Harry Finn, who had changed his name from Harry Fink — who could blame him — and who, as Duddy said, you couldn't trust because he had had his nose fixed. Leo Wasserman was up there, too: no brains, no heart, but a good Jew. And a hairy man! Duddy always said that the back of Leo's neck was like a carpet. Then there was Eddie Zachs, Max's third, same pinhead he had been as a kid. Back then he'd had a brush cut. Now, instead of hair, there were just filaments rustling on pink scalp.

Max threw some weight as president of the club, and as a businessman in Winnipeg: he could sell you a bridge. He sat next to the rabbi on the *bima* at the synagogue; he drove one of the little Shriner cars in their parades; he raised money; and, since some of his talents were still being wasted, he also organized junkets to Vegas every few months. He would arrange a couple of comps for guys from the QV, and that made them feel special. Just back from one of those junkets now, Max sported a tan that made his face shoe-polish brown. To show off the rest of his tan, he'd unbuttoned the top three buttons of his shirt and rolled up the sleeves of his Dean Martin cardigan to the elbows. He looked superb.

Apparently Max Foxman's announcement about the QV was big enough that he had to use the dais by the far wall, under the portrait of Queen Victoria. But getting everybody to shut up was taking time, time enough for Blackie to sneak another bite of his hot dog while not disrespecting Max. Nobody, nobody was paying attention except Blackie, and Max started shouting, his large nostrils reddening and expanding. Blackie could visualize Max's brain sitting on the urge to call them all good-for-nothings, to see if that wouldn't shut them up. Finally, Max turned on his glassy smile and his air of utter confidence and boomed:

– People! Guys! Guys! Can we have some quiet, please!

Blackie braced himself. And for good reason: the news was no-good lousy. The Queen Victoria Curling Club, the only Jewish curling club in the city, was running a deficit at the worst possible time. The roof had to be re-shingled, and the parking lot had to be repaved, which Max said was too small anyway because peoples' cars were getting bigger. He was referring to his own Cadillac Fleetwood Sixty Special and everyone knew it.

– There was so much financial grief that anyone would be disgusted, Max said. Where were the new members everyone promised to sign up? Where were the old ones? And why was Saturday night mixed curling in the pits? Dues were down and taxes and inflation up. In short, the QV was going to 'fold and fall by the wayside.'

Blackie relaxed: this was nothing new. At the beginning of every season, Max Foxman said the QV was going to fold and fall by the wayside.

Everyone went back to their conversations, ignoring Max, who stood there, taking in all the rough murmuring with a sadistic smile on his lips, lowering his eyelids and chewing up his next sentence into delectable and manageable bits.

– Dominion Stores, he said. – They've made an offer.

That got their attention.

A cramp ran through Blackie. The guys went mad.

– Dominion Stores. The Queen Victoria will be a new Dominion Store?

It wasn't Max who wanted the club gone. God knows he'd tried to keep it running? 'But the offer was good, guys: too good.' Blackie thought that Max was enjoying kicking them up the bum, shutting them up tight.

Max let the complaining rev up, but on his terms this time:

– We'll all get our initial investment in the club back, he told them. The deal will be sweet. Very sweet! Ever heard of a windfall profit? He'd flipped the burger now.

– Some of us are giving our windfall to Israel. It's what me and the Executive are going to do personally, as individuals.

– In person? someone heckled.

– You need rubber boots to wade in so much bullshit, yelled Duddy.

– We're going to post a list with the names of donors. Anyway, the Executive has decided to accept the offer. Negotiations should take time, so there'll be an announcement about the sale. Enjoy your curling tonight, he said, as he stepped off the dais. – And welcome back.

The initial look of enthusiasm Blackie had worn to the club that evening had been wiped off by Max Foxman. It was the first time that Max had ever mentioned there was a buyer. And Dominion Stores no less.

– Great way to start the season, Blackie said to Suddy, Duddy, Chickie and Oz.

Chickie Zabler, huge and doughy, with one lazy eyelid, put his forearm, big as a cushion, behind his head after dragging his fingers through his wavy grey and yellow hair. His ring, the one with the fat chocolate stone, had snagged a bit and he yanked hard. He lifted up one of his chins, stroked his sandy goatee and said:

– A *broch*. A real *broch*. He's talking crap.

– Now there's a word I haven't heard for a long time, said Oz. He looked at Blackie, and they both popped the butts of their hot dogs into their mouths at the same time.

– Oz, you look like a *broch*, said Chickie.

Oz did look like shit. He had blue sacs under his brown eyes, but he'd had those since he was three.

Duddy Joffe clawed Blackie's inside elbow to get his and everyone's attention.

– Now listen exactly to what I'm going to say: I've got his quote. Max's.

– Does that even mean half of anything? Chickie asked.

– Duddy knows the show, said Suddy.

Duddy and Suddy Joffe both had tremendous chests, like in advertisements for those chest expanders guys used when they worked out. They had square heads like all the Joffes, but Duddy was much taller, more robust, and saw himself as a prairie Johnny Weissmuller because of his height and looks. And while

9

Duddy basked in the attention of anybody, Suddy was born to be ignored, and happiest that way.

– Max Foxman, said Duddy. – He's always invited to the Negev Dinner for free. Notice that? He's won the door prize twice.

Chickie flapped his large wet lips to speak:

– At Milwaukee Kosher alone he has eighty workers or more under him.

– Why does he want to do this? Blackie asked.

– I'm baffled, said Oz, looking to Chickie.

– They're loyal to him. This you will not believe: he once said he could get forty of his employees to kill the other forty and no one would bat an eyelash. That's loyalty.

– Or murder, said Oz.

The room suddenly quieted down. Max was back on the dais. He had forgotten to say that the Executive was negotiating for the rental of six sheets of ice at a new rink to be built in the South End next year. It would have 24 sheets of ice and changing rooms. And *hot* showers. He said this as if they had never experienced running water. From his tone everyone knew 'they' meant that the bloody North Enders could drive south for a change, see how 'they' liked it.

– He talks so *fait a compli*, said Oz.

– That's French, said Suddy.

Blackie was pale, which Duddy was the first to notice:

– Blackie, you're spazzed out.

– I'm in shock.

– You're bumstruck.

– How can he sell the club? Blackie asked. – It's been good to us.

– You mean dumbstruck. Chickie said to Duddy.

– Not when you get it from behind by Max Foxman.

– You can't buck Max Foxman, said Chickie.

When it came time to play, Blackie and his team went easy on Hy and Brian Saltzberger's team. It wasn't league play so they let them score a few ends.

Standing alone by the door to his car, Blackie raised his arms in a gesture of helplessness. The frost had covered the car and windshield in a slim coat of hard tiny diamonds with his window scraper lying broken in the backseat.

On the first try the engine sputtered and knocked before stalling. On the second try, it turned over, and he felt as good as he'd feel the rest of the night. As he gunned the motor, he knew he'd have to change the battery now that the nights frosted over.

TWO

Without Deirdre, Blackie had no way of getting through · Friday and Saturday nights: he didn't want to impose on people when they were having family time, so he had to face those hours alone. Tino came over Saturday afternoons to watch TV with him and then eat supper at 5:00 o'clock before Michael MacGiligary picked him up to go out. Sometimes Mike would watch TV too.

There was no curling on Monday and Wednesday evenings, so Blackie went visiting right after work, sometimes to Suddy's house, sometimes to the Salisbury House to have supper with Oz, and sometimes to hang out with Chickie in his rec room till his wife Hazel told him to send Blackie home.

– You think Max is serious? Blackie asked Chickie one night.

– About selling the club?

Chickie pushed the lever of his recliner, went horizontal, and spoke to the perforated ceiling.

– He lies like a carpet. The only time Max Foxman tells the truth is by mistake.

– They just want to move the club to the South End, said Blackie, so they don't have to make the drive north.

– The bit about the parking lot being too small was rich, said Chickie. – It's all a bunch of shit crap.

– He says they'll give the money to Israel though.

– You take everybody at face value, Blackie. I bet you a ball he'll pocket the money.

– I raise you two balls that he won't.

12

– I call your two balls and raise you back.

– Raise me with what?

– He's a *shtunk*, said Chickie. – He thinks he's so high and mighty.

– The Foxmans were on relief once, said Blackie. – They didn't have a pot to pee in.

– No, they had money but went on relief anyway, to *schnor* things.

– Depression years, said Blackie.

– Fraud, said Chickie. – It's in his blood. Should I get you a coke?

– I'm good.

– I have a surprise for you, said Chickie, still focused on the ceiling. I might as well tell you myself because you're going to hear about it anyway: Linda's expecting.

Linda was Chickie's firstborn. She had just had her 'Sweet Sixteen' party. They'd rented the basement of the Rosh Pina Synagogue for it.

– That's for the shits! Blackie said.

Chickie's news left him feeling cold. If Deirdre hadn't left he'd have known about it already.

– Do people know? he asked.

– You know people.

– Not so sure I do these days.

– People are telling Hazel she should find Linda an Israeli to marry. They phone her up to give advice but they're enjoying her embarrassment. No standards, those people.

– How'd it happen?

Chickie pushed on the lever and the recliner springs almost chucked him into the air. He was sitting erect suddenly, looking Blackie in the eye.

– Intercourse.

– I meant who's the guy?

Chickie began the story.

– It was a ghoulish summer night saturated with mosquitoes. They'd just fogged. Outside the kitchen window, I see this *shagitz* skulking in the back lane, looking up at my Linda's window.

– They fogged last summer. Didn't work, said Blackie. – Never works.

Blackie pictured Chickie stepping trimly into the back lane, putting his hand into a swarm of mosquitos and grabbing the punk by the collar.

– I'm on top of him in a sec and I say: 'my daughter isn't coming out and you're not getting in.' The kid leers at me — I still can't shake that snotty look he gave me — and he says 'what makes you think I'm on my way in.'

They heard Duddy come in the back door and then Hazel hustle him down the stairs as quickly as she could. She couldn't hack him.

– What are you talking about? Duddy asked, stepping into the rec room.

– Linda, said Chickie. – She's expecting.

– I bet that's why Hazel looked pissed off.

– Linda's a good girl, said Blackie.

– I don't believe in good girls, said Duddy. – Should I keep it a secret?

– Everybody's going to know anyway, said Chickie.

– Blackie has troubles, too, said Duddy.

– No comparing, said Blackie.

– Is Deirdre coming home? Duddy asked him. – Not right for a woman to do what she's doing.

– She's still at Edith's.

– I had a dream that Max Foxman sold the club, said Duddy. – I'm calling it.

– He announced it last week, said Blackie.

– I went to see the Astonishing Kripkin the other night. He had thirty people up on the stage of the Winnipeg Arena clucking like chickens.

– I knew you looked different, said Chickie.

– Thirty people!

– You go up there? Chickie asked.

– I believe in hypnosis. It can turn your life around.

– I don't know what you mean.

– If you don't know what I mean, Chickie, it's because you don't try.

– It's faked, you know, said Blackie.

– I saw it! said Duddy. – When I left the Arena I had an illumination that Max was going to sell the QV. Then I dreamt it. Now I'm predicting it. I'm psychic.

– You're not psychic, said Chickie.

Duddy clawed Chickie's inner elbow.

– Who saved Bloomstock's house in the 1950 flood? I did. And I predicted the flood. I called it.

– Hello, Noah! said Blackie.

Chickie flicked Duddy's hand away from his elbow. – You knew the 1950 flood was coming?

– Who saved Bloomstock's house?

– That was some flood, said Blackie.

It was true, Blackie reflected. The 1950 flood had been biblical, the Red River swelling over the valley from Grand Forks to Lockport.

Duddy clawed Blackie's elbow instead of Chickie's.

– Listen exactly to what I'm going to say to you: eight dikes gave way in that flood, and I saved Bloomstock's house, didn't I?

– More than eight dykes gave way during that flood, said Chickie.

While shit and slime bubbled up through the sewers into the basements of everyone who lived near the Red River, Bloomstock's Tudor mansion, built too close to the banks, filled only with clear water. How come? Just before the waters crested, Duddy lowered a bag of flax seeds into Bloomstock's basement sewer drain. As the river rose, the flax seeds gorged on the muck of the first backup, puffing up like popcorn, keeping the shit down but letting clear water through. Bloomstock was ecstatic.

– He kissed me on the forehead and said: 'You're a maverick, Duddy.' – Twenty years ago, I knew from that kiss that Bloomstock had conveyed his talent to me. That I'd be a millionaire one day, too.

For a few moments nobody spoke. Blackie and Chickie had heard the story many times, and each time they paused out of awe and respect for Duddy's genius.

– So I'm predicting it, said Duddy.

– What?

– What happened in my dream? Max Foxman is going to sell the QV.

– You can't buck Max Foxman, said Chickie.

– A *shmear* here and there and no one bucks you. And now they're *shmearing* each other. Believe me, hear me, see me and feel me: *shmearing* and *re-shmearing*.

– I don't think Max Foxman is being *shmeared*, said Blackie. – He paid his way.

– The Foxmans started off selling vanilla extract to the Indians, said Chickie.

– He worked hard for his money, said Blackie.

– Hard stealing it, said Duddy. – The rich steal, too. I know the show.

– I guess Hazel will be wanting us to leave soon, said Blackie.

On cue, Hazel, from the top of the basement stairs, shouted down:

– Chickie! Tell the guys they have to go home. It's supper.

When Blackie got home he saw Michael's car in the driveway and found Tino in his old room, cramming his record player into a box that was too small for it. Blackie could have told him it wasn't going to fit, but he thought he'd let him figure it out for himself. See if studying physics had done him any good. In the end, Tino slit the box with a steak knife.

– I'm letting it out at the seams, he said, smiling wryly at Blackie.

The box wasn't a cube any more, that was for sure. Tino used a mile of electrician's tape to keep the cardboard snug around the record player: 'wrapped not boxed,' he said. He saw the kid look at his LPs and 45s and wondered how he'd get those in the box. Tino just taped them to the sides around and around till he got down to the spool.

– That's done.

His clothes he'd already moved into the *shmutz* back in September. Blackie wondered why Tino hadn't taken his record player with him the day he left home.

– I didn't have a plug in my room that worked. But Michael's fixed one up.

Blackie was jealous that Tino hadn't asked him to help with something like that; Blackie was handy.

There were a couple of boxes of books already taped shut and sitting on the floor.

– You need help with those?

– Michael will help me.

– You good for money?

– I got my stipend.

– Need a lift?

– Michael's got his dad's car in the driveway.

– Is he living there, too?

– It's Jerry Zubelsky and Heavy and me. There's only three bedrooms. Michael lives on the Crescent.

– Heavy? That's a name?

– A person.

Blackie didn't know Heavy, but he knew Jerry Zubelsky, or better, knew the parents. Jerry'd been to the house lots and was in BBYO with Tino. The kid had blond hair down to his chin and parted in the middle. Deirdre called him Christopher Columbus.

– You going to have supper first?

17

– Is there anything to eat?

– No. We could go to Kelekis's.

– I have a BBYO meeting.

– How's that going?

– Going to run for President this year.

– Hnnh.

Tino knocked on the window pane to signal down to Michael MacGiligary, who was ankle deep in snow, leaning against the fender of his father's Lincoln Continental. The kid came in and up the stairs and he and Tino carried down the books and record player and loaded them into the back seat of the Lincoln. With some quick thinking, Tino had grabbed two pillows and sheets and blankets from the linen closet, and now rolled them into a ball and threw them on top of the books.

Before getting in the car Tino turned to Blackie:

– Don't look at me like that.

– I didn't say anything.

– I'm a lot closer to university now. It's like an hour and a half from here by bus.

– You could have got in a carpool.

– I don't have my license.

– You could work on that. I could show you.

– Michael's giving me lessons. You could show me how to curl better. By the way, is it true they want to sell the QV?

Blackie had been trying to keep that miserable prospect out of his mind, but Tino's mentioning it made Blackie's bowels wriggle.

– That's what Max Foxman says.

– What do you think about it?

– You can't buck Max Foxman.

THREE

Curling nights were easier for Blackie. By mid-December, when there was already a thick crust of snow on the ground, the team had gotten off to a good start in league play. Although eager to hit the hacks, he liked having time to sit with Suddy, Duddy, Chickie and Oz before the bell rang.

Duddy clawed Chickie's elbow.

– Now listen exactly to what I'm going to say to you guys: it's tits up for the club. I predict it.

– It's *noch nila* for the club, said Suddy.

– He wants us to curl with the *shkutzim*, said Chickie.

– Maybe I should visit his face, said Duddy.

– Easy, Duddy, said Chickie.

Duddy snatched a roll from the basket Rita had given them and smeared it with a butter pad. When rattled, bread and butter soothed Duddy.

– Good night Irene, Duddy said to the roll and crammed it into his cheek. – Max Foxman. I know! I know! I have his quote.

– What do you know about Max Foxman? Oz asked.

– I know he can burp and fart at the same time.

– That's just an act.

The guys laughed.

– No. I saw him do it at Aberdeen School.

– He was always throwing me out the window at school when I was a kid, said Suddy.

– Lots of kids did that, said Chickie. – But just from the ground floor.

– Him and his friends: Harry Finn and Eddie Zachs. Harry's an alkie.

– I hated that school, said Oz. – Wasn't a day I learned anything.

– You know? said Duddy. – Even in the penitentiary, when I'd wake up, I'd be happy that I didn't have to go to school anymore.

– Amen, said Chickie.

– The only thing I liked about school was the smell of when you sharpened a pencil, said Duddy. – I'd sharpen everybody's pencil. They'd all bring me their pencils. Some kids I'd charge. It was Depression times. Minnie Mencken used to give me a dime. Her father committed suicide, and they buried him by the wall of the Hebrew Sick Cemetery. I used to neck with her behind the school after she gave me the dime, and before we kissed she'd lean on me and say, and I still remember this: 'Where are you going to take me with your kiss, Duddy?' She was poetic.

– She was wild, said Chickie.

– I've kissed so many girls just for pleasure. But not one was a poetess like her. She could write a poem in chalk on the sidewalk as she walked.

– What happened to her? Didn't she have a kid out of wedlock? Oz asked.

– I came away from that kiss like a victor.

– And a dime, said Chickie.

– Mr. Demkiw. Remember him? Oz asked.

– He used to put a Ping-Pong ball in my mouth to stop me from talking, said Duddy.

– Amen, said Chickie.

– I almost swallowed it once. I told my father and he said 'Good for you!' But Mona was irate.

– That's a good word, said Blackie.

– My father believed in the Fires of Gehenna. I once gave Demkiw his Ping-Pong ball back, and after he rolled it in two hands I told him I'd had it up my ass.

Duddy crammed another roll and butter whole into his mouth

and chewed vigorously so it wouldn't choke him.

They waited for him to swallow and take a sip of coffee.

– Nobody can burp and fart at the same time, said Chickie, shaking his fingers, thick as wieners, at Duddy.

– I saw him do it, said Duddy, after swallowing hard.

– Saw, heard and smelled, said Oz.

– It's *noch nila* for the club, said Suddy.

– He's finagling us into giving the club away, said Duddy.
– They're always finagling, those people. He shaves his *batzim*, you know? Max. All the way around. And under the sack, I think.

– You think? asked Oz.

– Okay. I know.

– Who told you? asked Chickie.

– Sophie.

The word Sophie pinged Blackie in the head. His cheeks flushed.

– She walked in on him one day in the bathroom and saw him shaving them with a razor, said Duddy. – He had shaving cream up to his *pupick*. Imagine the look on Sophie's face.

– Don't start with that 'imagine the look on someone's face stuff,' said Chickie.

– Imagine the disgust, said Oz.

– Were you there?

– It's in the public's domain, said Duddy. – I'd like to have seen the look on Sophie Foxman's face when she saw that.

– There's no way you can prove it, Duddy, said Oz.

– And his business is bent, and he has feathers on his balls, too.

– Not if he shaves them, said Chickie.

– That's why he shaves them. And did you ever notice he plucks his nostrils?

– He should pluck his balls, said Chickie.

Blackie made a moue of distaste, and Chickie taunted Blackie, who was famously prudish. – That's in his men's area.

– All I know is that it's *noch nila* for the club, as Suddy has pointed out, said Oz – whether he shaves his balls or not. Or plucks his nostrils. They have a buyer this time.

– Dominion Stores, said Blackie. – They're a big outfit.

– Max Foxman monopolizes conversations, too, said Duddy.

– Don't sully your lips with his name anymore, said Oz.

– I'm not out of jail a couple of months, and they want to close the club. This is worse than going to jail. He's out for me, personally.

– Wind it up and liquidate it, said Oz. – That's what they'll do come the spring.

– They want us to move into a bigger rink, said Blackie. – Share space with other clubs

– With guys who are just horsing around. Just renting ice, added Oz.

– That'll kill the club, sharing with the *shkutzim*, said Chickie.

– Next they'll want to move the synagogues south.

– You can't move a Torah without permission, said Suddy.

– It's in the Torah.

– Is it true your mother never found out you were in jail, Duddy? asked Chickie.

As the question was beneath answering, Duddy let Suddy respond.

– We kept it a secret from Mona. She's a shut-in.

– A secret. In this town? asked Chickie.

– Mona doesn't entertain.

Blackie didn't know whether to laugh or not.

– We told her Duddy was in Vegas. For his bronchitis, said Suddy.

– In Vegas? For two years? And she believed it? Oz asked.

– Since when do you have bronchitis? Chickie asked Duddy.

– I've always had bronchitis. Since forever.

– No, you don't.

– She believes what she wants to believe. Like everybody else. She has a belief system.

22

– A good mother will believe anything, said Suddy.

They all chewed on that for a moment.

Duddy started *shockling* his right leg, rotating his dickie, gingering his mole.

– It's tits up for the club, he said. – And I knew it was coming. I dreamt it. I know things. I'm psychic for the most part. You should know, he said. I know things.

– An oracle, said Chickie.

– Don't tease him, said Suddy.

– *A sol chen van* for the club, said Blackie.

Duddy opened his mouth as wide as he could and yawned till his jaw cracked under his ears. Then he snapped his teeth shut, adjusted his dickie, and gingered his mole.

– Let me tell you a few things about Stony Mountain penitentiary, he said. – Let me tell you things you *don't* know.

– What's more interesting is how you got there? said Oz. – Now that's a story.

– I got in like everybody else.

– Don't start till I get back, Chickie said. – I want to hear this again.

Blackie watched how Chickie's velvet step took him to the counter, where he ordered a jumbo hot dog with the works from Rita. He gobbled half of it down, then laid the rest on his plate in order to hike his pants up over his bum and tighten his belt. Chickie couldn't wear his pants under his belly or over it, so he was constantly fidgeting with them. The other half of the hot dog went the way of the first half before he got back to the guys to hear the story.

Duddy had held up the branch of the Royal Bank of Canada on Main Street and Kilbride Avenue. He just walked up to the teller, a Chinese woman, and he pulled out a revolver, handed her a Gunn's Bakery bread bag and asked for money.

– Those are good bags, said Suddy.

– Why did you have to use a gun, Duddy? asked Oz. – That just made it worse.

– I wasn't going to use a stapler.

The teller drew bills from her till, made a thick stack, bundled it with the thick elastic band that Duddy had rolled off his wrist, one of many he wore. She squeezed the bundle down to the bottom of the Gunn's bag, then scrunched the top like it had a kid's lunch inside.

She was so sweet to me, said Duddy. – In a poetic sense. So sweet, you know, and so polite, that I was proud to be Canadian.

– Polite or not, she buzzed the police, said Chickie.

The cock-up came when Duddy tried to get away on a bicycle, thinking that if he could make it to the monkey trails along the fence in Kildonan Park, he'd lose the fuzz. The cop car was confined to cruising the park drive, dogging him, while Duddy, his valiant legs pedalling madly, climbed and dipped and coasted the monkey trails.

– I was one of the best bike riders, as a kid, he said. – I invented riding double in the North End.

He was hidden intermittently from the cops by birch thickets, clumps of bush, and park buildings like The Gingerbread House, then he'd be out in the open, then concealed by shrubbery again. Duddy was really flying over the green banks, and when the cops vanished from sight he decided to exit the park, not on Scotia Street where he'd seen the cops waiting for him, but on Main Street. Bugger them, he thought, and pedalled like a maniac. Another squad car was waiting for him on the west side of Main. They nabbed him as he rocketed through the big gates and careened so low into his left turn that he scraped the asphalt with one knee and cheek before spinning to a stop.

– I should have taken the Aikens Street exit, but they probably had a third car there, too. I never figured them to use three cars to corner me. Didn't seem fair.

– You should've at least figured they'd have a car on Main Street, said Chickie.

– When I saw them there, I was so afraid — and I'm not afraid to admit it — my nuts went up my throat. I could have gargled with them.

– I don't know for the life of me why you did it, said Oz.

– If you've never stolen anything, you won't understand.

In no time he was in the cop shop, trembling in cuffs, getting banged in the head by two fuzz; not the arresting officers, but bigger cops who were already warmed up from having just punched out a native guy but good. When one of them, a head taller than Duddy, grabbed him around the neck, Duddy said to him: 'Watch the mole.'

With Duddy in a half nelson, the other cop jabbed him in the stomach. Then they tagged off: it was the turn of the cop who punched him in the stomach to grab him around the neck so the other guy could punch him.

Duddy said again: 'Watch the mole!'

Then they banged his head against the wall until he heard an orchestra tuning up. There was only one thing left to do: knee him in the business. Like a period to the sentence.

– You weren't so proud to be a Canadian then, said Oz.

Blackie noticed the tender wincing way Suddy had looked at Duddy while he told his story. It was warming to see Suddy's compassion for his brother. Pretty good as feelings go. Blackie'd known them both since they were kids and thought that's how brothers should be. Stella Avenue was no Gan Eden but there was no Cain and Abel either.

They were very close to their mother, Mona Joffe, their father Morris Joffe having died too young, and suddenly. Morris, strapping and in rude health, wasn't one for paying doctors. 'I'll bury them, you watch,' he'd say. But he didn't. One June day, he went out to work in his blue suit and came home sweating and pressing his side. He refused to see a doctor and by the next morning his eyes and skin had turned golden with jaundice. By evening he was dead. Poverty and loss of respectability swiftly followed the mourning and by fourteen both of the boys were already working, surrendering their wages every week to their mother.

While Duddy tried to be dapper, albeit in a brutish way, it would have been unfair to call Suddy a slob. And it was Suddy who had always held down a steady job, bookkeeping in a large firm, 'with a lot of family management,' he complained. Duddy used to joke that Suddy had five staff on top of him that were giving him a 'staph' infection. Suddy also did the odd bookmaking job for a guy named Abner and his brother, Bertie, who had a shoe shine parlour, with a bookie shop in the back. It was right off Main Street, kitty-corner from the police station: nothing fancy, just an '8-to-5 pick 'em' operation.

Suddy said that Bertie had two *vigorishes*: one for cops and one for people. Suddy also placed his own cautious wagers, banking a side income from kalooki and pinochle, and invested in a cab license and cab just in case something happened to him, and Duddy had nothing to fall back on. He coaxed Duddy to drive the cab once in a while, but Duddy was reluctant on many occasions because someone might see him; he would only do it as a favour to his brother. Duddy, from whom solvency ran screaming, just couldn't buckle down. He lacked *zitzfleisch*, Mona Joffe used to say, to which Duddy'd reply: 'Ma, I lack a job title.' As he got older, Duddy had less and less *zitzfleisch*, especially after he saved Bloomstock's house in the flood, since a powerful conviction had settled in his brain pan that he'd become a millionaire one day.

What Duddy actually lived off, nobody knew, but he always managed to have a wad of cash on him thick as a fist, wound tight, strangled in the middle by one of the thick rubber bands he wore around his wrists. Everyone suspected that it was Suddy who replenished this wad, but Suddy would never admit it. And yet it was Duddy who acted the role of Suddy's protector, making it look like *he* was watching out for Suddy.

Suddy was complicit in this.

– Didn't you feel the least bit ashamed going to jail? Chickie asked Duddy.

– I was a good friend in there, Duddy said, incensed. – To everyone, even the Indian guys, so I have nothing to be ashamed of. I was even friends with the Eskimo who shot that Mountie in the head up in Thompson. The Eskimo told me that the Mountie had shot his dogs, even the puppies. 'I eventually got *my* man', the guy would say, smiling, no teeth; they'd knocked them out in the Mountie car. So he was a soup *mensch* when it came to meals.

It was Oz who had Duddy and his overriding self-love all figured out. Whenever people scratched their heads about Duddy, Oz would sum it up:

– He has a superiority complex.

– Who was your lawyer, again? Chickie asked.

– Ralph Coren.

– Oh, that's right.

Duddy had another roll with butter and made the guys wait for what he had to say.

– But the Crown Prosecutor was mean, he went on. – He produced circumstantial evidence without needing it, just to get me. He represented the Queen.

– But he had witnesses, said Chickie. – He didn't need circumstantial evidence.

– The case was all circumstantial evidence. Just because I needed money, they assumed I robbed the bank.

Duddy then clawed at Blackie's elbow to get his and everybody's fullest attention.

– Now, listen exactly to what I'm going to say. Let me tell you something about jail. Everybody was so friendly to me, not like in the movies. Everybody: the Bohunks, the Indians, the Polacks, the WASPs, the Mennonites, Everybody.

– But personality will only get you so far, said Chickie.

Duddy continued unfazed:

– Some nights in there, I'd have dreams and nightmares. And some of the guys were always horny, so horny they'd get romantic.

– What do you mean romantic? Chickie asked.

– They'd neck. Blackie turned his head away. Homosexuality made him queasy; he couldn't joke about it like everybody else.

– Just neck?

– And then *shtip* each other. *Eyaculatio precox* in Latin, but the necking lasted the longest. They never wanted romance with me even though I was well-liked. I was only in for two years, but who knows what I wouldn't have done if I had been in for ten.

– Lenny Bruce said that if you put a man in jail that long, he'll *shtip* mud, said Oz.

– They weren't *shtipping* mud, Oz, said Duddy, with a superior tone.

– It's hyperbole, said Oz.

– They weren't doing hyperbole, said Duddy.

They all cracked up, even Blackie, who didn't like it when everybody pulled Duddy's leg too much. Blackie was three years older than Duddy, and he never forgot how Duddy had been the kid everybody on the street loved because he would share everything he had: candy, nickels and pennies, Mona's butter and brown sugar sandwiches, his few toys, and when he got older: shirts and sweaters and cash, whatever he had, anything, even the lint in his pocket.

– People can't help but like you, Duddy, said Suddy, even the *shkutzim*.

– You've always depended on the kindness of *shkutzim*, said Chickie.

Duddy ate two butter pads as if they were wafers; he'd already eaten all the rolls in the basket, save one.

– But the judge didn't like me for shit. He was meaner than the Crown Prosecutor, who represents the Queen. And he didn't have to be mean because he got his way. He lives on Wellington Crescent. I have his quote and number. Talk about *shkutzim*.

– Duddy never did anything if you think about it, said Suddy.

– He robbed a bloody bank, Suddy, said Chickie.

– But he didn't keep the money. Even though he was hard up.

– That doesn't matter, Suddy, said Chickie.

– It matters. He hid it in Kildonan Park but he told them where it was.

Blackie saw Suddy pull out a beer from his car coat pocket, pop the cap with his penknife, take a sip and then put the bottle between his legs. Suddy was feeling relaxed, his Hush Puppies were off his feet under the table, and he was massaging one foot with the other.

– You can't drink in here, said Blackie.

– Ah, nobody cares, said Suddy.

– Blackie's right, Suddy. I can't look after you all the time, said Duddy. – I can't blow your nose for you.

– Why would you want to? Chickie asked.

– You could get expelled from the club.

– He can't. He has a share, said Chickie.

– It's in the by-laws, Suddy.

– They're closing the QV anyways. Max said so.

Hearing it again made Blackie feel bad. He'd almost forgotten about it while listening to Duddy.

The first bell rang. Fifteen minutes to get on the ice, Blackie thought. Except Duddy, they all started untying the knots in the laces of their curling boots.

Duddy stretched out his legs under the table to bend the tip of his business into a more comfortable position, finally opting to point the whole apparatus up.

– Better get your boots on, Duddy.

Duddy kicked off his pointy shoes. He'd always worn pointy shoes, Blackie remembered. 'For kicking guys in fights until the daylights come out,' Duddy had said.

There were still some butter pads left. Rita was that generous. After he put his curling boots on, Duddy smeared butter on his fist and ate it that way. Tongue and teeth and the butter disappeared, leaving a shiny fist.

– Duddy! Manners.

– What?

– Don't do that, said Chickie.

– Don't do what?

– What you're doing.

– I'm not doing anything.

– With the butter.

– I'm a maverick, said Duddy, his leg toggling again. – Just look at them.

– Who?

– Max Foxman and Harry Finn and Leo. I'm sure they've been skimming. They have pyjama parties.

– Harry Finn's quite stupid, said Oz.

– He's got a large popcorn for a brain, said Duddy. – He's an alkie. They're crooks, those people.

– You're a crook, too, said Chickie.

– I robbed a bank, not my gal darn friends.

– And he paid for his malfeasance, said Oz.

– That's a good word, said Blackie.

– It's not really stealing, if you give the money back, said Suddy again, in Duddy's defence.

Duddy's face went wise:

– The real crime is getting caught is the concensus at Stony Mountain, said Duddy.

Then Suddy retrieved a point that had snagged someplace back in the conversation.

– And Duddy got caught because he was on a bicycle. If he'd been driving, it would have been a different story.

– Theft by misadventure, said Oz.

– Why didn't you? said Chickie.

– What?

– Drive to the bank?

– I'd lost my license.

– For that speeding ticket on Henderson Highway by the A&W?

– No, I lost it, misplaced it or something.

Chickie's laugh, which was made up of really long intakes of air through his nose, finally rattled the phlegm in his throat and then gave way to spiked snorts.

– Besides, the chain kept coming off. And it was a Raleigh!

– Raleigh's a good bike. It was new once, said Suddy.

– It should have performed better. They impounded it. I'm going to give it to Tino. I don't want the reminder.

– Thanks, said Blackie.

– When I get it out of the compound, said Duddy. – After winter. No sense now.

– Where did you get the bicycle? Chickie asked. – Did you steal that, too?

– Never mind where he got the bicycle, said Oz. – Where did he get the gun?

They all had a good laugh at that, except Duddy, who turned smug and snotty and looked at Oz as if Oz could learn something:

– Morris Silver. He can get a gun in a jiffy. I don't know if he'd be that fast for anybody else as he was for me. I had a chance to fink on him once when he robbed Pitt Lumber, but I didn't. Never told a soul. I could get you two guns from him. One for each hand.

– No thanks, said Oz.

– From Moe Silver? asked Blackie. – Ferne Silver's son?

– At least I don't steal from my friends, Duddy snarled. – Gal darn Max Foxman! They're skimming. That's why they've never re-shingled the roof. All the dues all these years? Think about it? I know the show. They give a *shmear* here and a *shmear* there, and everyone shuts up. I can bet you dollars to dogs' nuts that if they sell the club, the money won't end up in Israel.

– They're going to plant trees, said Chickie. – An entire forest of trees.

– Is there any other kind of forest? Oz asked.

– I was being sarcastic already. Pre-emptive strike.

– Vile man. He stooped to lie to us, said Duddy.

– He lies to *shtoop* us, said Oz.

– Taking from the rich Canadians and giving to the *shnorring* Israelis. They don't have flush toilets there, said Chickie.

– He's a *fertzeleh*, you know, said Duddy.

– Max's got two kids, said Blackie.

– I mean Leo Wasserman. Look at him, said Duddy. – Look at that lower lip! It's like a toilet.

They looked over at Leo Wasserman as if he was a stranger, though they had known him all their lives.

– He's always at Morris's *shvitz* on Selkirk Avenue, said Duddy. – I know what goes on there. I've driven cab some Saturday nights. I picked up a fare there I thought wanted to get cute with me. Said he'd put me up in business. Amazed by my acumen. He made me shiver, the way he said nice things about me: that I had a precious soul. The guy's thorax was like Jackie Gleason's. 'I always cab it home,' he said, 'and tonight was a more beautiful night for being in your cab.' He was so soothed by the *shvitz*. I think he would have written a poem in the back of the cab. He said he knew I'd go home alone to sleep and dream. He knew I was psychic.

– People like that need their heads examined, said Chickie.

– They need something else examined, said Oz.

– They get that examined, said Duddy. – I know what goes on there. That was the point of my story.

– I guess he had a man date, said Suddy, which is why he was so pleasant to you.

– Leo Wasserman is always running after those superior people, said Duddy.

– See his car? Chickie asked. – He must be doing good.

– I can't stand that, said Duddy. – And now that he's moved to the South End, he doesn't talk to me, the prick piece of shit. I'd slap him out till I reached his fillings.

– If you can't stand him, it shouldn't make any difference if he doesn't talk to you, said Oz.

– What'll we do if they close the QV? Blackie asked.

– We can curl somewhere else. Rent ice. That's what Max said.

– With the *shkutzim*?

– Or we can watch TV like everybody else, said Oz.

– All evening?

– People do it, said Chickie. – Or you get a video player thing.

– That's still TV, said Blackie.

The idea of spending an entire evening watching TV made Blackie's feet ice cold. Blackie never watched TV much, but he had made sure Tino could watch as much as he wanted.

– How do they get like that those people? Duddy asked.

Chickie coughed twice because he knew the answer:

– Hazel was at a Hadassah meeting years ago, and a child psychologist told her group that if the kid was too close to his mother he'd get like that and have inclinations.

– How old was that psychologist? Suddy asked.

Blackie remembered Deirdre telling him that, too. She was in Hazel's Hadassah group before Hazel switched to Pioneer Women. Blackie thought Deirdre wasn't being subtle; had told him that to get him to spend more time with Tino. He loved that kid, but he really didn't know how to play with him or talk to him. The best he could do was give him a big smacking kiss when he came home from work, or before going to curling, or at bed time, or when Tino showed him his report card. Or just whenever.

– He's such a suck, too, said Duddy.

– Who? Chickie asked.

– Leo Wasserman. Especially now that he lives in the South End. It all goes to their heads. Once they move to the South End, they think they're better than everybody else. No loyalty.

– How could he afford it?

– Leo's wife's got money. She was a Schecter. From Schecter Furs.

– He married her for her ugliness, said Oz.

– He can suck up to those people every day of the week, said

Duddy. – He carries a straw with him everywhere he goes. When he phones Max, he has to think about what he's going to wear, like for an important call. And now he says it's too far to drive here to the North End to curl. But I bet you he's at Morris's *shvitz* every Saturday night.

– He'll drive to the North End for that, agreed Chickie.

– The fun things, said Suddy, seriously.

– He's always sucking up to Max Foxman. Always sucking up. He doesn't say a word to Max without putting Vaseline on it first, said Duddy.

– On what first? Chickie asked.

They all laughed except Blackie. – Once they sell the club, believe me, the money will go to Israel. I can guarantee you that. He can't steal it. The club has auditors.

– You're talking like an accountant, said Chickie, patronising him, but in a friendly way.

The guys knew that while Blackie had passed his exams years ago to be a CA, and could sign accounts, he still worked as a book-keeper and office manager at the first job he'd gotten after the war. He could have moved up, but he was loyal to old man Shneerson, who made winter coats — double-breasted pea, toggle, and duffle — in a narrow four-storey factory on Albert Street. Maybe his lack of ambition was one of the rebukes Deirdre had concealed. She didn't like it that Shneerson never splurged on an elevator and still used a wooden paternoster that was a danger to the public.

Duddy wiped a few remaining globules of butter off his fist with his tongue. His arm shot across the table and clawed Chickie's elbow, getting everyone's attention.

– Who do we play tonight?

Chickie flicked Duddy's fingers away hard.

– Zyminsky, said Chickie. – And go *nudja* somebody else.

– Guess who we play Thursday? Oz asked.

– I don't have to guess. – I can read it on the bulletin board.

– Max Foxman, said Oz.

34

– We should play them skins, said Duddy. – Ten bucks an end. That would show the bunch of them.

The second bell rang, and it was time to get on the ice and *shmice* Zyminsky.

FOUR

D eirdre checked in at home the next day; there were traces of her consideration. She had done a load, and dried a load, and folded a load. She had left Blackie a note that said: 'Fridges don't clean themselves.' She had timed her visit so she wouldn't have to see him.

He had thought of leaving work early, to catch her off guard at home, to find out what was going on with her, whether her sister Edith was treating her well, how Tino was doing at his new place. But old man Shneerson had wanted to match invoices to payments, so he had to stay late.

As he drove across town in a winter sunset, the disappointment that Deirdre might be gone before he got home began to sink in. And just when the melancholy got so intense that he thought he'd have to abandon hope of her ever coming home, he decided to confront her. She'd be at the hairdresser's the next day, just like every Thursday, around 5:00 o'clock. He could go there before he went curling. He could sneak up on her when she came out.

On Thursday, it was cold enough for any remaining sparrows to freeze to death, poor guys. The sun had already set; Blackie wondered what had been the point of it coming out at all. The wind was howling and flinging specks of snow and sand against the windshield. He parked and opened his car door to get out, but a blast of Arctic air pushed it shut. He made a second effort; flung the door open so wide and hard it hit the telephone poll; the exertion itself kindled hope. Mounds of snow that were there to stay till April lay everywhere. It was already sandy and salted by the curbs, grey and dirty on the sidewalks. He got out of the car and stepped through a crust of bank he thought would be rock hard but wasn't: snow shot up his shins.

Deirdre emerged from the salon and began walking confidently down Selkirk Avenue, using her hands — in their grey cashmere mittens — to protect her 'do' against the wind. She looked fabulous in a shag cut with bangs, looked even younger than the last time he'd seen her, and that time she had looked younger than the time before. He watched her some more, realizing that what he was seeing had once been his. He caught up with her from behind, but she kept going; he pulled ahead of her and kept pace, but walking backwards.

– Are you following me? she asked.

She picked up her pace. Flecks of snow were hitting her cheeks.

– Where are you going? Slow down.

– To my car. I'm going to Tino's again. I started cleaning up where he lives. In the *shmutz*. I'm going back to finish. I bet the other kids' mothers don't go there to clean. I've never seen dirt like that.

– Stop for a second.

– I'm on the go.

Suddenly, one of Blackie's regrets popped into his mind. Years ago she had asked him to pick up a couple of chickens on the way home from work, because she was on the go, and he had said: 'why two, so they can fight?' She hadn't even goaded him. It was just a simple favour. He was going to eat those chickens, too. And he had said that to her? Made fun of her? – 'I was just joking,' he had said. And she had said: 'I don't like those jokes.'

– Stop for a second!

He actually grabbed her coat sleeve to make her stop. She mashed snow to keep warm.

– Thank you, he said.

– Have you seen how dirty his place is? she said, looking out at the traffic.

He hadn't been invited, but he didn't want to tell Deirdre that.

– Come back from Edith's, he said.

– I had to climb in the stove with a paint scraper to fight the grime, she kept on. The little shits watched. One called me a grime fighter. And the carpets were crawling. They don't even know how to vacuum. They said the vacuum was broken. The kitchen linoleum was full of crumbs, and I said – 'is the broom broken too?' I was against him moving out.

– So was I, I think.

– You think? Why didn't you say anything? Put your foot down?

Blackie had thought Deirdre would have been the one to stop Tino from moving out. She was the disciplinarian. Frankly, he was surprised she hadn't stopped him; she knew he didn't like confronting Tino! She knew that. He had rationalised instead: when Blackie was Tino's age he had been drafted, shipped overseas, ordered — amid the crump of cannons — to hide behind an earthen berm in Sicily; and, after all, what was a little *shmutz* compared to an aerial bombardment by your own side?

– Are you coming home?

– I'm on the go.

– I'm lonely.

– Six months tops you'll find somebody else. I know my customers.

He wanted to say right now that he'd die alone for sure.

– I'm so lonely I can't sleep.

– Blackie. I'm on the go. Believe me. Six months tops.

When he got to the rink, the smell of curling ice soothed his brain. He crouched in the hacks and then slid out as far down the ice as he could on his left foot, left knee bent, ankle crushed, right leg stretched out behind him. After Blackie came Duddy, his lead, chest out, sliding to the hog line. Then Oz, his third, followed him, then Suddy, his second. One, two, three, four, in a brocade, sliding gracefully past the hog line, opening their fists to release an invisible stone.

Chickie, who had subbed lead for Duddy while Duddy was at Stony Mountain, was now, after a summer of rich barbecues, too fat to get out of the hacks, and under doctor's orders to avoid exertion. He was just a curling *kibitzer* now, loyal to the team. He stood, hiking up his pants over his bum, on the little covered boardwalk to watch the game. It was cold enough for him to see his own breath, but he had a furnace in him and could stand faithfully in his thin V-neck to watch every end.

Suddy and Duddy practiced their sweeping. They were thundery sweepers, especially with their new foam brooms — Blackie and Oz still used straw — and could tease the curl out of a rock, or accelerate it to shatter the granite of the enemy's stone. When Duddy was in the pen members used to say the rink was quieter.

Blackie had missed Duddy's broom and the way he sometimes roared 'seep, sweep, sweep.'

Brooms and sweeping evoked for Blackie an episode when he was sweeping the kitchen floor lackadaisically last year and Deirdre out of the blue shouted 'sweep, sweep, sweep.' He didn't know it was writing on the wall.

The ice was beautifully pebbled, like an orange skin, Blackie thought.

– Great ice, he said to the new ice maker, Werner, a German immigrant who was stooping on the neighbouring sheet to pick up a piece of straw.

– What? Werner said, trying to hear above the clap of the brooms.

– Good ice!

– What?

Werner was as deaf as Beethoven.

– Good ice!

– Thanks, Mr. Blackie.

Werner was taciturn but gracious in that Old Country way. He had that going for him, which was important for a German guy making ice in a Jewish curling club.

Blackie slip-slid his way down the ice back towards the house, stepping down carefully on his hack shoe while sliding forward on his slider shoe. Step, slide, step, slide and in a jiffy he was back at the other end.

Blackie looked at Oz, Duddy and Suddy on the ice, and they made him happy. No way of explaining it but happy inflated into confidence and vision: not only would they *shmice* Max Foxman and friends but they'd go far this season with Duddy back and, if it was going to be the last season for the club, he wanted them to go out with a bang. They weren't a bad team. In their years on the ice they had twice made it to the sixty-fours in the provincial Brier, and had even gotten down to the finals twice in the B'nai B'rith Bonspiel.

Duddy too went over to Werner and shook his hand and complimented his ice.

As hysterical as Duddy was off ice, on ice he metamorphosed into a curling gentleman, and there was coincidence between what he said and what one should say. The ice was a place where Duddy found equilibrium and cool.

Max's team came on the ice in lavish matching white sweaters with the QV's blue crown embroidered on the backs. They all wore identical stretch pants with straps that fit snug under their insteps, and identical gloves. They all carried new foam brooms tucked under their arms. Their wool tams were a bit much. The only thing they were missing were kilts. Blackie couldn't stand it when Jews pretended to be Scottish.

Blackie, a good skip, always tried to be moves ahead of a mediocre skip like Max Foxman, who was the skip only because he could scream the loudest: Max's kind of self-confidence was just inexplicable to Blackie. Max's third, Eddie Zachs, was a much better curler and should have been the skip. But Eddie mumbled to the point of being inarticulate what with his head tilted and his eyes closed. He could never project himself as skip material next to Max.

Blackie gathered his team on the mat behind the house, including Chickie. They smoked while watching Max's team practice their pathetic slides.

– We should play them skins, said Duddy. – Ten bucks an end. I'm telling you. Shove their *punims* in it. Really bugger them up. *Mishlockt yiddin.*

– No swearing, Duddy, said Blackie.

– Right. Right, said Duddy. – But I mean it. Skins. Ten bucks an end. Blackie, go ask Max Foxman if he wants to play skins.

– I'm in, said Oz.

– Suddy? Blackie?

– Ten's too rich, said Blackie.

– A fin an end?

– I'm in, said Chickie.

– How can you be in? Duddy asked him.

– Blackie can lay half his bet off on me.

– Okay by me, said Blackie. – Five is too rich for me, too.

– Tell Max there's an extra fin a point if we skunk him, said Chickie.

Max Foxman, a betting guy, agreed, and so did Harry Finn, Leo Wasserman, and Eddie Zachs.

– Eddie will talk to you about the details.

Blackie also asked him about the club, about the sale.

– It's practically inked, said Max.

– That's going to disappoint a lot of people, said Blackie.

– There's no going back, Blackie. You know that. You know numbers.

Blackie slid back to the team and took out another cigarette.

– They flick each other's business with one finger when nobody's looking, said Duddy while giving him a light.

– Guess which finger. Go ahead. Guess.

– I'm not guessing.

Eddie Zachs, head on a tilt, eyelids shut, slid up to talk over the financial arrangements of the bet with Blackie, who couldn't hack him, especially with that way he had of mumbling, his eyes shut and head down. Leo Wasserman looked on, caressing the gold guardsman's moustache he had kept from the war, then rubbing the carpet of hair on the back of his neck.

Just before the game started, Blackie noticed Tino and Michael MacGiligary on the ice. He looked to see if Tino'd noticed him, but he hadn't. The boys were playing and talking. Always talking and talking, those two. He wondered what engrossed them so much. Life was not that complicated and it never got confusing until it got confusing. Whenever he tried to talk to Tino, he got nothing. It was like turning on a tap with nothing coming out, no matter how many times you turn the faucet. The other day he told Tino he read about the BBYO elections in *The Jewish Post.*

– Oh, yeah? Tino said. The conversation died there.

Max won the toss and gave Blackie a frosty smile when he chose the hammer. Blackie chose the blue stones, his lucky colour.

The first end started slowly, but well, for Blackie. He was lying one after his last rock, and although his rock was protected by three guards in front of the house they were too generously spaced apart. Max had the daylight in the channel for an easy takeout, which he was discussing endlessly with Eddie Zachs.

Blackie's team, plus Chickie, stood behind the house on the hack line, looking brainy, squinting at the action, until Max slid off to the hacks.

– He's marking it too far left, said Duddy to Blackie.

Zachs heard that, and twisting his head around, said:

– Bugger off, Duddy.

Duddy was about to say something, but Blackie cautioned him.

– You be the gentleman, Duddy.

With his glove, Max Foxman wiped and wiped the bottom of his rock, then he shot out of the hack, slid just halfway to the hog line, and slung his rock with might. He'd hit the broom but the broom was too far left to begin with and the rock couldn't hold the channel. Max had to start screaming at Leo and Harry: 'sweep! sweep! sweep!' His stone rocked and hurled like a meteorite until it annihilated one of Blackie's blue guards, which bashed into another of Blackie's guards. Three stones were now simultaneously careening through the twelve-foot, one of which, Blackie's, ended up kissing Blackie's shot stone, while Max's thunderball bashed itself against the boards.

Duddy killed himself laughing. It would've been better if Max Foxman hadn't taken the shot, he thought. Had just carried the stone on his head back to the hacks.

– I'm going to make you swallow that laugh, Duddy, said Max.

Duddy continued laughing until Blackie told him to get a grip, that it wasn't polite.

After scoring two in the first end and seizing the hammer, Blackie played as if in a trance: since Deirdre had left he was mostly living on half his brain anyway. Bliss engulfed him shot by shot, and he wasn't aware of anything going on around him, not even the score, until the ninth end, when Oz said:

– We're skunking them but good.

In fact, Blackie's team, playing the blue stones, was skunking Max eleven to nothing. No sooner had Max gotten a stone in the house than Blackie had it smashed out to eventually and prudently score one or two each end. They were up real bucks, and doublers if they kept Max Foxman scoreless.

At the beginning of the tenth and last end, Duddy knocked out one of Max's red stones and left a guard, and with his second shot he drew behind the guard stone to sit one in the four-foot. A beaut of a shot. The pen couldn't knock the curling out of Duddy's body.

The seconds threw their stones: Blackie's blues sticking behind guards, the reds smashed to the boards. For the first time Blackie let the house get lousy with stones, have a bit of fun, with blues in the twelve-foot and eight-foot until Eddie Zachs, who could actually curl, drew a red stone into the four-foot and sat shot rock by the time it came for the skips to shoot.

So Max was lying one, which could kill the skunk.

Skip's rocks. Incredibly, with his first rock, Max drew a golden stone to the four-foot to lie two. Blackie had no choice but to try to knock out both of Max's stones but he buggered his shot, and the rock sailed through the house. Chickie shook his head at him; Blackie felt ashamed as he slid home. He now figured Max, with his last rock, would try to set up a guard to protect his two points and save himself from the skunk.

Max's third, Eddie Zachs, held the broom for Max in the spot Max marked. Max, his face smooth and oily, Blackie could see, loved the moment when he walked backwards away from the house, examining where Eddie Zachs was marking the spot, registering a confirming nod before about-facing and sliding tall towards the hacks to make his climax shot, as if the whole rink was watching. Blackie admitted he could understand that vanity.

But Max's rock skidded in the channel and drew up short, and it wouldn't have been difficult for Blackie to sneak around his guard but he chose to draw to win the end and did. His rock nestled sweetly close to Max's to score one.

– We're shot rock, said Blackie to Max. – That's twelve points plus the skunk.

– I want the calipers, said Max.

Both stones did look to be pretty close, but it was obvious the blue stone was closer.

All eight players plus Chickie crossed the hack line to scrutinise which rock was closer to the button. They all stood in the eight-foot, up to their ankles in curling rocks as Werner walked gingerly over two sheets of ice with the enormous calipers he had taken down off the far wall.

Suddy was standing there, and his small boot came awfully close to Blackie's blue stone, which, as everyone could see, and the calipers would prove, was nearest the button. Point, end, and skunk.

Maybe Suddy's boot touched the shot blue stone, maybe it didn't.

– You burnt that! Leo Wasserman said to Suddy.

Suddy snapped to attention, scared.

– Me?

– You burnt that stone, Suddy.

– He didn't touch it, said Duddy.

Everyone was staring down at Suddy's toe, then they looked at the supposedly burnt stone as if it could talk. People look stupid when they're all looking at the same thing, thought Blackie.

– With his toe, said Harry Finn. – It's burnt. Scrub it.

– I didn't touch it, said Suddy, looking at Duddy and Oz.

– You budged it with your toe, said Leo. – It's burnt. I'm removing it. We get the end and the point. I'm ejecting it.

– Don't touch the stone, said Duddy to Max.

– It's burnt, Max said loudly. – Remove it!

– If I remove it, said Duddy, it's going up your ass.

– Remove it, Duddy, said Leo.

– He didn't touch it, said Duddy, coming chin to chin with Leo, sucking him into the Duddysphere. Werner was standing shyly nearby with the calipers, and Blackie was embarrassed that they were arguing in front of him.

– You're a liar, Duddy, said Leo.

With his massive gloved hand, Duddy swept Leo's tam off his head, causing Leo to start shuffling his feet for balance. To keep from falling on the ice he grabbed Duddy's curling sweater in two fistfuls, scraping his nipples in the process.

To get some purchase, Duddy grabbed Leo by the thick hair on the back of his neck the way you'd pick up a pup.

Leo grabbed Duddy's dickie and yanked.

– Watch the mole! yelled Duddy.

Leveraging, pushing, leveraging, Leo drove Duddy backward and banged him into Suddy, who fell down on his bum.

Suddy opened his eyes and started winking into the overhead fluorescents. On his face was a look of blank astonishment.

– Ouch! The bum, said Oz.

Max Foxman had laughed when he saw Suddy go down. The other curlers on the other five sheets stopped shooting or sweeping. Bunny Rabinowitz lit up a Player's Plain. Blackie saw Tino and Mike MacGiligary stop their talking to see what was going on. People looked down from behind the glass in the cafeteria. It had to look funny from behind the glass, Blackie thought.

Duddy had one of his sudden brain rages. As Leo put his tam back on, Duddy thumped him on the ear with a primeval fist, knocking his tam off again, making *shmark* run out of Leo's nose.

– Taste that!

Leo leaned to one side, sucked the *shmark* back up his nose, and with two fingers checked out his scalp for blood. Not once but twice. The second time made Duddy laugh. They grabbed onto each other's sweaters, slipping, planning punches, looking as pathetic as hockey players when they try to box.

Blackie dodged some rocks in the house to hoist Suddy up on his feet and then he gave Max Foxman and Leo Wasserman, who were standing over Suddy, a *shteff-mama* look. They backed off because they had nothing against Blackie.

Oz slid over to Suddy. He wasn't a doctor, but as a butcher he knew some rudimentary anatomy.

– I fell on my bum back there, said Suddy.

– On your tailbone? Oz asked.

– Just my bum. Did we lose the end?

– We'll have to scrub the end, said Blackie, thinking that would make peace.

– But they still owe us money, don't they? Suddy asked.

– How's the bum? Chickie asked, slapping the ice from Suddy's trouser bottoms.

– Freezing, said Suddy.

With hoary steam coming from their mouths, their bums resting on the matting, their feet fastened to the sticky ice, the five of them rested and waited for Max Foxman's team to walk off the ice first. But Max's team were taking their time looking for Eddie Zachs's tam.

– This stuff warms the bum good, said Suddy.

– You could get piles from it, said Chickie.

– You could get piles, too, said Suddy.

Max and his team gave up the search for Eddie's tam. As they walked past Blackie's team, heading for the staircase up to the cafeteria, Leo said to Duddy:

– Where's my tam?

– How should I know?

Leo, with clipped bully lunges, flicked out a bugger-you finger at Duddy, then at Blackie, then at Chickie and then at Suddy.

– Where're you going, Leo? You owe us money, said Duddy.

– I'm going for a piss.

– Wait for Max, he'll hold it for you, said Duddy.

Leo ignored him, and his team marched along the matted aisle, up the stairs and out of the rink.

Duddy stretched out one leg and adjusted his junk in his crotch, prickling from Leo's tam, which Duddy had stuffed down his underwear. It was wool, and his balls were starting to get hot. His shirt was soaked, his dickie, too, which he had stretched out to cool off. He let it spring back and then he twisted it around 180 degrees and gingered his mole.

– Let's go to Kelekis's for chips and gravy, said Suddy. Suddy loved those chips. He needed to eat them twice a day sometimes.

– You have a craving? Chickie asked.

– We have to collect our money, said Duddy.

– They'll welsh, said Chickie. – They'll welsh for sure on the skunk and swear Suddy kicked the rock.

– We'll see about that, said Duddy. – I have connections, too.

– What kind?

– I know a few guys. Guys that could teach Max Foxman a

lesson.

– We're scrubbing the end, said Blackie.

– You afraid to go Jew against Jew? Duddy asked. – They started it.

– There are kids watching, said Blackie. – You be the gentleman.

– We should go for chips anyway, said Suddy.

– How's your bum? Oz asked.

– Meh.

– Curling's not a contact sport, said Chickie.

– Did you know the most dangerous sport in the world is polo? Duddy said.

– Make that bullfighting, said Chickie.

– You know there was this guy once, watching a polo match, and a polo mallet flew out of a rider's hand and gave him a *knuck* in the head. Imagine the look on his face just before that mallet hit him.

The other curlers were now finished or finishing their last ends, ordering the stones, filing off red-cheeked along the walk, looking like they'd had a good time.

Tino and Michael MacGiligary came up to them. Blackie got off the mat and gave Tino one of his big smacking kisses. Tino looked uncomfortable.

– Where's *my* kiss? Duddy said to Tino, scrambling to his feet.

After Tino had been squeezed into juice by Duddy, Suddy, who didn't like to kiss, got up off the mat and gave Tino one of his shy smiles and a meek handshake. They had a little circle going.

– You win? Blackie asked Tino.

– Yeah. No thanks to me. I hogged a rock.

– Tell him I'm giving him my Raleigh when I get it out of the pound, said Duddy. – Tell him that.

– You just told him, said Chickie from below.

– Thanks, Duddy, said Tino.

– When it's spring, not now.

Out of the blue, Michael MacGiligary turned his fair head and said to Blackie:

– Is it true? Are they selling the club?

The kid had authority in his voice even when asking questions.

– That's what they say, said Blackie.

– *Cui bono?*

– What's a *cui bono?* Duddy asked.

– Who benefits? Oz said to him, getting up from the mat, leaving Chickie last man sitting.

– Are you going to stand for that? Michael asked them.

They thought about what to say to that.

– What are *you* going to do about it, Mr. Timmerman? Michael asked Blackie.

Chickie didn't like Blackie being pushed by this *shagitz pisher*, and seeing no one stick up for Blackie, he balanced on his fist to hoist himself up. A walrus would have made fewer attempts to get up and stand on its tail. After a final hoist, Chickie was on his toes, in the circle, and looking into Michael MacGiligary's face from close up to say:

– We're not going to have a rumble over it.

– You almost just did over a stone, said Michael.

– That was principle.

– I'm talking about the QV.

Chickie took time to think about what to say. He'd faced down *shkutzim* before, but this guy was different.

– I've got Max Foxman's quote, said Duddy.

– If it's what Max wants, it's what Max gets, said Chickie. – Nobody can buck Max Foxman.

– It's *noch nila*, said Suddy.

Tino looked at his father. No one was answering Michael seriously.

– Are you guys inclined to passive capitulation? Michael said.

Blackie wondered if 'you guys' meant them as a team or as a community: the Auschwitz thing.

– I've got his quote, Duddy said.

– They shouldn't get away with it.

They all looked at Michael as if he was selling hope.

– It's *noch nila*, said Suddy.

– What's *nock nila*? Michael asked.

– *Nila* is the last evening prayer, said Tino.

– And *nock*?

– *Noch*.

– 'Already.' Literally it means it's already evening prayers. He means 'It's too late', I guess.

– We're going to Kelekis's for chips, said Suddy.

– I've got his quote, said Duddy.

Michael looked puzzled; he wasn't used to so many non-sequiturs.

– They haven't sold the club yet, he said.

– Not yet. But you'll see. The money will wind up in a numbered account. I know these things. I know the show.

– He'll have to sway a majority of the curlers.

– You'll see. He'll get his majority. He's not a person in the people sense.

– And there's nothing more craven than a North End Jew, added Chickie.

– You're a North End Jew, Chickie, said Oz.

– So you mean the curlers have a say? Duddy asked.

– Of course we should have a say.

– You'll see, he'll convince everybody to vote his way, said Chickie.

– We're not having a vote, said Blackie. – They're the Executive.

– I don't know how he was re-elected, said Duddy. – Every year?

– He's a rube, said Duddy.

– Someone has to represent the rubes. Better a rube, said Oz.

– You voted for him, said Duddy, both index fingers pointing like a bull's horns at Oz.

– So did you, Duddy, said Oz, pointing back.

– How do you know who I voted for?

– It was unanimous, he volunteered.

– It's not unanimous if nobody else wants the hassle. But Max Foxman saw an angle.

– He loves the club, said Blackie, like we do. – His uncle was one of the founders.

– And pedophiles say they love children, said Chickie.

– So do cannibals, said Suddy.

– Cannibals aren't so bad after they've eaten, said Oz to Suddy.

– You can't buck Max, said Chickie. – The club is as good as gone.

– Let's not ice the puck just yet, said Michael. – To do what he wants to do, he needs a mandate. We have to defend the club.

– Easy to say, said Chickie.

– Easy to do, said Michael.

– How?

– We mobilize.

– Mass mobilization, said Tino.

– We'll smash Max Foxman.

From the way they looked at each other, Oz and Blackie had to be thinking how teenagers deformed reality so easily. They didn't know the world they were up against. All the Max Foxmans on every street corner.

– Nobody's going to make a to-do, said Chickie.

– We have to put the blocks to people, Michael said. – Resistance is a form of the sublime; it's irresistible.

Everyone looked confused.

– It's *noch nila*, said Suddy.

– Max Foxman owes us money, said Duddy.

– My advice? said Michael. – Get up a petition.

– A petition? Duddy asked.

– Get all the curlers to sign demanding a vote. Even the juniors and women curlers. This cannot be an Executive decision. Nobody gave Max Foxman omnibus powers. The QV is on the line. If you want to fight this thing, we want to help. We will formulate a special resolution. I will write the text.

– Do you know where Kelekis's is? Duddy asked Michael.

– I do, actually.

– We're going there.

– I had supper.

– Second supper.

– I could go for a hot dog, said Tino.

Blackie's car battery was iced dead. If Deirdre hadn't left him, she would have reminded him to change it. Duddy, who only had half a jumper cable, couldn't give him a boost, so they had to ride to the restaurant in Duddy's old Valiant station wagon, which was caked with filth. Someone had used their finger to write on the hatch window: 'wash me, pig.' Under the hatchback Blackie noticed pairs of fat white mice hugging together in sixteen loaf-sized cages with blue plastic floors, tiny doors, tiny drinking fountains, and tiny bins filled with sunflower seeds. The mouse smell made Blackie want to retch up Rita's jumbo hot dog and go straight home, but then he remembered that Deirdre wasn't there anymore, and it was a long time till bedtime. In the early days of their marriage, and after Tino was born, he'd sprint home from work like he was Jesse Owens. He didn't hurry home anymore.

– What's with the mice? he asked Duddy.

– It's my new business. Cancer research.

From Duddy's dazzled eyes, Blackie could tell he was embarked on one of his 'insatiable excitements,' as Oz called them, savouring attention, per usual, while showing off to Blackie about his business expertise.

– What do you know about cancer research?

– More than you.

– But I know 'zip.'

– I'm breeding white mice for this doctor out at the university: Dr. Davinsky.

52

– Toodle Davinsky's son?

– Mannie, yeah. He pays me two bucks a mouse. Delivered. Alive. Look at them. They're freezing, the little buggers.

– Are you breeding them in here?

– Over at Dee's. This is fresh cargo.

– Who's Dee?

– My lady friend. She's from the Cree nation. You should meet her, although it's winding down. I met her at the penitentiary. She was visiting some cousin she knew. Those people have lots of penal problems, you know. But they have seven different words for the word *goyim*. Even one for us. We're like *goyim* to them, too. They like to live near a river, she told me. So she lives on Scotia Street. She works for the March of Dimes, raising money for polio.

Duddy blasted the heat and drove leisurely at first, not wanting to bang the mice around too much. But when he got talking he started accelerating, taking a corner too tight. Blackie turned around to see if the mice were rolling on the cage floors. Maybe they'd hang on to the bars with their little paws? On one curve, the glove compartment fell open; Blackie saw enough parking tickets to wallpaper his front room.

– Your mice are going to freeze tonight. It's going below zero.

– If they're cold, they get cute, which is good for business. I'll leave the car running with the heater on while we're eating.

– If you leave it running, somebody might steal it.

– Not with mice in it.

Blackie glanced over at the gas gauge.

– You're almost out of gas, you know.

– We'll fill up at the Esso on Main. They've got Starburst of Bonuses there. I've got forty-eight tumblers already. But I gave Suddy a dozen.

– Those are good glasses.

– I always like a tumbler for a rum punch.

At the restaurant, Suddy and Duddy sat against the wall,

53

Chickie, Blackie, and Oz facing them. On the walls were framed photographs of Canadian and American celebrities. Liberace smiled hysterically from behind his white piano, his eyes directed at the wall opposite, at Nana Mouskouri in glasses with thick black frames.

– Do you think Liberace and her ever did it? Duddy asked.

– Liberace could get any woman he wants. Why would he *shtip* Nana Mouskouri?

– She probably gave him a BJ under the piano, said Chickie. – Look at that look on his face.

– The BJ is overrated, said Suddy innocently. – I could do that.

– Maybe she keeps her glasses on, said Duddy.

– If the owners hear you talk like that, they'll kick us out, said Blackie.

– My drive gets piping hot with a woman like that, said Duddy. – Dee looks a lot like Nana Mouskouri you know, but less Greek.

– Here comes your veal cutlets, said Suddy to him.

– Who's Dee? Chickie asked.

– And our chips, said Suddy. – Nice the way they brought it all at the same time. Only at Kelekis's.

– I'd love to have my portrait on the wall, said Duddy.

Everyone had ordered just chips and gravy, except Chickie, who was famished and had ordered a decent meal. They all went faux-gaga and emitted an exaggerated 'Ah' and raised their arms in the air as Chickie's breaded veal cutlets with gravy came off the tray first, followed by chips and gravy for the rest of them.

Chickie got ready to devastate his platter.

– Beautiful, he said.

– He can't eat all that, said Suddy.

– I should have ordered those, said Duddy.

– But you didn't, said Chickie.

– Let's switch.

– I'm not switching.

Duddy snatched Chickie's plate and Chickie grabbed it back

and, in the melee, Duddy managed to pinch, crimp, and scarf a cutlet.

– I'd have given you a bite, said Chickie to Duddy, and to the other guys:

– He always does that.

– I'm just horsing around, said Duddy, rolling his words around the wad of cutlet.

– It's just a cutlet, said Suddy to Chickie. – You have three more.

– It's not the cutlets; it's his getting his way.

– They gave you a generous portion.

There was silence at the table as they all began eating, each one of them into killing the thing that was going to kill them: hunger. They got into their thoughts as well.

The chips went down pretty fast, and they were left to watch Chickie work through his mashed potatoes and peas and cutlets with gravy on top. He trimmed the last two cutlets and cut them into perfect squares before dipping them in his extra gravy on the side. This only served to quicken everyone's hunger.

Oz said he was going to order a hot dog with the works when the waitress came back.

– You can't imagine how itchy this is, said Duddy, pulling Eddie Zachs's tam out through his fly and plunking it on the table.

– I'm eating here, said Chickie. – Chuck it on the floor.

Oz repeated that he was going to order a hot dog with the works when the waitress came back. Duddy, inspired, said he'd get a couple of hot dogs, too, and so did Blackie. Suddy thought he'd order some soup and saltine crackers.

– There goes the soup *mensch*. He'd order soup with soup.

– I'll get a hot dog, too, said Chickie.

– I thought Tino and Michael were coming, said Oz.

Chickie waved his hand wildly to call the waitress. His underarm sagged so much that it looked webbed to his ribs. The waitress came over and Chickie told her what to bring them.

– I'm not very happy about them selling the club, said Chickie.

– Gal darn Max Foxman, said Blackie.

– His wife Sophie has such a big mouth, said Duddy. – And she acts up at home. Nobody listens to her, so she acts up. She thinks because now she's got money she can say whatever she wants to him and people.

– She puts her mouth where her money is, said Oz.

– She falls asleep with her bank book in her hand. That's what I know, said Duddy.

– That's enough about Sophie Foxman, said Blackie. Duddy ignored him.

– Max doesn't even listen to her anymore. In fact, he got so mad at her five months ago at the cottage that he hasn't said a word to her since. He's that mad. She has no one to talk to.

– He should buy her a parrot, said Suddy, completely serious. They all cracked up except Blackie.

– She had shingles last year, said Duddy.

– That's enough, said Blackie.

– Who had shingles? said Chickie.

– Max Foxman's wife, said Duddy. – Sophie Foxman. Blackie got scrappy. – Stop. That's enough!

It was a relief when Tino and Michael walked into the restaurant and pulled up chairs, still talking to each other. Blackie wondered what had taken them so long to arrive but didn't ask. He didn't know whether anyone else had noticed Tino was always with Michael MacGiligary, and they were always talking.

They all stared at Michael in expectation.

– So, said Michael. – Passive capitulation to Max Foxman's simony or do you want to fight this thing?

The guys looked to Oz to say something.

– We should write that petition. Do something about the QV, like you said.

– No kidding around, said Blackie.

– We had to hear it from a *shagitz*, said Chickie.

– We should demand a special resolution and vote, said Michael.

– Did you order? said Suddy to Tino.

– Max is making an executive decision, said Blackie.

– We'd have to start canvassing, garner names to demand a vote. Fight this thing, said Oz.

– Make a real to-do, said Duddy. – And when it comes down to the vote, we'll be the ones sitting shot rock. I'd like to see his face. The look on it.

– It's all politics, said Chickie.

– Stay out of politics, said Suddy to Tino.

– Pearl would sign it, said Oz. – He's an activist.

– He's a fucking communist, said Chickie. – Pearl'd sign it just to not give the money to Israel.

– It's the communist line, said Blackie.

– He has a Zuken lawn sign in front of his house, said Suddy. – All year round. They embedded it in wet cement. I saw them pour it. A dog stepped in it and it's still there.

– I voted for him municipally, said Oz.

– The dog's still in the cement? Chickie asked.

– I meant his paw, said Suddy.

– So there's a dog with three paws on the street?

– Did you guys order? asked Suddy.

– At the counter. They're bringing ours.

– I'm treating you, said Suddy.

– You'll get no argument from me, said Chickie. – He might be a liability, Pearl; a guy like that.

– Still. It's a signature. It's a vote, said Oz.

– The North Enders won't buck Max Foxman, said Blackie. – He organises the junkets to Vegas.

– He used to throw me out the window at school, said Suddy to Michael.

– They're chicken shits, said Chickie.

– Who? Michael asked.

– The North Enders.

– We're North Enders, said Suddy.

– Who's going to write the petition? Blackie asked. – Oz?

– I don't really have time.

– Tino, you're the writer in the family, aren't you? Duddy asked.

– I'm studying physics.

Duddy, like Suddy and the other guys, had known Tino since before he could talk, and Blackie didn't know how many times he'd told Duddy that Tino was in sciences, pre-med. But ever since Tino skipped a grade, Duddy assumed that anyone that clever had to be a writer.

– We'll write it, said Michael.

– I think we ought to do it fast, said Oz. – We've wasted a lot of time already.

– Once they write up the petition, we can meet at my house tomorrow after work, said Suddy.

– They've got university, said Blackie. – That's giving them just one day.

– How long can it take to write a petition? Blackie asked Michael.

– We'd have to get the text just right, said Michael.

Once the hot dogs came, they were all sorry they didn't have any chips left to go with them, so they ordered more chips and more coffee, all except Suddy, who was happy with a coke float.

Blackie nibbled his hot dog slowly, knowing that when it was finished he'd have to drive with Oz to his car, get out the cables, open the hood, start his car, drive home, where he'd long for company: Deirdre's company. It would be nice if Deirdre were home, to have someone to turn to before falling asleep. The curling tonight, the snack, it had all helped winnow down the time, but he just couldn't adjust to this new routine of not having a routine, like when Deirdre and Tino were home.

Suddy's voice roused him from his thoughts, and he noticed his plate was empty. His coffee cup was being refilled and the guys were talking about Sophie Foxman again.

– What did she do wrong? Suddy asked Duddy. – How come Max isn't talking to her? You said she did something wrong.

– She did something bad. At the cottage. In Gimli. It's lakefront.

– How bad? Chickie asked.

Duddy prolonged the suspense that went with gossip of this calibre with squinting and wise nodding.

– Do you even know what it is? Chickie asked.

Duddy reached across the table to scratch Chickie's inside elbow, but Chickie was too fast for him this time, pulling back his arm.

– I know, said Duddy. – Any guy'd be mad, too. She argued with him in front of his family. She criticised him in front of his family.

– His whole family? said Suddy.

– The whole *mishpocheh*. Then she said something that ended the argument. He won't speak to her. Not now. Not never. She has to write him notes on paper.

– How do you know all this about Max Foxman? Chickie asked.

– He pries, said Suddy.

– So when can you get the *text* written by? Oz asked Michael and Tino.

The two kids exchanged looks.

– How about a week?

– That's a bit late.

– Thursday?

– We can meet at my house, said Suddy. – The *goya* comes in Thursday mornings. So it'll be clean.

– Can you get it to us before we meet on Thursday? asked Oz.

– I'll drop copies off at Shneerson's, said Tino.

– By Tuesday? – We have to read it first.

Tino looked at Michael and then they gave Oz an assenting shrug.

– I should go, said Duddy. – I left the car running with the heat on.

– Get the check, Oz said to Chickie. – It's late. Ruthie's going to kill me if I wake her up.

– I'm treating the kids, said Suddy.

Outside, in the freezing night, standing under the Kelekis's marquis in snow as hard as iron, they said goodbye and made it quick. Blackie thought it was odd that Tino wasn't coming home with him but going to the *shmutz* instead.

Tino and Michael MacGiligary, shivering because they were wearing only leather jackets, no toques, no gloves, thanked Suddy for treating them. Tino ducked Blackie's smacking kiss and walked off with Michael, talking and talking.

– Still want a jump or should I drive you home? Oz asked Blackie.

– I'd better. I'll need the car tomorrow to get to the office. I hope you won't wake Ruthie up.

FIVE

Blackie stood in fresh powdery snow up to his cuffs, a cigarette between his lips. He pressed the doorbell a third time.
The guys were meeting to discuss the petition that Michael
MacGiligary had written 'to save the club from Max Foxman's
simony.' Michael had crafted the petition in Bolshie prose, which
Blackie needed a dictionary to get through. There were lots of
good words, though.

He looked up at the sour December light and saw a hard kernel
of snow fall into the eaves above. Another hit him on the nose,
another on his lashes. It was only 4:00 o'clock in the afternoon
but the sky was darkening swiftly as a broad press of clouds
squeezed the remaining light out of the horizon. Suddy's porch
bulb, which he always left on, was burning out furiously with a
reddish twinkle and a crackle inside the globe. If Suddy didn't
open up soon, he'd have to go around to the back door. It was
always left unlocked, but there was a lot more snow on the walk
around the house, and he'd get snow in his socks.

– Suddy, open up! He rang again, then pounded on the metal
screen door.

– Suddy! Open the door! It's freezing outside.

– The door's open! Suddy yelled from inside.

– No, it's not!

Suddy unlocked the inside door and looked at Blackie through
the screen.

– You still have your screen windows on, said Blackie.

Suddy hadn't bothered, like every year, to take off the summer

61

screens in the fall and put up the storms, but that meant come spring he didn't have to take off the storms to put up the screens.

– Blackie. Hi. You look different through the screen. Are you cold?

– Cold? No.

A blast of hot air hit Blackie as soon as he stepped inside. He knew he was in for a charitable roast. Suddy kept the thermostat high: he liked to prance around barefoot in just a t-shirt, an open flannel shirt and Stanfield underwear that was stretched out at the crotch.

– Where's everybody? Blackie asked, slipping off his half rubbers on the doormat.

– You're the first. Don't step in your own slush.

Blackie followed Suddy through the front room — where purple drapes wailed — and into the kitchen, Suddy Joffe sensations hitting him one after the other like knocks on the head with a wooden spoon. They stirred childhood memories of Mona and Morris and Duddy and Suddy before Morris Joffe had died. Now Mona lived in the small bungalow next door with Duddy, a house Suddy had bought them when Mona became a shut-in. Blackie remembered what she'd called Duddy: maladjusted.

Andy Williams was singing *Moon River* on the record player in the TV console. That cheered Blackie up. There was a smell of last night's boiled perogies from what was once Bill Grod's diner. Bill had been a good friend of Suddy's, 'the ideal friend,' Suddy called him. After he sold the diner — something the family forced him to do — he'd moved to Toronto, also under instructions from his family. Suddy stayed in bed for two weeks after Bill left. He's despondent, Duddy had told Blackie when he went to visit. Blackie saw him just that once, on top of his bedspread crying, his face collapsed inward. He'd never seen Suddy cry like that. He'd never seen anyone cry from heartbreak like that.

– Where's Tino and Mike? Suddy asked.

– I don't know. They're coming.

Blackie looked at the back door, which gave way to the winter kitchen, and wondered who'd come through the front and who through the back. When he looked out the window, he saw Suddy's cab in the carport. It was plugged into a steel post, the sagging cable etching a sad smile against the snow.

He sat down at the Formica table, which pitched because the kitchen linoleum bulged under one of the legs. The table was piled up with food; bags of Old Dutch barbecue chips and maybe three pounds of fatty corned beef on butcher paper from Mellors Meat Market. Blackie's stomach grumbled and squirted.

– Oz is bringing the bread, Suddy said apologetically.

– How come Oz isn't bringing the corned beef?

– He always brings the corned beef. I don't like to take advantage.

Blackie knew that Tino preferred Oz's corned beef but that he wouldn't say no to Mellors either, which could get pretty fatty for Blackie's taste.

– Should I make room for the plates?

– Oh, plates. Sure, said Suddy.

There were some Star Burst of Bonuses tumblers out on the table for the bottled drinks lined up in bowling pin formation beside the corned beef. A single bottle of beer was the front pin.

– I'll run over and get Duddy. Maybe he forgot, Suddy said.

– Put some pants on first, said Blackie.

– I'm just going to the back door.

– It's cold out there, Suddy.

– It's only 10 below.

Suddy got his stockinged feet into rubber galoshes and buckled them up high and tight till they squeaked. Then he dashed into the winter kitchen and out of the house, crunching snow to Mona's back door. Blackie lit a cigarette and watched him. He smiled and batted ash into the sink. Then he put out the plates and went to the bathroom.

– Your teeth are chattering he said to Suddy when he came

back in.

– I should've put on a parka.

– Or some pants.

– Duddy is sleeping, said Suddy. – Mona's going to wake him up. She's not a hundred percent.

After Morris Joffe died, Mona never left the house; she thought people whispered about her when she walked past.

– So this friend of Tino's? This Michael MacGiligary? Is he coming or what?

– They said they'd both be here at 5:00 o'clock.

– I should put some pants on. What do you want to drink? Do you want a 7-Up? I've got Jersey Cream.

– I'm okay.

– Do you want a corned beef sandwich and some chips?

– There's no bread.

– Chickie's bringing it. Or Oz.

– How much corned beef is that?

– About four pounds when I bought it, but I think I ate a pound already.

– That kid knows how to write, said Blackie. – Did you read the petition?

– He's a good curler. Respects his skip.

– Tino says the girls at school think he looks like Glenn Gould.

– That's classical music.

– You're very erudite.

– Me and Mona used to watch Gould on CBC. She used to like the classics. He had his own show and orchestra to play Mozart or things.

– Michael plays Mozart on the piano too, said Blackie. – Tino says.

– Mozart was a genius when it came to music.

When the conversation ran out of gas, Suddy went to put some pants on.

Blackie heard banging on the front door and let Tino and

Michael in. Blackie gave Tino a big smacking kiss on his cheek, which made Tino blush. They stamped snow off their Beatle boots and walked along the plastic runner into the kitchen where the linoleum buckled and popped under them.

– There's corned beef on the table, Suddy shouted from his bedroom.

Suddy came back wearing pleated jeans with creases and cuffs just as Duddy pushed the back door open, stamping his galoshes in the winter kitchen to make a whirl of snow.

– I just dreamt that I was in a hollow log, he shouted.

Duddy shifted his body into a Sumo stance and opened his arms to hug Tino, like he had when Tino was a kid. Duddy hugged him till he was breathless. Then, when Duddy asked for his kiss, Tino had to give Duddy one on the cheek. That made him blush in front of Michael.

Chickie and Oz arrived next, neither of them in a good mood because they had trudged the unshovelled walk around the house.

– Don't you have a doorbell that works? Chickie asked.

– The back door's always open.

Chickie unzipped his parka and out tumbled loaves of rye bread onto the kitchen table. He hiked up his pants and said:

– Christmas lights are up everywhere.

– Bugger it's getting cold out, said Oz.

Chickie and Oz handed their parkas to Suddy, like everyone else was doing.

– Colder than Max Foxman's smile, said Duddy.

– When did you dream you were in a hollow log? Suddy asked Duddy.

– What'd we miss? Oz asked.

– Just now. Napping in bed, said Duddy.

– According to Freud, hollow things are vaginas, said Michael MacGiligary.

– *The Interpretation of Dreams*, said Oz, examining the

competition's corned beef on the table.

Suddy went off with all the parkas and jackets, and dumped them on the chesterfield in the front room.

– Women's tiny parts? said Duddy. – Really?

– Not men's parts, said Chickie, sniggering.

– Did you bring the bread? Duddy asked Chickie.

– What's this? A cow? said Chickie, pointing to the bread on the table.

– Sit, said Suddy.

– We're not dogs, said Chickie.

They all sat.

– I mean is there really a book about how to explain dreams? Duddy asked Oz. – Is there? he repeated, turning to Michael MacGiligary.

– Yes, said Michael. – Freud was one of the three Masters of Suspicion. He suspected that behind our actions stood the invisible mountain of the unconscious.

– He called it a mountain? Chickie asked.

– What we think we decide to do may be the unconscious desires that drive us, Michael answered.

– If Mohammed won't go to the mountain, it's because Mohammed prefers the beach, said Oz.

– I can interpret dreams without a book, said Duddy. – Did Freud make money from his book?

– Maybe you should write one, said Tino.

– I could write a book like that, said Duddy. – I'm psychic.

– You could.

– Make yourselves sandwiches, said Suddy. – What are you waiting for? I put the mustard somewhere here somewhere.

– Organization! said Oz. – Who's going to cut the bread?

– Me! said Duddy, appropriating the bread knife.

– Why you? Chickie asked.

– I know bread, that's why me, said Duddy – Where's the butter?

– It's right there.

Duddy vigorously sawed thick slices of rye bread, spraying crumbs like shrapnel, sending up puffs of flour.

– Ever been to bed with a Chinawoman, you guys? Duddy asked Tino and Michael.

– Duddy, Suddy said. – They go to university.

– Getting any action there? Duddy said to Michael and Tino.

– Didn't you work at a bakery, Duddy? Oz asked. – Duddy?

– My first job. I used to lick my fingers to roll the bagel dough. Old man Feld used to slap me silly when he saw me do that. But he knew how to make bagels. Fair is fair.

They improvised an assembly line. Duddy sliced, Tino layered on the corned beef, Blackie spread the mustard and Oz put the top slices of bread over the corned beef, then Chickie cut them in half and placed the sandwiches on plates.

They dug in. Duddy grabbed a sandwich and smeared butter on the top with the bread knife.

– Kosher topping, anyone? Chickie asked.

– This is how Max Foxman *shmears* people, said Duddy. – *Gib a kook.*

The others watched Duddy smear on more butter and then bite into a sandwich shellacked with the stuff. Butter, crust and corned beef disappeared into his mouth leaving a greasy trace around his lips.

– Is that kosher, Duddy? said Chickie. – Butter with corned beef?

Duddy's face cried out to answer but his mouth was crammed.

– He can't get it up to answer a question, said Chickie.

– It's perfectly kosher, said Oz, except for the corned beef.

– Mellors is kosher like Milwaukee Kosher is kosher, said Duddy, swallowing hard.

– Do you think kosher food is really kosher? Suddy asked. – Mona kept a kosher house.

– It's really a business, said Oz.

– Big business, said Duddy. – Goes to show. What's the point of keeping kosher when the kosher food isn't really kosher? And what do you do with food you ate ten years ago you find out was *traif.* You can't throw up what you ate ten years ago.

– You can't get real kosher in this city, said Oz who knew a thing about the butcher business, his own not even pretending to be kosher. He even sold bacon and Crisco.

– There isn't a critical mass of Jews in Winnipeg for true kosher, said Chickie.

– I know some critical Jews, said Oz.

– You can only get real kosher in Toronto, said Chickie.

– Thank God you can still get good bread here.

– At City Bread? I'm not going back there, said Duddy. – They look at me funny. Max Foxman shops there. He's a *shvantz.*

– Why aren't you eating? Chickie asked Michael, grabbing his arm.

Michael had started with a few courtesy nibbles.

– He's eating, said Blackie. – He's just not stuffing his mouth. Leave him alone.

– He eats like a sophisticate, said Suddy.

– Let him eat.

Michael was gnawing slowly because the sandwich was twice the size of how wide he could open his mouth.

– Look. Even he doesn't put butter on, said Chickie to Duddy. – And he's entitled.

– Max Foxman is a phoney guy, said Duddy to Michael. – You know that, don't you? If he wasn't rich, people'd think he was stupid.

Michael and Tino exchanged smiles, which didn't go unnoticed by Blackie. Suddy took a swig of his beer and put the bottle between his legs to save space on the table.

– Talking of *shvantzes,* said Duddy. – You know, once when Max Foxman was a kid, he told us he whacked off thinking of the Queen.

– Which queen? Suddy asked.

– Queen Elizabeth was just a child then, said Oz.

– King George VI's wife. The Queen Mother they call her.

– She's a lush, said Suddy.

– Max wasn't thinking of her in that capacity, said Oz.

– Anyway, didn't she have big tits! I mean big ones! said Duddy.

– Not nice talk, said Blackie.

– I have to admit, said Duddy, Max Foxman got me thinking after he told me that. Why not with royalty? I had her daughter once or twice. Once on the day of her coronation. So she wasn't a minor. I might have been the only one to do that to her on her coronation, said Duddy.

Everyone except Blackie stopped chewing to laugh at that.

– But she wouldn't know that, said Oz.

– How did that make you feel? Chickie asked.

– Happy and glorious.

Even Blackie had to laugh at that, but then he said:

– The shame is on you, Duddy. It makes you not so different from Max Foxman. That's what that makes you.

Duddy frowned.

– She would never know, so what's the harm?

– God save her from that, said Chickie.

– God save the Queen! said Oz.

Orange crush came out of Tino's nose.

– Her mother was a lush, said Suddy.

– Still is, said Chickie.

– Max Foxman doesn't shop at City Bread, said Blackie to Duddy.

– He doesn't do his own shopping. He has a wife for that, said Chickie.

– Miss Tuchus 1973, said Duddy.

Blackie felt mud in his mouth but managed to say – Don't insult Sophie. It's inappropriate. It's going too far.

– After what he did to the Queen? Chickie asked.

– She always wears a shift, said Duddy.

– The Queen?

– Sophie Foxman.

– She has a hefty profile, said Chickie.

– Glass houses, said Oz.

– And her tits come out the bottom of her cups, said Duddy. – I can tell a woman's bra size from that.

– Don't start, said Blackie. – I'm warning you.

She has a double chin like a bull's, said Duddy. – And what I know is that it's not only her ass that's fat. Go ahead. Ask me what I mean by that.

– The kids, Duddy, said Blackie.

– What do you mean by that, Duddy? said Chickie.

– Don't talk about Sophie Foxman like that, said Blackie. He blushed.

– I'm talking about the opposite of ass. She has such a fat one you can put it in bent. What about that?

– Feh, said Chickie.

– Why would you do that? Oz asked Duddy.

Everyone laughed except for Tino and Michael. They were adverse to that talk.

Chickie drummed the table with his palms.

– I mean, Duddy said, is you can fold it in like dough.

– I thought you once said you liked them like that, said Chickie.

– I'm just saying. You don't have to take a lot of stabs.

– But you like them like that?

– I do, said Duddy. – I like them substantial. You know, Max Foxman — the bum — always has something going on the side. He tells Sophie that her legs are too prickly when she shaves them.

– How do you know these things? Chickie asked.

– She told me.

– Big fib.

– He's getting it on the side. Sophie Foxman told me. On the side, from the back, in the front. She told me she would bite his

business off one night out of vengeance. In one bite. If I ever
wanted to get back at Max Foxman, I know what I'd do.

They laughed at that, even Michael MacGiligary and Tino.
Blackie's face started to relax.

Duddy, impervious to it all, said:

– Sophie Foxman hasn't done it in months, I know. Max doesn't
talk to her even. If I ever wanted to get back at Max, I'd . . .

– Bite it off? Chickie interrupted.

– I'd seduce her. I'm already getting her innuendoes flashing at
me. How she looks at me from those blue eyes! She could write
poems with them.

– You don't have the gumption, said Chickie.

– I have the gumption to do anything. She suffers from neglect.
Marital neglect. Mind you, that's a good word. Neglect. The click
at the end. Sounds make a word.

– What's in a name, said Oz. – A rose by any other.

Duddy thought that was a cue.

– Take Lilly Gales's name. She was married to Marty Lazer,
the big lawyer from Saskatchewan, and so Lilly Gales became
Mrs. Martin Lazer, or Lilly Lazer. People liked her until she had
an affair with Jack Minnick, but Jack Minnick dumped her and
handed her off to some of his friends, but even so, in comes
Abe Rosenberg, who was always in love with Lilly Lazer when
she was a Gales, and on his own wedding day, he and his fian-
cée, Diamond Mohen, were registered at The Bay. The Bloomstocks were invited, but they didn't know what to buy them, so I
suggested hand towels, but Mrs. Bloomstock said she wouldn't
know their size. That's how stupid she was. So on the same
morning as the wedding with Diamond Mohen, before the cere-
mony, Abe goes to see Lilly Lazer, and he tells her that if she says
she'd marry him he wouldn't marry Diamond Mohen!

– Lilly Lazer, Lilly Gales: neither here nor there, said Chickie.

– I'd seduce her, that's what I'd do, said Duddy.

– Who?

– Sophie Foxman. Even though she's no bar mitzvah mother anymore. Her kids are at university already. One has a gambling problem, and the other too. I'd seduce her if it wasn't for what's happened completely to her looks.

– You're no Adonis either, said Oz.

– I'd seduce her like a Mrs. Robinson. Woo her. It'd be no bother. She's sensual by nature. I'd give her attentions. I'd listen to her *tsouris*. I'd think up compliments she can believe in.

– You'd be using her, said Blackie.

– And then I'd get her in bed. And in the lie-behind-her position I'd feel her bosoms ripe and moist. And squeeze them. And feel up her front legs from the knees up, shaved properly or not, right up to her tiny parts. And, and, and . . . That'd make him suffer. Sophie told me that that'd kill him. She almost wrote me an invitation by hand.

– Doing a thing like that to someone will turn around and bite you in the ass, said Oz. – Mark my words.

Tino and Michael couldn't look at each other for fear they'd blurt out laughing. They found spots on the ceiling to focus on.

– That's such a bullshit story, said Chickie.

– He thinks he's a *macher*, said Duddy. – We'll see what kind of *macher* with his wife cheating on him.

– He owns Milwaukee Kosher, don't forget that, said Chickie. – Half the city buys his *versht*.

– So? The other half buys Chicago Kosher, said Suddy. – Why isn't there a Winnipeg Kosher?

– He's going to get away with closing the club, you wait and see, said Duddy. – I'm calling it.

– He buggered over the people who keep kosher and now he's buggering over kosher curling, said Chickie.

– He's buggered all of us with a summer boner, said Duddy. – He pretends he's a big Jew, big kosher guy. You know he has four sets of dishes. Milchedicka, fleishedicka, pesadicka . . .

– What's the fourth?

– He has a set for *traif*!

Michael asked Tino what *traif* meant. Tino translated and they all laughed again, this time Michael with them.

– They want to destroy our heritage, Oz said. – Closing the club. They have no respect.

– That's the callous rich for you, Mr. Oz, said Michael.

– Callous is Max Foxman to a T, said Duddy. – If he winds up the club, I'm going to seduce his wife on the QT. Believe you me! She's lonely for it. And there's nothing that would make him suffer more than finding out about it.

– So not on the QT? Chickie asked.

– I'm not going to do it when he's home in front of him in the front room.

– I don't like your fibs, said Chickie.

More sandwiches were made, thicker than the first batch because Duddy was still cutting the bread.

– They're too thick, said Oz.

– No one's telling you to eat the crusts.

– I have Jell-o for dessert, said Suddy.

The mound of fatty corned beef had begun to diminish. Duddy clawed Chickie's elbow, shoved a Duddy-thick sandwich with butter in front of his chin, and said:

– Taste that now. That's a sandwich.

– Go away.

– There's not going to be enough corned beef, said Oz.

– I got four pounds, said Suddy.

– That wasn't four pounds, said Oz, professionally.

– We didn't come here to talk about corned beef, said Blackie.

– I think we should get down to business, said Michael. – Have you all read the petition?

Chickie waved his sandwich at him.

– It's unsignable.

– Michael, let me tell you what we're trying to do here, said Oz. – We read your petition, and you write like an angel. We all

73

think that.

Michael's ears went red. Duddy swallowed some pop and smacked his lips.

Oz unfolded a double-sided three-page single-spaced 2,000 word manuscript and set it on the table after pushing aside the glossy butcher paper. He flattened the creases of the petition a few times.

– We're not criticizing your prose, but what I want to say is that we need this petition to be just right.

– I know, said Michael. – That's why we put so much work into it.

– We'll be the ones shouting BINGO, said Duddy. – We have to come out against Max Foxman with a gun blazing in each hand. Right from the line of scrimmage.

– I think we should say thanks to Mike and Tino first for coming, said Suddy, and for writing the petition.

– You do look like Glenn Gould, said Chickie to Michael.

They all looked at Michael MacGiligary to check the resemblance.

– Glenn Gould's Jewish, said Chickie. – His name was Gold. But from so much anti-Jewish hatred they had to change it to Gould.

– I heard that too, said Blackie.

– The Jews are excellent musicians, said Chickie. – It's in the genes. Horowitz. Perlman. Menuhin. Stern.

– Don't forget Mozart, said Tino.

– Musical genius is in the genes, said Chickie.

– They even had a band at Auschwitz, said Suddy. – I read that.

– Actually, said Michael MacGiligary – Glenn Gould's family wasn't Jewish.

They all stopped to look at him.

– Their name *was* Gold; they changed it to Gould so that they wouldn't be mistaken for Jews.

– Still, said Chickie, there's a connection somewhere there.

– What does that mean? said Oz.

– It means what it means.

– Oz, I know not a single Gold in this city who isn't Jewish, said Blackie.

– What about Ira Gold? His mother isn't Jewish, Oz asked.

– She acts it, said Duddy.

– Ira's father was from Toronto, said Oz.

– That's been my point for years, said Duddy. – Toronto's different. It took me 38 hours on the bus to get there, sitting.

– You can get a callus on your ass like that, said Chickie.

– That's the real Canada, said Suddy.

– It's a shithole, said Duddy. – They think they're better than Winnipeggers. And it's windy every day. It gets in your head that wind. Howling like a sick kid. It gives you a headache and drives you insane. Windy cities breed Nazism. Like Austria.

Michael bent a shoulder down and pulled Tino into an aside, murmuring.

– I don't think there's the opportunity for us here that I thought. Politically, I mean. – Why did we get into this?

– You wanted to. This is what the working class is like.

– I have no idea what social class this is.

Tino nodded, thinking of something cogent to say in reply, when he noticed Blackie watching. He whispered to Michael:

– Are you having second thoughts? You can always curl at the Winter Club.

– I'm not going back there. It's still restricted.

– I think this is a good cause, said Tino. – Saving the rink.

– My parents would get so smug if the QV closed.

Suddy went up to the fridge and opened it.

– I have chocolate milk, said Suddy. – I have BC apples. And, more pop?

He snatched out three more soft drinks between the fingers of one hand and popped the tops of a couple using the bottle opener screwed into the side of the counter, next to the cutlery drawer.

– Where's the pickles? Chickie asked Suddy.

– By Duddy's stone. Between the kettle and the bananas.

On the counter by the kettle, there was a 44-pound granite curling rock, dove grey with speckles, looming larger than it would on the ice because it was out of context.

– It's making the counter sag, said Chickie.

– Never noticed that stone before, said Oz.

– Duddy gave it to me, said Suddy.

Michael stood up to look at it and right away noticed it was from the Winter Club.

– They wouldn't serve me in the sit down restaurant because I'm a Jew. I had to have a grilled cheese at the sandwich counter. *Mishlockt yiddin*, said Duddy.

– How did you steal it? asked Oz.

– I put it up my sweater.

They were all on their feet now, bending in to examine the stone, holding their sandwiches in their fists, their cheeks bulging and chewing.

– Nice stone, said Michael MacGiligary swallowing hard, pointing to it with his sandwich. – It's like a Duchamp readymade.

– Beautiful, said Blackie.

– 'Winnipeg Winter Club,' said Chickie, swiveling his chin and reading the engraving. – 200 River Avenue.

– *Anti-semiten*, said Duddy. – *Mishlockt yiddin*.

– How long have you had that stone? Tino asked.

– Three years.

– That's a beaut of a stone, said Oz.

– What's it doing here? Chickie asked, meaning on the counter. – A paper weight?

– I like to have nice things.

– That stone was a gift from me, said Duddy with pride. – Mona doesn't like anything stolen in her house; it's against the Jewish Torah, she says.

– Mothers, said Oz.

– Anybody want another sandwich?

– No corned beef, said Chickie.

They worked on finishing their drinks.

– I think we should talk about the petition. Maybe the kids have to study, said Blackie, pointing his chin at Michael and Tino.

– Education is a great thing, said Oz. – I wish I had gone to university.

– You're smart enough without university, Suddy said to Oz.

– Just think of Einstein's brain for a second, said Duddy. – When he died and they took it out, it was so big the doctors were astonished. I'd like to have seen the look on their faces. Holding a big brain like that. Had to be Jewish. They took out Kennedy's brain, too. Big for Texas. In the end he preferred blondes to Jackie. Blondes have thinner hair, though, and not luxuriant like brunettes. I guess JFK knew that. And I'm talking top and bottom. But blondes aren't as phoney as people say. I once saw a cherry blonde canoeing by the banks of the Assiniboine River behind City Park. There was a mist-like fog over the river. But she saw me through it. She winked at me and paddled her canoe to shore. So I waded right in. You know what she said to me when her canoe bumped me?

– Don't get in? said Chickie.

– She said I must be some kisser. And she hadn't even tried my kisses. She was reading poems in a mini skirt.

– So not a canoe, said Chickie.

– Can we get back to the petition? Michael asked.

– With me leaning into the canoe, knowing where to touch with my hands, I had her breathing like a bellows.

– Shut up, Duddy! said Chickie.

Duddy made no attempt to conceal the fact that Chickie had hurt his feelings. He slung his dickie around to dissemble.

– The petition? Can we get back to the petition, Oz said, pointing to the typed sheets before him.

– Then I got attacked by a swan, Duddy said. – They're vicious, with their beaks. Bright red like blood.

– I've never heard this story, said Oz.

– Where did the swan come from? Tino asked.

– We should get up a petition to have a casino, said Suddy.

– We're talking about the petition for the QV, said Blackie.

– But the swan didn't deter me, said Duddy.

– Are you sure it was a swan, said Chickie. – Maybe it was a Canada Goose.

– I read your first draft, said Oz to Michael. – While passionate and well written . . .

– Kid writes like an angel, interrupted Chickie.

– This bit about the founder of the QV, said Oz.

– Benny Mendel, said Blackie.

Oz ran his finger under a line in the first paragraph. They all peered at the text like they were reading the holy scrolls.

– You say here that his father and grandfather were *rabbits* in Posen.

– *Rabbis*, said Tino, sticking a finger on the petition. – That's a typo. My fault. I typed it up.

– I for one thing think the start is too long, said Chickie.

– The preamble, said Oz.

– That's a good word, said Duddy. – But how come I don't have a copy?

– I gave you one yesterday, said Blackie.

– I think I left it at Dee's house. She's the reader. That's what's good about the March of Dimes. There's always reading material in the waiting room.

– But did you read it, Duddy?

– I had a glance at it. I read too much that day. She read it to me.

– What did you read too much that day? said Chickie.

– Lay off him, Chickie, said Suddy.

– What I'm getting at, Mike, said Oz, is that I don't really think it's such a political to-do. They, Max and those guys –

– The South End pieces of shit, interrupted Duddy.

– Just don't want to drive from the South End to the North End anymore, Oz interrupted him. – We don't want to drive from the North End to the South End. Now, don't take umbrage with me, Michael, but I have to be critical about your petition here.

– None taken, Mr. Oz.

– Why do you call him Mr. Oz? Chickie asked. – It's just Oz.

Then Blackie made a point straight to Michael MacGiligary:

– It's a laziness issue, said Blackie. – They're too lazy to drive to the North End.

– They're acting like communists, said Duddy. – They want to impose themselves on us because we're from the North End. They want to take the club away, like the communists in Russia. They want to show they're the ruling class.

– There's no curling in Russia, Duddy, said Chickie.

– Duddy's right, said Michael.

Duddy shone in his vindication.

– In an amusing way, this *is* a class issue. The rich guys are going to tear down the QV. They're going to ravage the community you have built. That is what capitalism does: it over-individuates and alienates. It devours its own traditions, dissolves them in false modernity, demolishes the 'sensuous human activity' that is invested in an object or in a tradition, and it turns you into one-dimensional man.

– I don't think we should say all that in the petition, said Blackie. – No one understands what you mean by one-dimensional man. I for one didn't.

– Keep it plain and *poshet*, said Suddy.

– We'll have to scotch a whole bunch of crap from it, said Chickie.

– We have to stickhandle the problem, said Duddy.

Michael MacGiligary stared down at his clean plate and then looked up into their attentive faces.

– Politics is power plus initiative. I think you have to motivate your side while patiently educating it. Patiently explain, as Lenin said.

– We have to thrash those bums, said Duddy. – Starting with Max Foxman.

– Who did you say he looks like? Chickie asked Suddy. – Glenn Gould?

– I'd like to meet him, said Suddy. – He used to have a TV show Mona liked.

– He's a hermit. He lives in Toronto. You can't meet him, said Oz.

– You're not getting me to go back to Toronto, said Duddy. – No way. I had enough of Toronto when I was there. It's not level, like Winnipeg. It's a city on a tilt, and you get 'dizzy Gillespie.' And you know what I think of Jews who move to Toronto. Don't start me up on that. But it's very similar to my thoughts on Toronto Jews. I was at the bus station at night there in the dark — they shut the lights off at midnight, not like Winnipeg's which has the lights on until dawn — and a big handsome woman with gorgeous pink cheeks and black black hair winked at me with both eyes.

– That's blinking, said Chickie.

– She was carrying a bag of chickens to fry up and we hit it off. We sat down on one of those bus benches and started getting cute in the dark. I think she had a small hatchet in the bag with the chickens, so I assumed she was from the farm and had brought the chickens to market. I remember it was Yom Kippur because there were no Jewish-looking people in the station. She told me that she liked my rawhide car coat, the fleece-lined one. That's the best memory I have of Toronto if you ask me. 'With *your* eyes,' she said to me, 'you could be a nature poet.'

– Are you the horniest man in Winnipeg? Chickie asked.

– I never heard that story either, said Oz.

– I did, said Chickie, but in the story it was Edmonton.

– I like love, said Duddy. – I'm going to be doing it until I'm 200. Next to getting money, the sweetest dream is to be in love. And nature poetry. I could have written that poem *Flanders Fields* in school. Soon as I heard it.

– He died young, said Oz. – John McCrae. Pneumonia.

– Poets should never die, Suddy said.

– Look, Michael, said Oz. – I think the petition just needs to be simplified. This is a friendly club. We can't call Max Foxman and his friends 'class enemies.'

– We have a friendly club, said Suddy. – Nothing like school at all.

– She said I was a sweet talker, said Duddy.

– Sweet talker is not a compliment, said Chickie.

Chickie flicked his hand with the chocolate ring, pointed a finger at Oz.

– You shouldn't have let them write the petition. See? See what happens if you let little kids get into your bed? You wake up in wet pyjamas.

– We have to stand up to them, said Michael.

– What if they have a nightmare? said Suddy. – You have to let them in your bed.

– The guys are too afraid of Max Foxman, said Chickie. – Especially the North End guys. Or anybody who wants to go to Vegas — South End or North End.

– Other guys organize junkets, too, said Blackie.

Michael turned to Oz. – As Marcuse said, this is a case of 'repressive tolerance for power.' We have to motivate our side so they can fight their own repressive tolerance.

– Michael, look, that's the problem with your language, said Oz. – Nobody understands what repressive tolerance means.

– Ask me what happened then, said Duddy?

– When then?

– With the girl on the bench in Toronto, said Duddy. – Because she was enjoying how I was petting her — her tiny parts were humming like a dragonfly — when all of a sudden her bag of chickens with the little axe started moving. Just when she started cooing and contracting because I was bringing her along, a headless chicken wriggled out of her bag and walked across the bus station. Didn't matter it was dark there.

– Sure it wasn't a swan? said Chickie.

– Chrissakes, Duddy.

– Well, maybe there's some language that could be worked on, said Tino. – We could titivate the text.

– You could learn how to spell *rabbis*, too, said Chickie.

– How long did it take you guys to write this up? Oz asked Tino.

– Days. Not counting the typing. It took days to write this text.

– We can't call Max Foxman's clique 'class enemies', said Blackie. – We're not Joe Zuken.

– Not even Joe Zuken would say that anymore, said Chickie.

– Because he's a Stalinist, said Michael. – And why can't we call Max Foxman and his friends 'class enemies'? They want to sell the club, don't they?

– We can't call them that because they're Jewish, too. A Jew can't be an enemy of a Jew, said Chickie. – We learned that lesson.

– That's class collaboration, or tribalism at worst, said Michael. – It dilutes the will of our forces if we claim an affinity with those we oppose. We'll lose the club that way.

– We're going to lose the QV, anyway, said Duddy. – That's why we're fighting this thing.

– It's all politics, said Suddy to Tino. – Don't get involved in politics.

– Our intentions are good, said Duddy.

Loftily, Michael opened his hand and plucked the invisible nub of his argument out from it and placed it in front of them on the table. They stared at the invisible nub.

– Here's the crux of the matter, said Michael. – It's not about intention; it's about motivation. Either we put up a fight by motivating and educating our side, or we'll lose the club. Take any working class action to defend its interests, like the 1919 General Strike.

Duddy ached to interrupt, and did.

– Like when I went on strike once at the CPR yards. Believe you me, it got nasty because of the fighting. Good thing I have pointy shoes. Some daylights came out of that day, out of the scabs. The police sided with the CPR. They should have been neutral; that's what we pay them for. You can get thrown under a train if there's a wildcat strike. But people liked me there; Labour and Management both. That day, the ants ate the elephant.

– It's called an industrial action, said Oz, not a wildcat strike. I worked there, too. It wasn't half as bad as Shore's slaughterhouse on Luxton, though. Now that was a shitty job.

– You should have worked at Thompson Tanners, said Chickie.

– Seven bucks a week. Six-day work week. Twelve hours a day. I still have the smell of rotted flesh in my nose. It made shit smell sweet. Even other people's.

– But you didn't have to kill anything, said Oz, not like at Shore's, with the *kelbelach* mooing for their mothers. The animals arrived dead at Thompson Tanners. You were lucky.

– In the war I had to kill *and* smell rotten flesh, said Blackie.

– And the guys you shot weren't mooing.

– That's trumps, said Suddy.

– When the workers seized the initiative in 1919, said Michael, the whole North End rose up as one man and came over to their side. And so, *mutatis mutandis*, by seizing the initiative, we can save the QV.

Blackie saw Duddy's eyes light up when he heard Michael say *mutatis mutandis*.

– It just makes us sound fanatical, said Chickie.

– Trotsky said 'Nothing important in history has ever been accomplished without fanaticism,' said Michael.

– We're not in the working class, Michael, said Suddy.

– Certainly not, said Chickie.

– Yes, you are, said Tino. – You don't own property, commodities, capital, or the means of production.

Duddy put on his insulted face and scoffed:

– Suddy owns two houses. Including this one we're in.

– And the cab, said Chickie.

– We're in that together, said Duddy. – It's a joint adventure.

– We all own our own homes, except Duddy, said Chickie.

For Michael's benefit, Duddy balked, fluttered his hands, and chuckled as if Chickie was just kidding.

– My father, said Michael, owns a thousand houses and apartments, a stake in the Blue Bombers and four seats on the Grain Exchange. And three islands in Lake of the Woods. And half a nickel mine in Flin Flon. That's what I meant by owning capital and property and the means of production.

– Holy Moly, said Suddy. – He's like a Bloomstock.

– He could buy and sell Bloomstock ten times over with that equity, said Chickie to Suddy, before turning to Michael. – So you're from those MacGiligarys?

– Suddy, he's not talking about the Jewish rich; this is the WASP rich, said Oz. – He's talking Richardsons.

Suddy looked from Oz to Chickie like he had two teachers telling him how to colour within the lines.

– I'm not a WASP. My parents are Scots Catholic, said Michael.

– And they invented curling, said Suddy.

– Look, if you don't have that sort of property, and if you work for a living, then you're working class, said Michael. – Being ashamed about it doesn't change your social class. It is just being subaltern. And if anyone should be ashamed, it's the parasitical rich. You don't want to know the viciousness of the elite of a money-grubbing society. And what is their money for anyway? For their big parade of riches. To show off their wealth. Show off the things they have, especially the ones other people don't have. The parade of riches.

– Adam Smith, said Tino, adding the footnote.

– A nickel mine! You're the *hoi poloi*, said Suddy to Michael MacGiligary.

– I have to take issue with your use of the term *hoi poloi*, said Oz to Suddy.

– Did I pronounce it wrong?

– The *hoi poloi* doesn't refer to the rich.

– The literal translation from the Latin means 'the many,' Michael MacGiligary said to Suddy.

– I've been using the word wrong for all my life?

– We're the *hoi poloi*, said Blackie.

The Bloomstocks have cake from Jeanne's bakery in the fridge, even when it's nobody's birthday, Duddy said.

– That's how you'd make class distinctions? said Tino. – If you can afford Jeanne's cake between birthdays?

– How do you know what Bloomstock has in his fridge? said Chickie.

– He could buy and sell the Bloomstocks ten times over is what Chickie said, said Suddy.

– His father could, you mean, said Chickie.

Duddy grabbed Michael's arm with one hand and clawed his inner elbow with the other.

– I see you in a new light. I saved Bloomstock's house on Scotia in the flood. I admire the capitalists. That's why I'm not working class. I'm a maverick. You know, Bloomstock has two freezers with whole cows inside.

– You admire my father's stinking millions?

– He should let them out of the freezer, said Chickie.

Duddy was holding Michael's elbow in two fists now, like a towel he just might wring, but the kid looked at Duddy squarely and said:

– The capitalist world is empty. It's existential nothingness, Duddy. My dad's millions signify nothing because money means nothing. Real economic value, which comes from exploiting the workers, is invisible until it turns into money, which is meaningless until it turns back into means of exploitation. Read *Capital*. But really, is there anything less important than money? A single genuine feeling of compassion for someone who is suffering is worth more than all his millions.

Astonished, Duddy unlatched his grip from Michael's elbow.

– 'He who wears shoes of gold, tramples on the weak and old,' Michael said.

– Bertolt Brecht, said Tino, adding the footnote.

Duddy grabbed Michael MacGiligary's elbow again:

– Where do you get those quotations?

– Books.

– We're flying in the face of adversity, said Duddy. – We're going down. How can you buck Max Foxman?

– Duddy, I thought you were a maverick, said Chickie.

– You should read some of our literature, said Michael MacGiligary. – And, if you want us to help with your campaign to save the QV, and we want to help, you have to know we're Young Socialists. We're in the youth group of the Canadian Section of the Fourth International.

They all looked at Michael as if he had said him and Tino were brown bears.

Blackie, flummoxed, tilted, and pointed his forehead at Tino. Their eyes met for only a second because Tino looked down and away. The kid was blushing.

– What's the Young Socialists? Blackie asked.

– What's the Fourth International? Chickie asked.

– Do they know me in your group? Duddy asked.

– Trotskyites, said Oz. – They're Trotskyites.

– Trotsky*ist*, said Michael MacGiligary.

– The suffix *-ite* implies religious feeling. It's derogatory, said Tino to Oz. – And we're not just atheists, we're militant atheists.

Ten years of Hebrew School for that kid, thought Blackie. And it wasn't free. Him and Deirdre went without for that.

– The dif? Chickie asked Michael.

– We go out of our way to convince people not to believe in gods. Not to believe in that for which you have no evidence.

– Bertrand Russell, said Michael, it being his turn to footnote.

– I don't care what you are, said Oz, if you want to help us save the club. I thank you for your honesty.

– Honest as the Masters of Deceit, said Chickie.

– But we have to tone the petition down, said Oz. – It's not Depression times.

– So no one objects to us working on this action because we're Young Socialists? Michael asked.

– As long as you're not communists, said Chickie.

– Trotskyites are communists, said Oz.

– Trotsky*ists*, said Tino.

– They're socialists and communists, revolutionists, but not Stalinists, said Oz. They follow the teachings of Leon Trotsky, *née* Bronstein.

– Age of majority! said Duddy.

– Did you know your son was a Trotskyite? Chickie asked Blackie.

– Trotsky*ist*, said Tino.

Blackie thought he had a fever, but just in his face. And now his throat got constricted. He guzzled the last of his warm Jersey Cream. He felt under scrutiny by the guys and barely managed to pump the words up his throat:

– I did not know that, said Blackie. – I thought he was in BBYO. Is it true, Tino? Are you a Trotskyite?

– I am, said Tino. – A Trotsky*ist*.

At least he answered square without being wry.

– Does this mean we have to be Trotskyites? Suddy asked Michael. – I always vote NDP.

– The NDP are sheep in sheep's clothing. The Stalinists are sheep in wolf's clothing.

– Only once I didn't vote for the NDP, said Duddy.

– You were a Trudeaumaniac for a week. Mona gave you good shit, said Suddy.

– You know, Tino, Mike, if they find out, you won't be able to work in the United States, said Chickie.

That hadn't occurred to Blackie. Doctors were better paid in the States.

– You can't buck the system, said Suddy.

– As long as you're not communists, said Duddy.

– Trotskyites are communists, said Oz again. – Trotsky and Lenin were the architects of the Russian Revolution. They nationalized the means of production in Russia. You can't get more communist than that. Trotsky was the founder of the Red Army. One of the founders of the Third Communist International. Although he came late to Bolshevism. Which was his downfall. And then, after Stalin's betrayals of communism and the Third International, Trotsky founded the Fourth International. Stop me if I'm wrong.

– A functional summary, said Michael MacGiligary.

– An obscure political figure now, said Chickie.

– But an important obscure political figure if you'll pardon my oxymoron, said Oz. – Don't you remember when Stalin killed him in Mexico? We were on Selkirk Avenue in front of the White House when the news came over on the radio and people were crying. I remember Mayer Palter bawling, the *shmark* running down his nose. He was in Workmen's Circle. I didn't know there were any Trotskyites left.

– Trotsky*ists*.

– I'll still vote NDP, said Suddy. – I voted NDP when it was the CCF.

– You seem to know a lot about it, said Michael to Oz.

– *Mishlockt yiddin*. They killed him because he was a Jew, said Duddy.

– Does Deirdre know about this? Blackie asked Tino. – About you and the Young Socialists?

– She's known for months.

– What about all those BBYO meetings last year? Blackie said.

– I was going to meetings of the Young Socialists.

– I thought he said he was a Trotskyite, said Duddy.

– Trotsky*ist*.

– Communist, Socialist, Trotskyite. It's all the same thing, said Oz. – They want to socialize the means of production. They want Capitalism dead and the State to wither away.

– We did a good job on the corned beef, said Suddy.

– So you're not running for President of BBYO? Blackie asked Tino.

– I'm not even in the BBYO anymore. I dropped out last year.

– So is a taxi cab a means of production? Suddy asked.

– No, said Tino. – A piano neither.

– We're getting off track, said Oz. – My point is, can you tone down the petition? We need to get as many signatures as possible to force a vote against an executive decision. Otherwise the club's kerflooey. I did like your history of the club. We can keep that, on the verso of the petition. You write like an angel.

– He's a sophisticate, said Suddy.

– Some people have to be hypnotized to write that well, Duddy said to Michael.

– I thought you didn't read it, said Chickie.

– Dee's the reader, said Duddy. – Bloody Max Foxman. He wears seven different *mezzuzas*. You need to carry a vomit bag from Air Canada when you're around him. And he pees sitting down.

– I think it's called an airsickness bag, said Chickie.

– We're going off topic again, said Oz. – And this here, the 1919 General Strike and Emma Goldman and Nelly McClung and Mr. Jacob Penner, is immaterial.

– What do you mean immaterial? Suddy asked. – I had an uncle who went to jail during that strike.

– I didn't mean it personally, Suddy, said Oz.

– You said it was immaterial.

– I meant immaterial vis-à-vis the QV situation.

– It wasn't immaterial for my uncle. He lost his house. He

couldn't cross the line to get into the States after that.

– Who wants to get into the States? said Tino.

– What if you had a bonspiel in Grand Forks? Or Thief River Falls? Suddy asked. – And you can't lie on the forms when you cross the line.

– Amen, said Chickie.

– Okay, I'll rewrite the petition, said Michael.

– Thank you, said Oz.

– And make it something guys can sign their name to, said Chickie. – You don't want to alienate our supporters.

– Yes, we wouldn't want to alienate the coward vote, said Tino.

– Some North Enders might not back us, said Blackie.

– I can see some of them even betraying us, said Chickie.

– La Malinche, said Tino, looking at Michael.

Duddy look puzzled. – La Malinche?

– Aztec princess who betrayed her people to the Spaniards? said Tino.

– The North Enders will betray us for sure, said Chickie. – It's human nature.

There wasn't any more corned beef or pickles or drinks or much more left to talk about. And Tino and Michael had two Young Socialists meetings that night, one was a pre-meeting to prepare for the meeting and then the meeting. They'd had enough corned beef and pop, too.

– We've got to go, said Michael.

– The revolution beckons, said Chickie.

Everyone started shifting their bums to get up from the table, except Duddy, who looked up at Michael. – If you're so rich, how can you be a Little Socialist?

– It's Young Socialist, said Tino.

– What did I say?

– Little Socialist.

– Don't take amperage with me for saying that, said Duddy.

–It's umbrage, said Tino.

– None taken, Duddy, said Michael. – But in answer to your question, I can only say that there are times when one betrays one's social class out of an ethical imperative.

– So you're La Malinche? said Chickie to Michael.

– It's not like that, said Michael. – Try to go beyond Aristotelian logic: the betrayal of my class is not for my material gain, like in the case of La Malinche.

– But to your parents, you are La Malinche, said Chickie to Michael. – A Malinche is a Malinche.

Oz's sigh could have sunk a boat.

– I know you guys have to go, but how are we going to coordinate all this?

Michael opened his diary to a fresh page, pressed it flat with his fist, and made a few annotations.

– I'll rewrite the petition with Tino and get it to Oz, and he'll okay it. Oz can give it back to Tino, and Tino can get it printed up and give it back to Oz or Mr. Timmerman to vet. Mr. Timmerman, can you divide up the names on the curlers' roster into seven groups?

– Sure.

– Then Oz gives us all a set of petitions to circulate amongst the list of members that Mr. Timmerman gives us.

– What should I do? Duddy asked.

– You have to get into Sophie Foxman's pants, said Chickie. – She's lonely for it.

– Titillating she's not, said Duddy.

– If titillating she's not, how can you get off?

– I'll imagine someone else, said Duddy.

– The Queen?

– I'll think of someone. Plenty of fish in the sea. Anyway, all a woman needs is something that works for me: a nice ankle, nice fingers. I just need one thing, and then I can get over the rest. And Sophie has big blue eyes, like Elizabeth Taylor. Do people with big eyes have bigger eyeballs than everybody else? Duddy asked Chickie.

– I bet you don't get a boner. You'll have no choice but to fold it in.

Duddy held his hands over his ears.

– I can't hear you.

– You'll need a shoehorn, said Chickie. – Or a spoon. You'll see.

– I still can't hear you.

Blackie banged his fist on the table:

– Would you stop that! It's really disgusting in front of the kids.

– Even not in front, said Oz.

– Can we move on from Sophie Foxman? said Michael.

– It's immature, said Tino. – And sexist.

– The eggs teaching the hens, Chickie said.

– We each take a group of names Blackie gives us, Michael continued, and get as many people in our group to sign. When we get a name, we call Blackie and he checks it off against the curlers' roster.

– What about juniors?

– Everybody.

– And women curlers?

– Everybody.

– Who gets Max Foxman's name? said Duddy.

– A fool's errand, said Oz.

– The person who gets Max Foxman's name should get an extra name, said Duddy. – Fair is fair.

– Nobody's getting Max Foxman's name, said Blackie.

– Why not? I'd like to see the look on his face, said Duddy.

– He's not going to sign it, so it's a waste of energy.

– You just do your names, said Chickie to Duddy. – Without buggering it up.

– I have pineapple slices and red Jell-o in the fridge, said Suddy.

– You and your pineapple slices.

– He puts them on steak, said Chickie.

– I've seen it done, said Suddy. – Hawaiian steak.

92

– We can't start arguing amongst ourselves either, said Oz.

– Yeah, said Duddy. – We can't step on the hose.

– Well, there are going to be lots of people who won't sign it, said Chickie.

– But they should read it first, said Suddy.

– They still won't sign it. A lot of people will line up behind Max Foxman.

– Even people in the North End, said Blackie.

– The Malinches, said Duddy.

– People are moving south. Or their kids live south, said Chickie.

– It's not going to be easy, said Blackie.

– What's Glenn Gould going to do? said Chickie.

– He's rewriting the petition, said Oz.

– I'll sign up the people on my list, said Michael to Chickie. – Like everybody else.

– Michael's very convincing, said Tino. – A Bolshevik has to be the best student, the best worker, the best canvasser. Tino made a wry smile to share with Michael.

– He should get Max Foxman's name, said Duddy.

– But Michael doesn't really know a lot of people at the club, said Chickie.

– What kind of remark is that? Oz asked.

– Chickie means that he's not Jewish, said Blackie. – Maybe he should just organise behind the scenes.

– Just give me my names, said Michael. – I'll get them to sign.

– Put the blocks to them, said Duddy.

– No vote, no peace, said Tino.

The guys got up from the table. The kids put on their leather jackets, folded up their collars Elvis high, to the cheekbone.

– Hey, said Duddy.

– What? said Tino, just about to move to the back door.

Duddy grabbed Tino at the elbow. He palmed him a fin after peeling it off a thick roll.

– That's enough for pizza at the Pizza Place. A fin's the best bill to have on you. You can buy anything in fives. Nobody has to change you.

– I'd bank that if I were you, said Suddy.

Tino and Michael said 'Little Socialists' to each other and laughed themselves out the door into the winter kitchen and then all the way down the back stoop.

O n Thursday, Blackie was waiting for Deirdre outside the hair salon again, holding onto his hat in a bluster of snow. It was bloody cold: the temperature had to be in the minus high teens. But Christ, he didn't know how else to find her and talk to her. Whenever he phoned her sister's, they said she was out or couldn't come to the phone.

– Are you following me again?

– Did you know Tino isn't in BBYO?

– I knew last year. As if you cared.

– Did he tell you or did you find out?

– Better than that: I know when he's lying. But I found out from Belle Shore anyway. She made sure of that. Some people!

– Did you know he was a Trotskyite?

– Trotsky*ist.*

Blackie groaned.

– He explained the whole thing to me. We had a long talk about it.

– Him and his friend are both in it pretty deep.

– Michael MacGiligary?

– They're always talking. Even when their skip is throwing his rock. Chickie says they'll never be able to work in the States.

– Chickie's an idiot, she said. – And I know lots of things about Tino you don't. Lots.

It was as if a bird had swooped down in front of him, startling him, making his face go hot.

– You know who you look like right now? Just now? she asked.

– Who?

– Your mother. *Alavasholem.* Always worried. Always worried about what people will say. No wonder your father died young, *Alavasholem.*

Deirdre and his mother had shared a reciprocal animus until his mother followed his father into his neighbouring plot at the Chesed Shel Emes Cemetery.

– So you know Tino better. Good for you.

– Is that my fault?

– So what's going on with him?

– It's freezing here, she said.

– So let's go get coffee. And a bun.

– I'm on the go, Blackie.

– I'll make this short. Him and his friend? Him and Michael MacGiligary? What's with those kids? Are they dating?

– Each other?

Blackie felt sick. The air smelled like medicine. He could hardly countenance what sort of acts might be going on if they were dating each other. Even imagining them holding hands made him turn off the imagination tap in his brain. He knew about Suddy and Bill Grod, but Duddy told him that had been just a crush. Suddy and Bill never got going with the physical part because Bill's family made him move to Toronto. Or so Duddy said. But Suddy took it pretty hard for a crush.

– No. I meant girls? Are they dating girls? Does Tino have a girlfriend?

– Ask him, Deirdre said. – Ask him if he's dating.

– But if you already know.

– You see. That's what I'm saying.

He didn't see what she was saying, and he had nothing to say to what he didn't know she was saying. The wind filled in the gap with a lashing sound and then died down.

– I don't see what you're saying, Blackie said.

– They're in a war on monogamy, Deirdre said.

96

– Never heard of something like that. And I was in a war that had everything in it.

– Tino says nuclear families are dead, Deirdre said.

– I know one that is.

Deirdre stopped and began mashing and stamping snow.

– My toes are numb, she said.

He looked down and liked her pointy boots, which came up to her knees, but he didn't know if they were new or not. Didn't matter: she looked appealing in them. And to think she had once been his and no one else's.

– It's way too cold to discuss the nuclear family outside. I told you I'm on the go. I left your clothes on the dryer this morning.

There was silence, and into it, Blackie thought of something bold but too dumb to say, but he went ahead anyway:

– If you don't come back home, you'll never find someone else like me.

– That's the idea.

That was uncalled for, he thought. She'd never said anything like that ever. Blackie, deflated, could tell it tasted new to her, too, and also that she'd regretted it.

He went home feeling like shit until Duddy called him up.

– Hello? said Blackie into the receiver.

– Where's the action?

It was Duddy, interrupting the TV show that Blackie, Tino, and Michael MacGiligary were watching in the den. It was *Monty Python's Flying Circus*, and the two kids screamed every time one guy on the screen said: 'No one expects the Spanish Inquisition.' Blackie didn't get it, but it was nice of Tino and Mike to come over before they went curling.

– I think I hypnotized myself bad, said Duddy. – Can you help me?

Blackie had picked up the phone in the kitchen and now cradled the receiver in his collarbone as he lit his cigarette. Outside the kitchen window, across the backyard, a deer up to

97

its bony knees in a snowdrift, looked back at him. Must've come up the river, Blackie thought, and through the back lanes looking for food. Poor guy: January was a bugger.

– There's a deer in the backyard.

– I was constipated so I hypnotized myself to soften my stool.

– With that Kripkin hypnosis book?

– I think I did it right. I used two mirrors, like Kripkin said the old masters did when they painted themselves.

– So what's the problem?

– Death by success. I over-hypnotised myself. I softened my stools too much. I'm getting the runs intermittently. I have to go to the Garden City Mall. I need more mice cages. They're getting cute day and night. Especially when the stars come out. Gerbil cages would do, too. So I need help. After their TV show finishes.

– I was going to watch Tino curl tonight.

– You call that curling?

– And I'm really tired. I don't know why. I'm just not sleeping right lately.

– Wasn't right what Deirdre did, said Duddy. – Do *we* curl tonight?

– We curl Tuesdays and Thursdays.

– Right. Right. I knew that.

– Have you signed anybody on your list?

– I canvassed.

– But did you sign anybody?

– I'm still canvassing.

– Michael MacGiligary signed fifteen guys already, Blackie said. – You want him to take some of the guys on your list?

– What about you?

– I signed up seven. Yesterday I signed up Frenchie Litman at the Grain Exchange.

– Litman's only got one toe on his right foot.

– He used his hand to sign.

– Give me time and I'll sign everybody up. They all know me.

I'm well-liked. Listen, it'll just take a sec to help me out. Just up to the Garden City Mall.

Duddy put a snow shovel of pretty please into it.

– I'll pick you up and then drop you off at the club to watch Tino. It'll be two secs.

– Can't you take two trips with the cages back and forth?

– You'll be a better friend for it.

– So you think the hypnosis did it?

– Overdid it. You know, Mona used to get constipated. So it's genetic.

As it turned out the hypnosis must have been working because Duddy had to ask the floor manager of the pet store twice if he could use the bathroom before they finally went through the cashier. After Duddy paid, he gave Blackie a hug for helping, and they both lit up before going into the cold evening, into what Duddy called snow light.

–Maybe I shouldn't smoke. Smoking makes me go too, said Duddy.

Duddy's leather car coat squeaked as they crossed the icy parking lot together, carrying about ten cages each. Duddy had a cage hanging from his lips and let it drop when they got to the Valiant.

– Hamster cages are just as good as mice or gerbil cages. Oh. And I lifted a bag of pet food.

– Where is it?

– Under my sweater.

Blackie had to be really drowsy because the heat blowing out of Duddy's dashboard put him out like a light. The night before he had one of his sleepless bouts, which went bad around 3:00 a.m., the ugliest hour. He had to go down to the refrigerator for some cold milk. He didn't use a glass, just drank it from the quart. Deirdre wouldn't have allowed that, but it was one less glass to wash.

When Blackie woke up he thought he was airborne. The radio was pulsating just beneath Blackie's consciousness and then on top of it. When he looked down, out the window, he saw the frozen river below was clogged with thick sharp crystals tinged purple. Duddy was flooring it over the Midtown Bridge.

– Where are we going? I thought you were taking me to the rink.

– A cannon couldn't have woken you, you know that.

– Not even if I was shot out of it? I'm sleeping for the shits these days. Why are we on the Midtown Bridge?

– I could hypnotise you. You'd sleep a lot better — so as you'd never wake up.

– Where are we going?

– Tuxedo. We're going to Max Foxman's first.

– I'm not going to Max Foxman's, said Blackie.

– Just for a second.

– Not even for a second.

Max is in Vegas.

– I want you to leave Sophie Foxman alone.

– I have an excuse to see her again. I'll just run in for a sec. You can wait in the car.

– What excuse?

– I've got the petition. I'm going to say to her that I've come over to sign Max up. She won't know what I'm talking about. He doesn't talk to her anymore. He hasn't talked to her for months. Since the summer. She criticized him in front of the whole family. Said something horrible to him. He shuns her like a Mennonite.

– You told us.

– I'll have an 'in.' I'll just start seducing her.

– *Fuld mir a gang.* It's a stupid idea, Duddy. And what about Dee?

– It's about the QV, Blackie, said Duddy, as if Blackie was slow.

– And it's winding down with Dee. I told you. But she has the cutest kids. When I saw them, I wanted one, too. I made them tinfoil hats. They loved me for that.

– If she finds out, she'll be hurt.

– I've been hurt, too. People have been false to me. Women,

too. Do unto others. That's why I don't get married. I'd rather sleep with Max Foxman's wife than him sleep with mine, because that's what a woman can do. They should put that in the Jewish Torah. Take you and Deirdre. Deirdre's a *shtikgelt* and *she* left, so imagine what lesser wives and women can do. I'm not saying I know why she left.

– Do you know why she left?

– No. But it wasn't right. And you shouldn't have let her go. But from being disappointed by girls, I learnt how to numb pain, even before hypnosis. If you say to yourself that nothing means anything to you, yourself, or anyone else over and over, that's how best to numb pain. She could learn that. Dee, I mean. If I dumped her.

– What would Mona say about you doing this?

– Mona has suffered too. She knows what it's like to suffer. And this is about the QV, not Mona. You know Mona's not a hundred percent right now.

– It's demeaning to Sophie, too, you know.

– It's an esteem builder to be wanted. Sophie should look at it that way. And if she doesn't want to, she can always say 'no.' But this is about the QV, Blackie. That's what's on the line. By any means necessary.

– We have the petition, said Blackie. – We'll force a vote. Oz says lots of guys are signing it. If you canvassed someone, you'd see.

– I'm canvassing. But Max Foxman is playing dirty.

– Impatience. That's your problem, Duddy.

– No *zitzfleisch*. I know.

– And it's a dumb idea.

– It's psychological warfare. Max'll be devastated. What's bad for Max is good for us.

– Tell me how it's good for us?

– I'm going to patiently explain. Just a second.

Duddy pushed in the lighter and simultaneously stuck a pack

of cigarettes between his teeth. With one hand on the wheel he managed to draw out two cigarettes between two fingers, without any of the other cigarettes falling out.

– You want one?

– Sure.

Duddy lit up and then handed the lighter to Blackie. Blackie inhaled: the spicy taste sizzled in his mouth.

– If I seduce her and Max Foxman finds out, it will unnerve him and he'll make mistakes. I've seen how cuckolds react. I've been there. It's like when another man spits in your *kasha*. Your nerves go kerflooey. I've observed that personally in people. And that's if he catches me in the act. His mind will loop over and over the same scene. You go sexually mad.

– What if he doesn't find out?

– Now, that's the best part. If he gets away with selling the QV, I'll make sure he finds out about me seducing Sophie. He'll be punished by my contingency plan. Either way he loses.

– Makes no sense, Duddy. You're trying to catch two butterflies with one net.

– In terms of Aristotelian logic?

– You're talking differently, Duddy.

– Too fast, you mean? I talk at the speed of words.

– And just how are you going to seduce her?

Duddy took a long drag.

– In three steps: One. There's surprise on my side. She'll never expect it.

– Nobody expects the Spanish Inquisition, said Blackie.

– Why should they?

– Seriously. How are you going to seduce her?

– True. A better man would go for the inner core, but I can't get past women's looks. It's a shortcoming of mine. That's why I liked Dee off the bat, based on how she looks in glasses. She's a doll. And she reads. Says she'll help with my book on dreams.

And number two?

– I'm banking big on her loneliness. Listen exactly to what I'm going to say: I know these women. I know how miserable they are. I've never met a married woman who was happy. Only their kids make them happy or summer holidays.

– And three?

– Ring her bell. Charm. *Mutatis mutandis.*

– And if all that doesn't work?

– Hypnotic techniques. I can recognize women who can be hypnotized. Girls with low metabolisms are good. Low blood sugar, too.

– I don't want anything to do with this, said Blackie.

– You can wait in the car.

Duddy slid the Valiant up in front of Max's house, scraping the snow- and sand-crusted curb with a battered hubcap. The cages in the hatch rattled when he came to a stop, and the car sputtered when he pulled out the key from the ignition.

Max's house was vast, taking up two city lots. You could have planted sugar cane on the front lawn and made a go of it, thought Blackie.

– This is what *shmearing* can buy, Duddy said. – But it can't buy you fidelity. You don't know how devastating infidelity can be. Was Deirdre unfaithful?

– No.

– It's hardest on the man.

– You're not playing fair with Dee if you ask me.

– You see a ring on this finger? Or my nose?

– What are you going to tell Dee if she finds out?

– Like last time. I told her I was in great demand with people. Guess what she said? She said I was in great demand with her too. Sweet, eh?

– How can I ever use the word sweet again? Blackie asked himself.

– And it's got nothing to do with Dee. Dee's appealing. She looks like Nana Mouskouri with her glasses off or on. This is

103

about the QV. It's got nothing to do with pleasure either; it's the opposite of pleasure when the person is not appealing.

Duddy ran from the Valiant with the rolled petition and his gloves in his right fist and hopped over the curb into a low snow drift. He kept running. The Foxman path carved through the snow was pretty smart; someone had scraped the snow completely down to the flagstones. In a jiffy he was knocking on the Foxman's door and stamping his feet on the swept stone steps.

Without the defroster on, the Valiant fogged up quickly. It was going to get cold fast in the car without the heat on. If only Duddy had left the keys Blackie, could put the heater on, even listen to the radio to distract himself.

Blackie wiped a hole with his thumb in the steamed-up glass and saw Sophie Foxman open the door wearing a paisley silk shift. Duddy had exaggerated a smidgen about how fat she'd gotten. Her hair was in a beehive wrapped in toilet paper. Her pretty face stopped Blackie's heart.

Ten minutes later Blackie was as cold as a lettuce in the crisper, and his teeth were chattering. He weighed two options to get Duddy to come out: honk the horn long and hard, or run to the house, ring the bell, get inside, and drag him out. There was a third option: if a cab came by, he'd hail it. And if that didn't happen, he could walk to Corydon and catch the bus.

He couldn't find the bell, so he knocked, and waited, stamping his cold feet. This time the Jamaican maid came to the door and let him in.

He attached the house smell to something intimate with Max Foxman, and he almost gagged. Blackie had been to the Foxman's house on Stella Avenue when he was a kid, and he recognized the same smell that had impressed him so many years ago.

The maid pointed him downstairs to a lavish rec-room. One wall was floor to ceiling mirrors; another was upholstered in black leatherette with big buttons tacked in the middle of bulging rhomboids. While the main floor had that distinctive lush

Foxman family odour, the rec-room smelled neutral and fresh as a cave.

Duddy and Sophie — she'd peeled the toilet paper off her beehive, letting her hair hang loose on her shoulders and forehead — were having mixed drinks on stools tucked under Max Foxman's famous Hawaiian bar. They were taking it pretty easy, nodding at each other and laughing.

So, he thought, Duddy was already on good terms with Sophie. Maybe Duddy did know about Max and his depilatory habits in his men's area. He wondered if Duddy was phoning her or coming over to see her.

— It's like the bar in *Mrs. Robinson*, Duddy said to Blackie when he saw him standing there.

Blackie watched Sophie pretending to be befuddled, pretending to take her time recognizing him, but he could tell she knew right away who it was.

Blackie had known her when she was little Sophie Wolfman, going from being a Wolfman to a Foxman when she married Max. As a kid she had a gentle but fearless soul in a tiny frame that smiled out of a high blush, her lips always chapped in winter because she licked them without remorse.

She was good at games. She hardly ever got caught in hide-and-seek; she saved the bunch often. Blackie must have liked her even then because he always liked hiding with her. After her parents died suddenly, she had to go live in the Jewish orphanage, which made her wilder. Blackie remembered that she was the only girl who had ever jumped into the Red River on a dare and almost drowned. Who'd have thought she'd marry Max Foxman. Blackie always thought she'd marry him, as he had yearned, as she had once yearned too.

In their teens Blackie had loved her without a shadow. That was many years ago and years before Deirdre. Sophie had loved him back then; he had felt it, before the separation that overtook them, 'the force of circumstance', as Oz termed it; the war,

Blackie called it.

And to think he had thought all memories and feelings for Sophie had been eradicated from his brain and that he had felt he had been a better husband for it.

Sophie slid off her stool, shakily, catching the seat with the hem of her shift, so that it wobbled and almost fell over had it not been for Duddy's reflexes. Blackie wondered if she was drunk.

– Hi, Blackie, Sophie said. – What have you been up to?

Blackie noticed that Sophie's make-up had gold dust in it. And her eyelids were painted blue, as blue as her eyes, so blue that King Tut came to mind. Maybe one eyelid was droopy. But her lashes were still how they had been: short, black, and stiff like whisk brooms.

– Look at this bar, said Duddy, going behind it and turning on a furry mechanical gorilla dressed as a sommelier in a spotless tuxedo shirt bib.

The Foxmans had other bottles dressed up like monkeys in tuxedos, and others with simulated volcano rims, but the mechanical gorilla stole the show. It began whirring and pinging as it lifted a wine cup on a chain to its lips and drank. Blackie thought about where the purple water went.

– Blackie? Don't you remember me?

Sure he did. He could still remember the sting of her rejection. He looked down at her little grey-stockinged feet; they stirred buried longings for her. He wondered if she could tell how hot his cheeks felt. Or what would happen if he fainted?

More of Blackie's memories of Sophie flooded in. She'd had a black bicycle with a beige seat. And in their teens they'd go to lots of movies and neck till the lights went up and started up again when the next feature started. Sometimes she'd come to his place when his mother was home. His mother was always pleasant to Sophie, something she never was with Deirdre.

That was before the war. He'd thought Sophie would wait for him. He never asked her to because it felt unnecessary. That's how much he'd thought they were in love, the type of love you're afraid you'll never get the chance to have again. After Blackie was shipped overseas, he was stuck in hell for three years: first in Sicily, in 1943, and then Belgium, in 1945. Meanwhile, Max had evaded conscription, got rich, and stepped in; Blackie knew that Sophie hadn't been born so pretty for nothing.

Now he wondered where all those days between Operation Baytown and finding her drinking with Duddy in a rec-room had gone. Time made no sense when it bent like that, from one instant to another, obliterating everything that came between: fighting in the war, getting rejected by Sophie, meeting Deirdre, having Tino. And maybe ten thousand curling games.

– Blackie Timmerman, Sophie said again, almost querulously.
– You do remember me?
– Sure.

He was disappointed that she wasn't as pretty or as delicate as she once was. He was also enjoying the fact that she had lost some of her looks. Her eyes were watery now, with crows' feet around them, and her facial bones had grown thicker. And she hadn't plucked her eyebrows in months. She moved like she had an illness or was recovering from one. Or she'd been drinking all afternoon.

It was actually beyond him why Duddy wanted to seduce her.

Oddly, guiltily, it crossed his mind that if he had fought harder for her, hadn't just given up when she'd written him about Max sniffing around, he could have saved her from coming down to this: slipping off a bar stool in a rec-room, *shickered*.

– Blackie, she said. – There was something I was just going to say to you. Now I can't remember.

How about sorry? he wanted to say.

Her mouth was shocked, slipped to one side. He saw her blue eyes talking with remorse: 'I never liked any of this, this house.' Isn't that what Deirdre might have thought before she left: that she 'never really liked any of this.' It taught Blackie a thing or two about making assumptions about people; he had always thought things were going well with Deirdre.

– Can I get you something?

– We have to go. It was nice seeing you again.

– Let me get you something.

– I'm good.

Blackie watched her walk behind the bar, her cheeks blazing, as Duddy squeezed by her to get out.

– After I finish with her in bed, whispered Duddy, she'll think she was run over by a fire truck.

– Can we go? I want to watch Tino curl. You promised me. I promised him. I can catch the last few ends.

– I can get off, I think, Duddy said. – I just have to sympathize with her problems for a bit. She's been drinking all afternoon.

They heard a tap close and glasses clinking and suds swishing.

– What are you guys talking about?

They didn't answer her and she opened the tap again to rinse.

– Let's go. It's not right, said Blackie to Duddy.

– What's she to you anymore? And Max is in Vegas.

– I knew her when she was a nice kid. You know that. Let's go.

Sophie twisted the faucet shut.

– What are you guys talking about?

– We've got to go, said Blackie.

Sophie looked at Duddy for confirmation. Duddy put force into a shrug of resignation and regret.

– Blackie's kid is curling.

– Say hello to Deirdre for me, Sophie said to Blackie, slurring her words.

– She doesn't know that Deirdre and you are busted up, said Duddy. They'd made it out of the house and were walking off the landing onto the walk.

Sophie had come to the front door to watch them leave.

– No one in the South End knows about me and Deirdre, said Blackie. – We're nothing to these people.

108

is nights were more restless after seeing Sophie in Max's rec-room; but he found calm on the ice.

On a lane all to himself, Blackie threw practice rocks before the meeting: drawing one to the button, then smashing it out with the next, then drawing to the button again. In just a few minutes, Oz would present their petition, and then there'd be a showdown with Max Foxman.

The night before, after some wracking yawns, Blackie had managed to sleep right up to the ugly hours, from 3:00 to 5:00 a.m. Awake and marooned on his bed, he was delivered to a swarm of shadows. Sophie was one. And then he was anxious about the QV and had to tell himself over and over what Oz had said earlier in the day: the guys had come through. They had signed up more than a hundred men, plus juniors and women curlers, to demand a vote to keep the QV. So they already had a majority. Why should he worry? He went downstairs for a glass of milk from the refrigerator, but drank out of the carton. Then he went to the front room and drank from the carton there, looking into the street, watching it snow, thinking.

Michael MacGiligary had signed up twenty plus guys himself, even the guys that Duddy was still canvassing. Oz made his quota, and so did Chickie. And Rita got some but not all of the lady curlers to sign; some had to ask their husbands first. Even Tino came through. Blackie got his guys, of course, but they were easy: he'd curled with them for years. A couple of them had even been shipped off overseas with him. They had Max Foxman *shmiced*, Oz said. So why did Blackie have a sense of doom? Was he worried about Tino? He had told Oz he was concerned about the kid. 'A guy will worry about his boys even when their balls have beards,' Oz had responded.

Back in bed, and just as he was about to fall asleep, Blackie remembered that after the meeting they'd have their first Manitoba Brier match, a home game against Rossmere who could really curl and would probably knock them out of the Brier right away. He threw a hundred rocks in his sleep that night: trying to draw to the eight-foot only to watch them all sail right through the house.

Morning brought exhaustion and pins and needles to his curling arm. Outside his window he saw fresh snow, maybe half a foot more. Snow is the most beautiful thing, he thought, until you had to shovel your way to your car.

At work he spent the day preparing Shneerson's January payrolls, but he was still anxious about the vote. His one focus: to get straight to the rink after quitting time and throw some rocks to stop his mind from buzzing, perhaps have a hot dog or two, and see the guys.

He was at the lunch counter with Oz. The air was thick with cigarette smoke and steam from onions and hot dogs spitting on Rita's griddle. After a time she turned around to him.

– I got the rest of the lady curlers to sign. The ones who had to ask their husbands.

– Thanks, Rita.

– The petition was beautifully written, she said.

– Nice crowd, Blackie said to Oz, looking for assurance.

Guys were sitting impatiently at the counter, their bums swivelling on the red and chrome stools as if they were screwing them into the floor. There were guys on bridge chairs set up in meeting formation; other guys standing, pressing their rear ends delicately against the large slabs of glass that slanted down onto the sheets of ice. A few more bums and they'd go through the glass and fall into the hacks. Guys were talking and laughing while

110

changing into their curling boots or picking broken straw or lint out of their brooms. Even guys who weren't curling that evening had come for the meeting and were standing near the entrance.

It was a full house. Everybody was waiting for Max.

Blackie had already lost the calm he had felt throwing rocks, and his QV anxiety inflated with worries about Tino's politics and Deirdre's absence. For no reason at all, he even had a quaking sense of guilt about a yearning for Sophie Foxman and about Duddy's plans for her.

Life wasn't all curling.

Blackie saw Chickie come in and he thought about asking him how Linda was doing, how he and Hazel were handling things, but just then Max arrived. There he was: up on the little dais, kitted with a table and two bridge chairs, facing fawners and detractors. Sitting stiff, tall, and strong to chair the meeting, Max panned the large hall, first along the lunch counter, the tables and chairs, then across to the windows. Then he made a self-important gesture to Leo Wasserman, who occupied the other chair and was already taking minutes — of nothing — and pulling on his moustache hair. Max leaned over and whispered something in Leo's ear. Leo answered him and Max placed a finger under his nose to pretend hide a snigger. Blackie knew it had to be not a what but a who they were talking about.

Curling boots already laced up, and sweaters and brooms between their legs, Suddy and Duddy had taken up seats in the next to back row. They had saved three bridge chairs for Blackie, Chickie and Oz, who came over from the counter to sit with them. Squeezing by knees and managing not to get a broom up the bum, Blackie ran the gauntlet down the row, making sure he sat beside Duddy so that he could stop him from rising to the baits he'd get if the meeting got hysterical. Chickie made Suddy vacate his chair so he could sit on Duddy's other side: this way him and Blackie had Duddy hemmed in should he act up. Oz followed and sat on Blackie's other side.

Tino came in late with Michael MacGiligary, engaged in serious conversation, no doubt about socialism. Blackie wondered, and not for the first time, if they were dating, if they were in love. Again, he remembered Suddy crying on his bedspread after Bill Grod left Winnipeg: that wouldn't be a happy life for Tino. He wondered whether Deirdre knew the real situation and wasn't letting on.

The two kids found seats right behind him and Duddy and Oz. Up on the dais, Max had his self-confidence percolating and his I-could-make-you-all-jump-in-the-lake-if-I-wanted-to look on his face. As usual it was hard for Max to get the guys to shut up, and the last thing Blackie heard before he did was Duddy saying to Chickie:

– I'm psyched for this meeting. Watch me. Michael MacGiligary gave me *Robert's Rules of Order*. Dee read it to me.

Tino leaned forward, his face poking between Blackie and Oz's ears, and said:

– The Foxmanites are out in force.

– Foxman*ists*, Oz said.

– Am I going to get hair like that in my ears?

– If you live long enough, said Oz.

Would everybody take their seats! Max Foxman banged his gavel and then gave a little shpiel mentioning once again that the roof needed repair, and how that would cost every one of them thousands of dollars *de minimis*. Then he drew the balance sheet of the club's finances and talked about amortization and depreciation and stuff. He concluded:

– There's no way the club can survive.

– A lie you can believe, said Duddy.

– Shut up, Duddy, Leo Wasserman snapped from the dais.

– Leo's the head of the anti-Duddytariat, Tino said to Michael, loud enough for Blackie to hear.

The building will be sold and each member will receive the cost of their share back, plus a windfall.

– You'll all be plenty compensated for your share.

– My ass, said Duddy.

Max's hand swatted Duddy's heckle down.

– Don't you have any other place to be, Duddy?

Duddy rubbed his dickie against his mole, then clawed Chickie's inside elbow and whispered:

– In his wife's pants.

– How's that going?

– I'm cranking her up.

Jack Sanders, who had taught Blackie how to curl and was sitting on one of the stools at the counter, got up and said:

– What kind of windfall are we talking about exactly?

– At the price we've been offered, Max said. – About $3,000 for each member.

The guys murmured, and not in a way that pleased Blackie. $3,000 was real cash.

Max continued:

– And those who want to donate their share to the State of Israel are encouraged to do so. The Board and I have come up with an honour roll for those who want to plant a forest in the Negev Desert that would have the QV name on it. On a bronze plaque.

– The Nevada Desert, you mean, said Duddy.

– Don't be a *nudnick*, said Harry Finn, sniping at Duddy from a row back.

– Don't minute what Duddy said, Max said to Leo Wasserman and then continued.

– The QV *qua* club won't disappear, but instead of owning our own rink we will just rent ice four days a week at a new 24-lane rink. I have brochures on the place. They're breaking sod in March, and we're already negotiating our evenings and lanes. We'd still be the QV, something that'd still be Jewish, and some members wouldn't have to drive all the way across town anymore. Let you North End *shmoes* drive across town now. Ha.

113

Max was endearing himself insultingly to the North Enders by calling them *shmoes*. Blackie heard some of the guys give oily laughs.

– He's giving us a rigmarole. I knew it, said Duddy.

– That's big bucks, said Chickie. – You could put a down payment on a cottage in Winnipeg Beach with that. Or do lots else.

Duddy stood up, holding his broom like a mic stand, and said:

– For all we know . . .

– You haven't been recognized, Duddy, interrupted Max.

– You didn't recognize Jack Sanders when he asked his question.

– Sit down, Duddy.

Duddy sat down and scoffed:

– Big bucks. We won't see a dime of it.

– Don't be a *nudnick*, Duddy, said Max.

– He's double dribbling you guys, said Duddy.

– Shut that *pisk*, Duddy! said Harry Finn.

– Who's heckling me? said Duddy, turning around to identify the voice. – Harry Fink?

– *Sha,* Duddy. You're the heckler, said Blackie.

– Duddy, don't let them bait you, said Chickie.

– Don't shush me, Chickie. They're heckling me.

Blackie saw Duddy bite his lip hard, rotate his dickie 90 degrees to the right and then 90 degrees to the left, and then *shockle* his knee up and down, which set his broom in motion tick-tock, tick-tock, before whispering as loud as he could:

– Just you watch, he'll pocket the windfall.

– Duddy!

That came in a chorus from several directions simultaneously.

– It won't end up in a forest, said Duddy. – Or in State of Israel Bonds.

– Don't minute that, said Max Foxman to Leo Wasserman.

– I said it won't end up in State of Israel Bonds either, said Duddy. – Don't minute that either, he yelled toward Leo.

– Nobody mentioned anything about bonds, said Leo. – We're talking about a forest.

– Your pants pockets, that's where it'll end up, said Duddy. – That's as close as it'll get to a bush.

– I resent that, Duddy, said Max Foxman. – The club's books are open to everyone.

Duddy gave a sick scoff:

– The books. Right. Books can prove anything. Even the truth.

– Anyone can see the accounts, said Max.

– I'd like to see the accounts, said Duddy.

– The Chair still doesn't recognize you, Duddy.

Max Foxman got on to the details of the windfall, wanting to make mouths water, Blackie thought. He then unrolled a poster-sized picture of a forested expanse: The Queen Victoria Forest. Max continued to explain that the windfall would go into escrow after the sale. Come spring, by the time of the Father and Son Banquet, the QV would be wound up and liquidated.

– So that's how the Executive sees it, said Max.

– Motion to adjourn, said Harry Finn.

– I'd like to speak to that, said Oz.

– Is there a seconder? Max asked.

Duddy got loud:

– Into escrow, my ass. You mean into your pocket. He'll keep the windfall. You'll see. He'll be sucking it down from both tits in each hand.

A voice boomed from the back:

– I move that Duddy Joffe, the shit disturber, be thrown out of the meeting. We can't hear Max back here.

– Is there a seconder?

– Why don't you get your mother to second the motion, Leo? Duddy asked.

– What?

– I was with her last night and she asked for seconds.

– Leo's mother passed away last year, said Blackie to Duddy.

115

– What's wrong with *you*, Duddy? said Chickie.

– What's wrong with you? I didn't know Leo's mother died. Why didn't you tell me?

– So it's my fault?

– Not that she died.

Max asked if anyone wanted to speak to the motion.

– What motion? said Duddy.

– To expel you from the meeting, said Harry Finn.

– The motion to adjourn came first, said Chickie.

– Point of personal privilege! shouted Duddy.

– Duddy, let Oz talk, said Blackie. – It's his turn.

– Point of privilege. My name's been mentioned, said Duddy. – I have the right to speak. It's in the *Robert's Rules.*

– You have the right to remain silent too, Duddy, said Harry Finn.

There was a roll of laughter from the Foxmanites.

– Apologize Duddy, said Max, and you can stay for the rest of the meeting.

– Point of privilege, Duddy repeated.

– Duddy, you've *bakukt* this, said Chickie.

– Nothing's *bakukt.*

– They're going to have you thrown out. Apologise and shut up, said Blackie.

– Okay, I'm sorry! shouted Duddy to Max and Leo. – Sorry for interrupting. Sorry for living.

– Is that an apology? Max asked.

– Sorry! said Duddy.

– Thank you, Duddy Joffe.

– No need to be sarcastic, said Duddy.

– Are you sorry or not?

– Can I have the floor? Oz asked, taking the petition, stapled to pages of signatures, from a veal-coloured leather pouch. – I would like to say something.

All the guys, except for Duddy, were listening.

– Did you see how fast that prick piece of shit Leo Wasserman seconded the motion? he asked Blackie.

– Get a grip, Duddy, Blackie said. – It's Oz's turn to speak.

– I have a petition here from a majority of the curlers that says we should vote on liquidating the QV, said Oz. – So I would just like to say a few words about not selling the QV.

– The wheels are in motion Oz, said Max. – We already have a buyer. The Executive is handling it.

– I think we should discuss it first. – You can't ram something like this through.

– There's nothing to discuss. There's a signed letter of intent, smiled Max.

– But I have a petition here signed by the majority of the curlers. – We want a discussion and a vote tonight.

There were nods and murmurs from the curlers. Even thuds of curling brooms banging on the floor.

Max Foxman, looking out with contempt, played his trump card.

– Of course you'll get a vote, he said. – It's in the by-laws. You didn't need a petition for that Oz.

Oz went red in the face.

– Once all the details are worked out, it'll be put to a vote of the *shareholders*. But we can't have the vote tonight since a shareholders' vote has to be advertised in two newspapers. And let me add one thing: you might have a majority of the curlers, but do you have a majority of the shareholders? The lady curlers and juniors don't count. Nice try.

There was commotion amongst the North Enders. Blackie felt his brain catch fire from confusion. He looked at Oz, and then behind at Michael, who was leaning forward with Tino. They all looked just as puzzled.

– Shareholders, curlers, the dif? said Oz. – All of us here. We're all members of the club. Well, maybe not the juniors. Or the ladies.

117

– Big dif, said Max. – You'll get your vote when things have been worked out. But it's the shareholders who'll vote.

– We had the wrong information, said Michael to Tino, loud enough for Blackie to hear.

– So you can put your petition away, said Max.

Blackie felt the familiar Max Foxman snideness addle him. Then he heard Michael say:

– I'm such an idiot. Such an idiot. Did you know Lenin called Béla Kun an idiot 50 times for his *putsch* in Budapest 1919? I could do that to myself.

Blackie didn't know who Béla Kun was but he too felt the sting of embarrassment in his cheeks for being so stupid, for not having realized that it would be the shareholders and only the shareholders that could wind up the club. But he'd always equated curlers with shareholders. Who else'd have shares in the QV?

The embarrassment and humiliation were shared by Oz, who stood up and started stammering again:

– What? What? What do you mean?

– What a boo-boo, said Suddy.

– Sit down, Oz, said Max.

– Don't sit down, said Chickie.

– He told me to.

– It goes by shares, said Max. – That's in the by-laws. You're in business, Oz. You should know better. More than the other *shmoes*.

– Don't let him patronize you, Michael said to Oz.

Oz sank despondently into his bridge chair while Blackie, on the edge of his wobbly seat, found the courage to say something.

– Everyone that curls here has a share, said Blackie. – Except the juniors and the lady curlers. Okay. So we're asking for a vote now so you don't pursue this any further. You'd be wasting your time. There was some authority in Blackie's voice, but that was an act: his heart always pumped and pounded whenever he had to speak in public.

– Consideration, said Max. – That's what I like. But the chair hasn't recognized you, Blackie. Don't minute that, Leo!

Blackie stood up and raised his hand sarcastically and asked Max if he could speak.

– What? Max said impatiently.

– Can I speak?

– Say what you want to say if you want to speak to the motion.

– What I just said. Everyone that curls here has a share, everyone knows that. Except the juniors and the women curlers. We concede that. But the shares were non-transferrable, if I remember correctly.

– Not so, Blackie, said Max Foxman. – The by-laws have been amended; one of those meetings you guys never came to. Now they're transferrable and alienable. Some guys have sold their shares to other guys. Even some ladies have a share, actually. And some people bought shares for their kids, but then their kids never curled or stopped curling. If you saw the register of current shareholders, you'd be surprised.

Blackie eased his body slowly down into the bridge chair like he was sinking into lava.

– Too many moving parts, said Duddy to Chickie. – Do you understand this?

– That *bakukts* us, said Suddy. – It's *noch nila*.

– This is all phoney, said Duddy.

– It's got to do with Articles of Association, Chickie said to Duddy.

– I don't know what those are.

– You're ignorant. You're ignorant, said Chickie.

– I don't know about that stuff only because I don't want to know, not because I'm ignorant.

– I'd like to see that register, said Blackie, standing up again and then sitting down right after speaking.

– Who sold their share? asked Duddy, also standing up, his

broom clattering to the floor. He adjusted his dickie, gingered his mole, looked around and pointed a finger here and there, and said:

– Who of youse sold your share?

– Sit, Duddy, said Chickie.

Duddy sat down again, put his broom back on his lap, the tip of the shaft almost taking the ear off the guy in front of him.

– Enough members sold their shares over the years to give the Executive a majority, Max said. Believe me. I can count.

Blackie stood up again and said:

– How do we know that? How do we know you have a majority of the shareholders on your side? You didn't ask me, and I'm a shareholder.

– Should I minute this? Leo asked Max.

Max shrugged.

– Sit down, Blackie, you don't have the floor anymore.

Blackie didn't sit down but turned around to see Tino look up at him with a large proud smile.

– You didn't ask me neither, said Sammy Ostrove, sitting next to Jack Sanders at the lunch counter.

– We have more than enough votes in favour of selling, said Max. – Trust me.

– How do you know which way I would vote, Max? asked Duddy, getting to his feet beside Blackie.

– You don't have a share, Duddy, said Max. – You never had a share. So I know how you'll vote. A *gournisht* vote.

Max's clique laughed at him. He sat back down, his ears burning red with embarrassment. Suddy had bought two shares way back, one for each of them, but one was in Suddy's name and the other in Mona's name for some reason.

– Are you going to sit down, Blackie? Max asked. – You'll get your vote in April.

– When in April?

– After the Father and Son Banquet.

120

– We'd like a copy of the Shareholders Register. Can you do that?

– I can do that if you can sit down.

Blackie sat down and Duddy rose to his feet again, his broom clattering to the floor.

– It's *mishlockt yiddin* with you people, said Duddy. – Can't you see! He's going to keep the money.

– Only a thief thinks everybody else is a thief, said Eddie Zachs, mumbling into his own shoulder.

Duddy blushed and gingered his mole up from underneath his dickie. Tino thought that Duddy was about to start baying for Max Foxman's blood. He saw Duddy's lips crimp, his fingers splay and then clench.

– Sit down, Duddy, said Chickie.

– Move to adjourn, said Leo Wasserman.

– An ass licker can't make a motion, said Duddy. – *The Robert's Rules of Order.*

– Sit, Duddy.

Blackie clawed at Duddy's elbow in a Duddy way, while Chickie, tugging on Duddy's sleeve, said:

– I said sit, Duddy! – Sit!

– Don't talk to me like I'm a dog, Chickie.

– Get a grip, said Blackie as he tugged Duddy's trousers and pulled him back down into his chair.

– They're not closing the club without a vote if I can help it, said Duddy to Blackie.

– We're getting a vote! said Chickie.

– But the meeting's going to be adjourned, said Duddy. – They're going to abscond with the money.

– Do we have somebody to second the motion to adjourn?

Duddy lurched forward out of his chair, turned around, grabbed his chair, folded it with a creak and raised it above his head like the tabernacles:

– Does this second the motion?

The bridge chair soared over everyone's heads and landed behind Max, who had ducked just in time. Duddy then got pelted with boos from the Foxmanites.

– So that seconds the motion. Meeting adjourned, said Max.

People started folding up their bridge chairs and stacking them behind the coat racks. Michael said to Duddy:

– Individual acts of violence will get us nowhere, Duddy.

– Like mass violence will? said Chickie to Michael before turning to Suddy and chuckling:

– And you have to control Duddy's ejaculations.

Suddy looked blankly at Chickie.

– No vote, no peace, said Duddy.

– But there's going to be a vote! said Oz to Duddy. – We just need now to get a majority of the shareholders and win that vote after the Father and Son Banquet.

– What about the petition? We already have the majority on the petition. I canvassed.

– You explain it to him, said Oz to Michael.

– Patiently explain, said Chickie.

– The petition is moot now, Michael said to Duddy.

Blackie could tell Duddy liked that word moot.

– It doesn't matter, we're *bakukt* anyway – they'll have more shares, said Suddy.

– But we have the curlers, said Duddy. – Even the ladies. If you call what they do curling.

– Ladies don't slide out, said Suddy to Michael. – It's the hips.

– It's the shares that vote, not the people. – The QV is incorporated.

– Trotsky would have known that, said Chickie to Michael.

– I don't understand that part, said Duddy.

– We have to find out where all the shareholders stand, said Michael.– We have to sway a majority, or their proxies, to vote against the sale. We'll have to have a meeting about this.

– This is a meeting, said Chickie. – We're meeting now.

– We made a mistake, said Michael. – We're in the process of self-criticism now, but we can't get discouraged. We thought it was going to be a war of maneuver but it's turning into a war of position.

– Antonio Gramsci, said Tino.

– So why did I run around canvassing people, said Duddy.

– Who did you canvass? Chickie asked.

– I canvassed.

– I think Max is bluffing about having so many shareholders on his side, said Oz.

– If he doesn't, they'll start pressuring people to sell them their shares to him, said Michael.

– Maybe he's started already? Maybe he's in cahoots with the buyers, too?

– Dominion?

– That's a big outfit.

– They're *shmearing* him, said Chickie. – Same old story.

– So Duddy's been right all along? asked Suddy.

– We can pressurize people and buy up shares too, said Duddy. – Let them eat that with chips.

– With what money? Chickie asked.

– Where's Max getting the money?

– Maybe from Dominion, said Oz. – Maybe he's underselling the club. Go know.

– We can stop people from selling, said Tino. – Put the blocks to them politically.

– I'll get the money, said Duddy.

– Where are you going to get the money from? Chickie asked.

– I meant it in a general way, said Duddy.

– Let's just get the list of shareholders, said Oz. – See what's what.

– I'll get the list, said Blackie.

– Put the blocks to them all, said Duddy.

– The *goyim* are here from Rossmere, said Chickie.

Blackie saw four huge guys from Rossmere walking towards the lunch counter looking relaxed. They wore matching sleek, black sweaters that hadn't stretched out like theirs, and they all had new flat foam brooms too, with black broom covers that matched their sweaters. Their curling boots were black and polished.

– I feel like a real *shleper*, said Blackie, pointing at them.

– Good thing they didn't see what just went on, said Oz.

– Bloody humiliating, said Duddy.

– Those guys look like they get down to the sixteens every year at least, said Blackie. – They might knock us out just when the round robin begins.

– You underestimate yourselves, Michael said to Blackie.

– Their sweaters match their brooms, said Chickie. – That's a first.

Blackie noticed that Tino and Michael were putting on their jackets – still no parkas, no gloves, and no toques – and getting ready to leave. He felt let down; he wasn't a show-off, but he would have liked Tino to watch him curl against Rossmere, what with their matching brooms and sweaters.

– I've got go, Tino said to him.

– Back to the *shmutz*?

– We've got a meeting.

– BBYO? Chickie said.

– Little Socialists, said Duddy. – I see they get that look in the eye.

Tino gave them a mock:

– Adam Buday is giving a lecture on Marx's theory of the *falling* rate of profit.

Blackie thought Michael and Tino would explode with self-irony so he gave them back a dose:

– Oh. – The falling rate of profit is it?

– Yeah. What did you expect? Tino asked Blackie.

– Not the Spanish Inquisition.

Tino and Michael liked that one.

– Good luck, Blackie. Guys! said Michael.

– Don't you have a toque? Blackie asked Tino. – Or gloves. It's freezing out.

– Michael's car's just outside, said Tino. – I lost my gloves.

– Where's your scarf?

– With my gloves.

– Kids just want to look cool, said Oz.

– If that's true, how come they don't wear denim jeans? Suddy asked. – What's with the pleated pants?

Michael MacGiligary looked down at his pleats and got into his patient explaining mode:

– Jeans are examples of repressive de-sublimation. Their false modernity only confirms conformity.

– Herbert Marcuse, said Tino, handy with the footnote.

– You good for money? Blackie said to Tino.

– Yeah. I'm good.

Before Tino and Michael could get out of range, Duddy, who was trying to foist a fin on Tino, had to get the kid in a fierce headlock. He went in for a noogey, working through Tino's mound of curls until locating and knuckling his scalp.

– Duddy!

Duddy gave him a dramatic release, throwing his arms open. Tino acquiesced and pocketed the fin before adjusting his hair, which didn't need adjusting because it just sprang back.

Michael turned to Blackie and Oz and Chickie and Suddy and said:

– You guys still in for the fight? This is where character tells.

Blackie wanted to give him character where it hurts.

– We've made ourselves look this foolish, said Oz. – Why not continue?

– We finish what we start, said Blackie to Michael.

– Are the Foxmanites going into the dustbin of history? Chickie asked.

– Foxman*ists*, said Oz.

– Blackie and me will organize a meeting, said Michael.

Where'd that kid get his confidence? Blackie wondered.

Blackie gave Tino one of his big smacking kisses in spite of his disappointment that Tino couldn't stay to watch him curl Rossmere. Tino left, but not before Blackie pressed a fin into his hand, too.

–Maybe you'll go for chips or something.

Tino did go to watch Blackie's second Brier game a few days after Blackie, much to his surprise, beat the Rossmere guys. He and Michael said 'hi' to Blackie, who was a bit spazzed out and fatigued from sleeping for the shits. He noticed Tino and Mike were pretty quiet for a change; Michael was looking sad and like he couldn't make his mind up about something.

– Where are we? Blackie asked Oz.

– Elmwood. Are you okay?

– I'll be okay. These clubs all look the same.

Elmwood was a nice clean club with a long spotless lunch counter and friendly staff that split their wieners and fried them in sizzling lard, plastering them down with a spatula, then serving them with the works and generous portions of chips with gravy.

Who are we playing?

– The Grain Exchange. Those little guys over there.

– Is Michael okay? Blackie asked Tino.

– His mother wouldn't let him give his piano away to the Indian-Métis Friendship Centre. The movers were there and she stopped them. Sent them home. Pretty embarrassing for him. It's a Steinway.

– Mothers.

– It was his to give, said Tino. – His grandmother gave it to him.

Michael was hungry but like rich kids he had no money on him so Chickie treated both kids to chips and battered black cod. They ate with their fingers and soon had oil running down to their wrists. If one of them lit a match he'd lose a hand. The grease and salt worked wonders, and Michael's mood did a 180 turn, and soon he and Tino were talking their heads off again.

Watching the kids eat their fish and chips made Blackie realize that if, or once, they liquidated the QV, Tino would be practically out of his life. Going who knows where?

On the ice, Blackie made a full recovery and they shellacked the Grain Exchange guys to win their second Brier game.

He slept pretty decently that night because of it.

EIGHT

Tino's eyes filled with excitement when he told Blackie that there was no end to Michael MacGilligary's audacity, or Danton's. Michael would shrewdly await the 6:00 o'clock news, when the whole world was watching TV, and then pounce. Each evening he would phone up a different shareholder on the list Blackie had given him and put the blocks to them.

Tino had dropped by to borrow the toaster for a few months because one of the comrades at the apartment had stuck a knife in theirs to retrieve a whole bagel stuck between the grills. He should have cut it in half, Tino said.

– He could've been electrocuted, said Blackie.

– He got a shock, that's for sure. His finger is blue. It's funny because he's in electrical engineering. He's Egyptian. He and his wife are crashing in Heavy's room till he gets student housing.

– Where's Heavy?

– No one knows.

Max had kept his word about letting Blackie have the Share-holders Register. Max could be fair, Blackie thought; he'd even had the Pink Lady Courier bring it to where Blackie worked. Old man Shneerson offered the Pink Lady a coffee because she was shivering in her short pink parka and little furry pink booties. Blackie walked her out to Shneerson's creaking paternoster; he saw her smile and yip like a cowgirl when she jumped on and rode down out of sight.

Tino told him that Michael, when applying the blocks, would even ask the guys to go check and see if they had their share certificate. He'd hold the line and the guy'd stop watching the news and go peek in his sock drawer where he kept his mortgage and stuff. If it was there, Michael'd come out with it: are you going to sell it or keep the QV alive?

– He calls at supper time? Blackie asked.

– Michael doesn't take 'no' for an answer.

– I can see that.

– He hopes you guys aren't quitters. He says we need to meet again.

– He already called me. At work. Shneerson said I was busy with inventory but he told him it was urgent. Talking like that to Shneerson.

Blackie told Chickie they had to meet again and mentioned Michael's 'quitters' remark, and Chickie said that that Mike was an arrogant prick who loved meetings. But his canvassing inspired Blackie, so one Saturday he and Oz decided to do Michael MacGiligary one better and visit QV shareholders in their homes to see if they had their share certificates and keep them from selling to Max and his clique. Oz came over in the morning and together they picked the easy ones first, guys they thought would be loyal, so as not to get discouraged. Oz's idea. They would first hit on Sammy Ostrove, Oz's best friend. There was some trepidation about it since Suddy said he had seen Sammy talking to Max Foxman and it wasn't about curling.

– My car or yours?

– Mine, said Oz. – Or did you replace that battery?

Blackie hadn't.

And bugger it if it wasn't freezing out. January was like that. Maybe twenty below. But in the splintered glare of sunlight and the sky so blue it hurt his eyes, and with Oz by his side, for a moment he didn't miss Deirdre so much. Blackie had always hoped a Saturday would warm up a bit — justice for the workers — but that's not what things depended on: there is no justice, his mother used to say. And after the Holocaust the world should have ended. But it didn't.

They walked through fresh snow to Oz's maroon Olds. Blackie had been remiss lately about keeping the walk clear because without Deirdre telling him to shovel it he didn't even think about it until the snow got in his socks, giving him that cold jelly feeling. She was still coming over to check on things: do a load of laundry, tidy up, leave him notes, but she made sure he wasn't home when she did. He thought about leaving her a note, but he didn't know what to say. He wondered if he should ask Mike to write one for him.

Sammy Ostrove's house smelled of cottage cheese, Blackie thought, as he and Oz opened the door to the winter kitchen without knocking and walked right into his kitchen.

– What's that smell? Oz asked.

– You smell it, too? said Blackie.

Oz gave a shout.

– Sammy!

Sammy came into the kitchen and stood as erect as a plinth and greeted them:

– What's it going to be?

Sammy pointed them in the direction of the front room and beckoned them to follow.

They followed him to the living room where the smell of cheese got stronger. It was coming Marilyn, the baby. Blackie had no idea how Sammy was going to start looking after kids, not at his age. But Sammy was always a non-conformist. He wore sandals to work in the summer. He went to Israel in '48. He lived on a kibbutz with an aunt who believed in free love. He married a younger woman when he came back to Winnipeg. And now, at 45, he was looking after a baby. And a girl, yet; she'd give him all kinds of headaches when she got older. He'd have to worry about her getting raped, or pregnant out of wedlock, or end up married to a piece of shit guy.

– We should have brought something for the baby, said Blackie.

– Deirdre brought something, said Sammy. – Said you'd chipped in.

– She didn't tell me.

Blackie bent down and stuck his head into the crib. He fake spat on her to ward away the evil eye like his mother used to do, especially when a baby was so delicately featured, and baby Marilyn was that except for the big baby pores on her nose filled with a cheesy substance. She wasn't one of those flat-nosed, bald, pointy-headed kids, who looked like an ironed potato. Marilyn already had looks, and a head of rich starter hair.

– Look at all that hair. It's Rita Hayworth, said Blackie, his head now out of the crib, letting the kid breathe. – She's going to break hearts, Blackie said, putting his head back in again.

– They could have pulled her out by the hair, Oz said, his head out now too.

– They say it'll fall out.

– You'd better get stronger locks on your door, said Oz.

– Who locks their door?

Oz leant inside the crib again and puckered a fake spit against the evil eye. The kid stared up at the two adult fake spitters, their faces hovering above hers. She fidgeted like she had the shakes, little arms and fists jerking up and down like a drummer. Blackie had forgotten about how babies did that spazzy thing. His eyes smarted, remembering Tino when he was that little.

– What's that smell? said Oz. – It's coming from her crown. It smells like cheese.

Blackie pushed his head back in the crib and smelt her crown. In came Oz's head after his. Cheese alright.

– We're breastfeeding her, said Sammy.

– Both of you? said Oz.

– Get your heads out of the crib, said Sammy. – You'll suffocate her.

Blackie gave the baby one of his big smacking kisses. Deirdre hadn't breastfed Tino, not even in the hospital. None of her friends breastfed their kids either. The kids went straight to the bottle. Something about getting cracked nipples they were told at Hadassah meetings, Deirdre had said. Blackie wondered what that would have been like, seeing milk come out of Deirdre's breasts. Did it come out of both at the same time? The Hadassah women would know. But now with women's liberation they were all doing it: breastfeeding on demand. Blackie didn't know what liberation there was in that.

– Where's the wife?

– Yoga, said Sammy.

– Why do they do that? Blackie asked. – Deirdre goes to yoga, too.

– She likes it.

– You know why we're here? said Oz.

– Come in the kitchen. The kid's supposed to sleep.

They sat around drinking instant coffee out of mugs. They could hear the baby gurgling and cooing from the front room, then laughing for no reason.

– She'll have a *pisk*, said Oz.

– She's got a lot to say already, said Sammy.

Blackie was resting his cup on his bottom lip when Sammy said:

– I know why you're here. You didn't just come to see the baby.

– I saw you talking to Max Foxman the other night at the curling rink, Oz said. Sammy looked shifty. Oz continued:

– What'd he say to you?

– He offered to buy my share. I'm not the first guy he's approached.

– How much did he offer you?

– $3,250. Cash money. If I sold now.

Blackie had been afraid that would happen, Max slapping on more money if a guy sold before the vote. Duddy was right about him *shmearing*. But it was also a sign that Max didn't have a majority of shares, not if he was out shopping.

– Are you tempted?

– $3,250 is pretty tempting, Blackie. I've got bills. Sammy's head nodded towards the noisy kid in the front room.

– You do okay, said Oz. – You don't need the money.

– We won't have our own club anymore.

– I don't know if I'll have time to curl anyway.

Blackie and Oz looked disappointed. If Sammy had been flipped, it was *ois* QV. Blackie couldn't conceive of the curling club without Sammy. He was a fixture, and a good skip. He never lost his cool; he could draw to the button nine times out of ten; and, despite his height and thin frame, he could sweep.

– What do you mean you won't have time? Blackie asked.

– Because of the kid?

– I'm supposed to be involved.

They gawked at him.

– Involved?

– With the baby.

– That's not right, said Blackie.

Blackie didn't remember Deirdre making him stay home with Tino, or using Tino as an excuse to make him miss a curling game. That, and how he'd drop his clothes on the floor wherever he took them off to put on his pyjamas, was for Deirdre what made him the perfect husband, as she had called it. Mind you, she had said it to be funny.

– You realize if you sell to Max now, the money won't go to Israel, said Oz.

– He told me it would anyways if I wanted it to. He'd put it in escrow. Or I could keep the money and no one would know.

– That would be a moral issue for you, said Oz.

– Don't moral me. – I fought the Arabs in '48. They would attack us with swords!

– I fought the Nazis in Sicily in '43, said Blackie. – And they weren't carrying swords.

– Anyway, said Sammy.

– Anyway, what? said Oz.

– I told Max Foxman to eff off.

Sammy got up and fetched his share certificate from the bread-box.

– You guys want to hold onto this? Just in case.

– Deliver you from Temptation? Oz said.

– Just in case. I know you want to.

As they left Sammy's, they felt the wind starting to bite at their cheeks and ear lobes. In the car, Blackie checked off Sammy's name on his list. Minnow Pasner was next.

They drove further north, to Garden City, to see Minnow Pasner, where they got lost because the streets were all screwy with crescents and circles and drives, not a straight street or avenue in sight. Still, it was nice and warm in Oz's car, and he drove providentially over ice.

– So if Max went after Sammy's share, it means Max doesn't have a majority, said Blackie.

– If he's looking to buy people out, it's because he's worried.

– Duddy's right. He's *shmearing* and being *shmeared*.

– He's probably getting a kickback from the buyer.

– Dominion?

– They have nice stores. Well lit.

– Still. Not fair to tear down the QV. Lots of other land around.

– But the QV is already zoned commercial, said Oz.

– Did you phone Minnow and tell him we were coming?

– He told me to honk and wait in the car. He doesn't want us coming in the house.

– What are we? *Schnorrers*?

– He doesn't want Adelle to see us. You know Minnow. Always hiding something from Adelle.

They pulled up in front of Minnow's house, honked the horn and waited.

The wind was blowing snow around now, in whorls about a foot off the ground, scooping here, making a bump there.

Minnow, looking like a pirate, with his pyjama bottoms tucked into unbuckled galoshes, ran out of the house through the powdery drifts. He had on earmuffs, and his wife's black seal coat was hanging from his shoulders like a cape, which he held fast in his fist at his neck. In his other fist was a manila envelope. He skidded down a high snowbank from the boulevard to the street and slipped. He fell but managed to keep the envelope in the air. When he got back on his feet, his seal coat looked like it had been painted white.

Oz rolled down the window just to a small slit, but even so a vicious gust sucked the heat out of the car.

– What's with the pyjamas? Oz asked.

Minnow twisted the steel band of his earmuffs to free one ear.

– What?

– You're in pyjamas, said Oz.

– I called in sick.

Minnow worked at Canadian Tire, and Saturday was his busy day, so he must've been real bad.

– What's wrong?

– I'm sick.

Minnow looked sick. He had cotton batten coming out of his left nostril and his throat was so swollen you could see the outline of his tonsils.

– It's freezing out, said Oz. – Go back inside.

– Here's my share. I'm not selling. You guys hold on to it.

Minnow started feeding the envelope through the window gap, as if he were posting it. Oz didn't know what to say and began pushing the envelope back out.

– We trust you, said Oz.

– Trust no one. Take it. Take the envelope.

– You don't have to give it to us.

– I don't trust myself. Here. Take it. Take it already.

The wind writhed around the stripling sticking up out of the snowbank; then it ripped with enough power to flip Adelle's fur coat up and make it flutter over Minnow's head. Minnow's side was exposed and his pyjama bottoms shimmered. Just so Minnow wouldn't catch pneumonia, Oz took the envelope as it came through the gap for the last time. He opened it and read the certificate and the bearer's name. It was Minnow's alright.

– If Adelle knew, said Minnow, she'd want me to sell. So keep it for me.

– It's a lot of money, said Oz. – Even for a woman.

– You guys hold on to my share. We're still paying off Shelley's wedding. We had to pay the liquor and flowers.

– Fair is fair, said Blackie.

– I had to take out a second mortgage, said Minnow. – Cost me a thousand bucks just for the liquor. And I thought Jews didn't drink. They drink like *shkutzim*.

– So much for reputation.

– You'd better get inside, said Oz.

Minnow clutched Adelle's fur coat around his body in two fists, one at the neck and one at the waist, and ran back through the snow into the house.

The stubby pencil came out.

– Minnow's a good guy, said Blackie, putting a check next to Minnow's name.

And that went on most of the afternoon. They were doing good. Nobody was selling, or at least that's what they were telling Oz and Blackie. Some guys, like Minnow and Sammy, gave them their shares to hang onto. The more Blackie and Sammy heard from people about guys being approached by Max Foxman or his minions, the more they felt Max was bluffing and that they could put up a fight. At 5:00 o'clock, Oz called it quits:

– It wouldn't be nice to bother guys now. They're getting ready to go out with their wives.

– It's Saturday night, said Blackie, feeling sad.

When Michael MacGiligary got wind from his skip that Hy and Brian Saltzberger were thinking about selling their shares, he phoned Blackie at work to call an emergency meeting. The Saltzbergers were of historical import; if they succumbed, the QV would fall.

– It's for you, Shneerson said to Blackie. – Says it's urgent. I said I'd get you, but he insisted even more. He wouldn't take yes for an answer.

Blackie knew it would be Michael MacGiligary.

– Oz says we're sterling, Blackie said.

The line crackled as Michael said:

– We can't close the umbrella just yet. Hy and Brian Saltzberger are iffy. You should know this.

The Saltzbergers were on Chickie's list and Chickie had said they were sterling. He wouldn't be very pleased with Blackie if he told him what Michael MacGiligary just said.

– What can I do about it?

– We need to meet, said Michael.

– Chickie's not going to like having another meeting.

– Then there's Jack Sanders. He's thinking of jumping ship.

Jack was on Oz's list, but Oz had said Jack was sterling too.

– Jack's solid.

– Not what they're saying.

Blackie got the guys to meet at Oscar's on Main Street to powwow over lunch the next day. He walked instead of waiting for the Templeton bus and when he got to Oscar's he was miserable because his toes were half-frozen and his trouser cuffs wet. But the smell of rye bread cheered him up; he knew he'd feel better after having something to eat.

They had sat down to corned beef sandwiches and half a quart of truly sour dill pickles on a big plate in front of them.

– The QV's on the line, said Michael. – It's the big grab. Max Foxman's big grab. It's happening. The kickbacks are flying.

The guys were subdued.

Oz took a generous bite from his pickle. It was so sour it made him squint. He waved the other half as he spoke:

137

– Dominion *shmears* Max, Max *shmears* Jack and Hy and Brian.

– All for what?

– For his fire pit of riches, said Tino.

Blackie's toes were warming up and he was feeling better after he'd started eating, licking mustard off his knuckles, nibbling off the rags of corned beef sticking out from between the two slices of rye bread; he figured as long as there was food, meetings weren't so bad. You had to eat anyway.

– I'm not one to complain, but some of us are busy, Chickie said. – We don't need all these meetings.

– Then what are we going to do about Hy and Brian? Michael asked. They're on your list. Are you going to firm them up?

– You can't be sure they flipped. It's innuendo.

– This is about the QV, said Michael. – It's information.

– Ok. I'll phone them. But they'll think I'm pushy.

– When? When will you phone them?

Chickie got flushed. He hacked like he was going to spit, but then he swallowed. He guzzled some of his coke.

– As soon as I get a chance. I don't want to bother them. They had an unveiling last week.

– The AGM is coming, said Michael. – It's March already. Just seven weeks away. You can't go into a meeting without knowing the outcome. Something tells me you're not taking this seriously.

Chickie was about to put his knuckles into his mouth but he looked first to Oz and Blackie for sympathy.

He got none.

– I'll call Hy tonight. I'm not calling Brian. I won't go *shnorring* to him. It's embarrassing.

– Who had an unveiling? Suddy asked.

– Hy's always been the easiest to talk to, said Duddy. – He sponsored me to get into Glendale.

– He's not in Glendale, said Chickie. – And they'd never let *you* into Glendale.

138

– Hy Saltzberger neither, said Blackie. – Too picky there.

– What the hell are you getting at? Duddy asked Chickie. – Hy always liked me. He said he'd get me in. You can use Glendale for cocktail parties if you don't golf. The facilities they've got!

– Hy's not a member of Glendale, Oz said. – And he doesn't golf for sure.

– That's not what he told me, said Duddy.

– I think we have to re-canvas everyone, said Michael. – And report back to Blackie.

– There's a Malinche or two or three out there, said Tino.

– You guys see Malinches in your soup, said Chickie. – I wouldn't characterise neither Hy nor Brian as Malinches.

– Either we take this seriously or we don't, said Oz.

– I'll phone Hy but I'm not phoning everyone on my list again, said Chickie. – I don't take shit from anybody.

– Neither do I, said Duddy.

– You haven't phoned anybody, Duddy, said Michael. – I have half your list.

– I'll call my guys again, said Oz. – What are you so afraid of, Chickie? Getting a guy off his ass to answer the phone.

– Who said I'm afraid? – I just don't like being pushy. Asking them for something. And getting shit from them. Getting their remarks. I'm no *shnorrer.*

– You need to know how to pose the question properly, said Michael.

– I know how to 'pose' the question.

A few days later, Blackie went to the Sals on Matheson and Main right after work. He wanted company and he knew Duddy'd be there; Duddy was always there on Fridays around 5:00 o'clock.

Duddy was sitting in a window booth, enjoying a nip and a cup of hot coffee. He had a pencil in his fist and a large red scribbler opened beside his coffee cup. Blackie ordered a cup of scalding coffee and approached Duddy's booth. A big greasy parka with a fur-lined hood had slid on to the floor next to Duddy.

– Your parka's on the floor, said Blackie.

– Thanks, said Duddy, without picking it up. – Didn't see you pull up. Where did you park?

– Right in front.

They both looked out the window onto Main Street at the snow falling gently in big flakes on the roof and hood of Blackie's car. The wind was picking up gently, then came a big gust.

– If it keeps snowing like this, your car'll be buried by the snowplows, said Duddy.

– It's just flurries.

– It's supposed to really to come down.

The streets were already white.

– We'll see. But that's March for you, said Blackie. – That's a big scribbler. What are you doing?

– Writing that book on dreams. Dee bought me it.

Blackie noticed Duddy hadn't gotten much down on the page.

– I parked the cab in the lot behind, said Duddy. – That way it won't get buried by the snowplows. They'll be out fast enough. Now it's snowing.

Blackie started on his nip and let his coffee cool. He didn't want to burn the roof of his mouth.

– Max is still in Vegas another few days. He took his kids. Did I tell you that? He's crazy about those kids, for a piece of shit guy. One of them has a gambling problem. Only because he loses though. Sophie's miserable about it. She babies that kid; she still shaves him.

– How do you know he's in Vegas?

– Sophie told me on the phone.

– You shouldn't call her. That's in the Jewish Torah.

– She called me. She asked about you?

Hearing that made Blackie's nip taste better.

– She said we should come over again.

– We?

– She stressed the 'we.'

Duddy suddenly remembered to pick up his parka from the floor and put it on the bench seat.

– I went to Chickie's yesterday, said Duddy. – Did you see Linda lately? I did. She's like a balloon already. If he catches that guy, it'll go to show.

Blackie remembered he still hadn't asked Chickie about Linda. He'd been avoiding dropping by, afraid he'd see Linda pregnant.

The wind started whining and winding up good. Kernels of snow pecked at the big windows of the Sals; it wasn't just flurries or flakes. It made Blackie glad to be inside where it was warm, with a nip in his hand like he'd never let it go. He was crushing the bun he could see.

– Max Foxman's in Vegas, said Duddy.

– You just said.

– It's happening, Duddy said with a wink.

– With Sophie?

Blackie regretted asking that; it made Duddy's plan to seduce Sophie Foxman sound like a normal thing, and normal meant sanctioned.

– What's happened with her that you're not telling me?

– Pants-wise?

– Or otherwise.

– Meh. She says I'm not sincere.

– You aren't.

– She said I had no way of showing that I was sincere to be trusted.

– Send her flowers.

Blackie was being facetious, but Duddy was impervious to it.

– I did. From the florist's on Main and Belmont. From a pail. I splurged on the price.

– Have you been back at Max's house?

– I've been around. We've had a few drinks in the rec-room. She's never let me in her front room. That's the acids test.

– You're not sincere. You told me yourself she doesn't titillate you. You told everybody.

– I keep that covered up from her. She's a master of suspicion. I admit I knew it would be a challenge without appeal. So now I know how a prostitute feels.

Blackie pressed his coffee cup against his bottom lip and watched Duddy pop the last of his burger into his mouth, getting relish and mustard on his fingers. He licked those and then got started on the courtesy butter pads, which he smeared on his fist. Watching Duddy working with the knife and butter pads — scraping and smearing — was mesmerizing. If he didn't restart the conversation, Duddy could end up hypnotising him.

– Oz did a new tally, said Blackie.

– A tally of what?

– Our lists. The North End is pretty solid.

– What about Hy and Brian?

– Chickie says 'sterling.' Mike just panicked.

– And Jack Sanders?

– Oz talked to him.

– You have to put the blocks to those people.

– What I'm saying, Duddy, is you can stop bothering Sophie Foxman. The QV is safe.

– Not what I heard.

– What'd you hear?

– I heard Major Midgie sold his share. Cash money.

Duddy was referring to Manny Mizhkinsky, who everybody had called Major Midgie since he was a kid. He was one of the founders of the club, so Blackie found Duddy's claim hard to believe.

– Who told you?

– Major Midgie himself. Coming out of Canadian Tire. He showed me a cashier's check for $3,250 bucks. Cash money. So I think the QV is far from safe. How's your nip?

Blackie's nip wasn't tasting so great now.

– Max is getting grubbier, he said.

– How come they call it a nip? Duddy said.

– Two syllables shorter than hamburger, said Blackie.

– I could go for another nip, said Duddy. – They put just the right amount of grease on the bun here. They use a brush. He slid out the booth, knocking his parka to the floor again.

– Get me another one too, said Blackie, pulling a fin from his money clip.

Duddy took out his roll and flashed it like he was waving a flashlight into Blackie's eye.

– Your money's no good here.

– Thanks, Duddy.

Duddy came back to the booth with two more nips. He had chatted up the girl at the counter while he waited.

– They love me here.

Duddy took the first bite and waved his nip under Blackie's chin and then in a circle around Blackie's face:

– The maid has the night off, Duddy said. – Goes to show.

– Goes to show what?

– It's coming down good. Like it did at Christmas.

– That was a big snow, said Blackie.

– That snow was good for the *shkutzim* and their Christmases. All the little Christian kids like that.

– Santa and the reindeer and all that, said Blackie. – We can't compete with Christmas.

– If you ask me, said Duddy, Santa Claus has actually got to be a Laplander. How else would he know so much about reindeer? Dee says they're Cree, too. She says that's anthropology. Books.

– There's a point.

– So let's go over there.

– Where?

– To Sophie Foxman's. The maid has the night off. Max is in Vegas with the boys. He told his kid with the gambling problem that if he stopped gambling he'd take him to Vegas.

– That's parenting.

Hearing about the maid and Max and the boys again gave

Blackie a bad feeling.

– Look at that. I should get going.

A snowplow, its shovel brimming, went by scraping the curb. Then it swerved hard to the left of Blackie's parked car and built a snow fort around it up to the fenders. Bugger. He should've known that would happen.

– I'm going over there, Duddy said. – I'm getting off with her, tonight or never. On a wink and a prayer. And you're coming. Max neglects her. You're the proof I'm sincere.

– No sense driving in that, said Blackie. – It's really snowing now.

– The cab'll make it. It has studs. And chains in the trunk.

– It'll get stuck, said Blackie.

– I'm going.

– This whole idea of yours is demeaning to her.

– I've been demeaned and plenty. You don't think I wasn't ever demeaned?

– What about their kids?

– The boys are in Vegas with Max. Don't you listen?

– I meant in the other way. You could break up the family.

– One of their kids is really hooked on cards. She told me. They took him to the Rabbi to straighten him out.

– I mean what about their kids and their feelings? That's what happens when you break up a family. Consequences. The kids suffer.

– She's not going to tell her kids if I get into her pants.

– What about Dee?

– I don't spend all my time with her. Even last Christmas, I had something else going on. She thought I'd spend it with her and her kids. They're crazy about me. I'm teaching them hypnosis. She said: it's Christmas, Duddy. So I told her about Hitler and what he did to us. He went to mass, you know. She already knew about that because someone at the March of Dimes told her. And its common knowledge because of the Auschwitz camps, she

144

said. But I personalized it for her: you know. She got a real shock our first time. It started off like flowers and poems at night, but then she realized I was circumcised. That came as a shock. She put her glasses on like Nana Mouskouri to see it properly. She thought something was wrong with me! She thought it'd hurt if she rubbed it. She flicked it like a lighter to see my threshold for pain. Nothing's wrong with me. She found that out, and how! Did I tell you she works for the March of Dimes? Maybe I did or maybe I didn't. I like to keep girls mysterious. She has white shoes for there. I met her at the pen, I told you that, but when I wanted to date her after my release, I went around to where she worked, hoping she'd bump into me by accident. And she did because either I'm psychic, or sooner or later she had to leave the building for lunch. When she came out, I didn't recognize her because she was wearing a white uniform and I'd met her in normal clothes. She told me a lot of people didn't recognize her when she was wearing her uniform so that didn't make me a first. That was great though, that uniform, the way it fit. And then when we went on our first date, she wasn't wearing her uniform and I didn't recognise her again. And I know people.

– You should just go to her house. Appreciate what you have.

– No. I'm going to Sophie's, said Duddy. – My mind's made up. Weather or no weather. Look. Cabs are out there. What if people have to get somewhere and they can't take the car, like to the hospital or a viewing. If other cabs can be out so can mine. And you're coming with.

– So you saw Major Midgie's cheque?

– If Major Midgie sold his share, you can bet other guys did, too. It's up to me to save the QV. I can do this.

– But she thinks you're insincere.

– She just thinks it.

– And she's right.

– But she doesn't know it.

– Yes, she does.

– But not why I'm being insincere. The real reason. And if I go in this weather, it'll be proof I am sincere.

– Or stupid.

– That's Chickie talking.

– Does she even know you have a girlfriend?

– It's winding down with Dee. Always happens after things begin so hot and all your feelings for the girl are outside your body for the taking. Dee's a princess. She doesn't get hysterical. She knows how to hold her head high.

– So you'd really drive there in this? Look at it come down.

– It would make it romantic for her.

– So why do you need me?

– She trusts you. She's always grilling me about you. About you and Deirdre. She wanted to know if Deirdre was with someone else romantically. She thinks I'm your best friend, which raises me in her consideration. She always says nice things about when you were a kid. I bet after Max stopped talking to her, she must have had regrets about not waiting for you when you went overseas. And her son, the gambler? He'd be different if you were the father. Or when that woman phoned her anonymously and demeaned her.

– What woman?

– The woman Max was getting something on the side with. 'You're reliable,' she said. I know what she's been going through. Life hasn't been easy for her. Sophie has an inner self-respect and she recognizes that in you. You're innate. Doesn't matter how she gets it from me but she needs this for her ego after Max stopped talking to her. I'm saving her ego in the dark.

Duddy held out his arms and cupped his hands together as if he was saving a half-frozen bird.

– I'm saving her. With my hot hands. And you're coming with. She trusts in you. Be a friend.

Duddy's studded tires barely got them over the Midtown Bridge, but they couldn't get much traction by the time he got to

Corydon. He was crawling through more than two feet of it, up to the headlights, when he decided to pull the cab to the curb and put on the chains, managing to press the front fender into a snowbank with the rear end angling out.

– We can't leave the cab screwy like this, said Blackie.

– I'll back up and we'll put the chains on. The studs weren't enough. Goes to show.

Duddy backed out of the snowbank.

They got out of the car into snow falling so thick and fast they could barely see each other. An attempt was made to put the chains on the front tires: they had scuffed away the snow with their feet and were standing in the flare of the front headlights in eddies of snow while they looked down at the chains, one set lying flat in front of each tire, figuring out how to wrap them around the treads. The snow kept coming down fast, and soon they couldn't see the chains.

They jumped up on a snowbank as a city plow bore down on them and pushed a stiff dike of snow against the cab right up to the door windows.

– He did that on purpose, said Duddy. – *Mishlockt yiddin.*

– We're really stuck now, said Blackie.

– We should call a cab. We can call from the drugstore.

– Do you see any cabs out?

– Then we're hoofing it, said Duddy. – We're almost there. It's just a mile down Corydon. It'll be a cinch.

– In your world.

– It'd be a cinch with snowshoes. They sell them at Nelly McKelly's. In March they go on sale.

– What's that got to do with anything for Chrissakes? said Blackie.

– Come on. Come on. We can walk to Sophie's. It's twelve miles to walk home.

– Let's go in the drugstore. It's open.

– And when it closes?

147

– They won't kick us out if there's a blizzard, Duddy.

– It's just a snowstorm.

– Look at it. It's really blowing. I think it's a blizzard.

– Put your hood up. It's just me and you, Blackie. We've gotten this far. You want to spend the night in the drugstore?

He didn't.

They put up their parka hoods and tied each other's scarves around their mouths and nose and knotted them from behind like schoolkids. The wind blasting, they walked south down Corydon in the direction of City Park and the Zoo, where they'd turn left somewhere to get to Sophie's. Duddy's pace was driven and relentless; natural adversity lit a fire under him, so did the call of the wild. They were both breathing heavily into their scarves. Blackie sucked up the smell of wet wool.

– What do you think the animals at the Zoo think when it snows? Duddy said. – I mean the African animals, not beavers or weasels.

– They're smart enough not to leave their dens, said Blackie, panting. – They stay inside.

– You know, a monkey has more square feet in the zoo than we had in jail. What does that say about people?

– Nothing good.

– You're panting, said Duddy.

– Don't make me talk.

– I go to the Assiniboine Zoo with Dee's kids. Puts me in her good books for when I want action. I take them tobogganing. It's great to look at the animals with them. You know those people have more than just *he* and *she* than we do.

– Like *it*?

– No. They have a special another *it* for things that are far away and close up. So they get in closer to things than we do. It puts them inside the animal or the thing, she said.

– Don't make me talk. And wait up.

Blackie thought he'd soon be gasping for breath. But if he didn't

148

keep up he'd lose sight of Duddy. Visibility was nil. He ran to catch up.

– It's like in Kripkin's instructions, said Duddy. – When you hypnotize someone you actually stand in their head. Very still, at attention, and with authority you say: do this, do that.

Breathing hard, Blackie said:

– I thought you said that book was a rip-off.

– Don't talk if you're out of breath.

Blackie nodded. He felt sharp pains in his chest. Maybe he was panicking. People had been known to die in storms like these.

– You'd think the animals'd want to see snow like this, said Duddy. – Maybe animals are not driven like us. They don't quest like us.

They trudged on, Duddy swinging and twisting his arms from side to side as the wind screamed.

– There's romance here, Duddy said. – A single hair from their tiny parts pulls a guy as strong as steel cable through a snowstorm. What a guy will do for a woman!

– To a woman, Blackie said weakly into his scarf. He had wool hair on his tongue and in his mouth.

– We're almost there, said Duddy, twisting to look at Blackie. Look. There's Max's house.

– What if she's not home? Blackie asked.

– Na. Who'd go out on a night like this?

NINE

B lackie thought Sophie Foxman sparkled when she opened the door. There was health and warmth and shyness in her look. She hadn't been drinking, Blackie noticed. She was wearing her hair down, with a couple of locks across her forehead, just as he remembered it from long ago. But she couldn't have been expecting them?

– Where's the action? Duddy said, barging in.

Sophie winked and Blackie thought it was for him. – Come in, Sophie said. – You look like a snowmen.

Blackie and Duddy kicked off their galoshes and took off their parkas and scarves, which were scabbed up with snow. Sophie brought out a whisk broom and swept the snow vigorously from their parka hoods, scarves, and zippers, and then she went at the clips of their galoshes until every fleck of snow was removed. She made them take off their shoes too, which meant they'd get to sit in her front room. She looked at Duddy's pointy shoes twice.

Sophie offered them spots on her lavish chesterfield set on carpet coasters sinking into the plush ivory broadloom. Blackie's eyes took in the expanse of the front room and wondered if this was the kind of house Deirdre had wanted to live in when she had campaigned a few years ago for Blackie to be more ambitious, make more money, and move them to the South End: another fault of his he hadn't seen soon enough.

Blackie sat down on one of the chesterfields, wishing Sophie had let him keep his shoes on; he didn't like going around in socks in a strange house, but at least he didn't have an egg on his heel, like Duddy's did. His toes were numb from the cold.

Blackie could feel, taste, and smell the lush Foxman family and all its happy and disappointed moments. There was a smug studio photograph of Max in a silver frame on a teak sideboard: in a very manly pose, his angled shoulders in a Perry Como sweater over a turtleneck.

Duddy grinned cheerfully and moved right in on Sophie, sitting close to her, his nose near her ear.

– Where's Max? Blackie said, feigning innocence like a guy who'd never visit a married woman when her husband wasn't home.

– Vegas. With the boys.

– How come you didn't you go?

– I get on a plane and I can't breathe. Last time, I got off before the plane took off.

– Max doesn't talk to her anymore, said Duddy, as if no one knew this, including Sophie. – It's ostracism like in the Torah.

Sophie looked spry and gay: she was wearing a one-piece blue lounging outfit with Capri-cut pants that showed off her ankles. The whole thing buttoned up the back from the bum, and Blackie caught himself wondering how you'd get something like that on, or off.

Blackie told himself it was not only humiliation he was saving Sophie from. Infidelity could have economic and social consequences if Max divorced her. She'd lose all this: the front room you could play lacrosse in, the matching chesterfields arranged in a U, the glass coffee table, the teak furniture, and the three-car garage, probably with skidoos gassed up to race across the frozen river. Worst of all, a divorced woman lost all her status. She'd be worse off than an old maid in the eyes of the community, and she'd end up bitter and frustrated and pitied. No way was Duddy getting his hot hands on her: Blackie felt himself worthy and on a mission, numb toes and all.

– I'll mix some beverages, said Sophie.

After a few big gulps of their drinks Duddy had Sophie in stitches.

– You make me laugh, she said, her big violet eyes darting back and forth between the men.

– If you can make a woman laugh, you can make her do anything, Marilyn Monroe said in a quote, Duddy said.

They finished their first drink and Sophie got them another.

– Did Marilyn really say that? Sophie asked on her return with the beverages.

– It's a direct quotation, said Duddy. – She said it to JFK.

– We'll see about that, said Sophie, looking sceptically at Duddy.

– She overdosed on pills, you know, said Duddy. – She was talking to Jack Kennedy when she died. Long distance.

– Very, very long distance, said Sophie. – I mean, when she died.

Sophie turned her eyes on Blackie again. Her mouth was slackening slightly.

– JFK was a good husband, said Duddy.

– Ach, husbands. Where's the *rachmonis*? Don't get me on to that topic. Max doesn't even talk to me. No. He doesn't even look my way. He's shunning me.

Now Sophie, instead of sparkling, pouted at Blackie. Blackie didn't know whether that meant he was included in the husband reference, but he might as well have been.

– Husbands are useless, she said, taking a sip of her second drink.

– There are no bar mitzvah fathers, Duddy said, eager to agree with her. – That's for sure. Who's making the egg sandwiches Saturday mornings? Where are the fathers?

– They're at Oscar's having breakfast like sensible people, said Blackie. – Or throwing rocks.

– Don't get me started on curling, Sophie said. – Thank god Max's getting rid of the club. It's a drain on his time. When that's

152

out of the way, maybe he'll be home more.

– To ignore you? said Duddy. – Don't forget that.

– Maybe he'll talk to me again. I never could understand what he saw in that game.

– You curled, too.

– One season. It was a fad.

– I, for one, don't think the QV is finished, said Blackie.

– I know it is.

– I thought Max doesn't talk to you.

– He doesn't. But we had dinner at the Old Bailey with these people who own Dominion Stores. He needed a wife there to show he's serious. Listen, if it's not over, people should tell them at Dominion.

– The shareholders have to decide, said Blackie.

– Max has been buying up shares. Even you North End people are selling your shares.

– How do *you* know this?

– I've seen the shares. They're in his den. It's a lot of money for some people to resist.

For Blackie, this didn't mesh with Oz's tallies, even taking Major Midgie into account. Either guys were lying to them out of shame or Sophie was. But why would she?

– Got anything to eat? Duddy asked.

– Icecream? We've got six tubs in the chest freezer downstairs?

– I'll have white.

– You mean vanilla?

– That's white.

– Blackie?

– White's okay for me.

Sophie came back with a tub of vanilla ice cream, three bowls and spoons, and a professional scoop.

– I nearly fell in the freezer, she laughed, a laugh that transported Blackie back to old times.

She refreshed their drinks while Duddy scooped and filled

the bowls to the brims. Blackie didn't know if it was going to be his second or third drink, which is the same as a warning. Outside the wind buffeted one of the large windows, making it rattle. He had thought South End homes were built to a higher standard. The ruckus reminded him the storm was still mad and that Suddy's cab and Blackie's car had to be buried up to their antennae by now.

– This is creamy, said Duddy. – I hate it when it has ice crystals.

Blackie tried some from his dish. Duddy wasn't kidding; it was really buttery and there were no frost particles. On top of the rich portions that Duddy had scooped out for them, Sophie had put sprinkles and shredded peanuts. Blackie felt guilty eating Max Foxman's ice cream, drinking his liquor, and entertaining his wife while he was in Vegas

– Do you guys do yoga? Or meditate? Her cheeks were getting a peach bloom on them.

– I wouldn't do those, said Blackie.

He linked yoga to Deirdre's transformation. Before that he'd only seen it on TV, where men in turtlenecks and corduroy blazers and women in pantsuits planted their bums on a shag rug next to a tray of wine and cheese. He'd seen other things on TV about yoga: people in India wearing silk shifts and long scarves. He couldn't see himself squatting into those positions. When Deirdre first started going to yoga, he'd laughed at her, so if she saw him do it now, she'd sneer but good. No way he'd get down on the floor.

– I can't crouch in those positions, he said.

– If you can curl you can do yoga.

– No I can't, said Blackie.

Come on. You'll like it, she said and slid off the chesterfield onto the thick broadloom, landing with a laugh. She crouched on her haunches and then she got into a yoga position.

–Duddy? she said, patting the carpet.

Duddy was wild to assent, winking at Blackie as he roosted on the carpet, crossing his legs in the position Sophie showed him, which pulled Duddy's groin, as Blackie could see from Duddy's expression.

– You have dancer's legs, Duddy said to Sophie.

– Don't talk. Just close your eyes.

Duddy shut his eyes and clenched his fists. Sophie instructed him how to breathe, and the two of them sucked air in through their noses and held it for five Mississippis.

She patted the carpet beside her thigh.

– Blackie?

– I don't do that sort of thing, Blackie said. – I'm fine where I am.

– It's not against the Torah, said Duddy.

– It's not in the Torah, said Blackie.

– That's what I'm saying, Duddy said.

– Don't talk. Keep breathing. Big breath in. Hold it. Breathe out.

Sophie left Duddy to his breathing, turned to Blackie and patted the carpet again.

– Blackie. Don't be cranky.

Blackie, feeling cold and sozzled, his toes defrosting in pain, got on the floor and crossed his legs and shut his eyes. He sank into the plush carpet and worried about the ice cream melting in the tub on Sophie's coffee table.

He inhaled when Sophie said. Big breath in. Hold it. Breathe out. Stuffing his lungs with Foxman family air wasn't that bad. Smidgens of anxiety about this and that, such as Deirdre's contempt, Tino living in the *shmutz* and being a Trotskyite, attached at the hip to Michael MacGiligary, and the QV winding up all just seemed to give him gas. The drinks helped too, he supposed. Had he had two or three? Would Sophie start humming, as he had seen on TV? Would he have to hum?

– Don't think of anything, Sophie said as if she could hear his anxiety. – Just breathe and empty your mind when you exhale. Think of nothing.

Is that even possible? To think of nothing, which is thinking, isn't it? He'd give it a try. He listened to hear how the other two were breathing, Sophie in even breaths, Duddy like he was in an oxygen tent.

He repressed his urge to think by wondering if there was someone equivalent to Duddy in yoga countries like India. But wondering like that had to be thinking. And still the ice cream was melting, wasn't it? There was no way of getting out of the activity without offending Sophie, so Blackie rolled with it, listened to his own breathing for about ten minutes, which made him even more *shickered* and squizzy.

Literally lacking *zitzfleisch*, Duddy said:

– I can't sit still like this any longer.

– *Sha*, Duddy. You have to relax.

– I'm relaxed. Too relaxed. I have to drop a few friends off at the pool, that's how relaxed I am, Duddy said with his eyes shut.

– *Sha,* Duddy.

– That's it. I gotta go.

Duddy bounced up to go to the powder room to take a crap, leaving Blackie and Sophie alone, their knees barely touching, listening to their own breathing and each other's, their eyes shut tight. From so close up, Blackie could smell her good perfume. He was feeling drowsy and emotional with her voice soft in his ear. It would be nicer if he didn't feel thumbtacks in his toes as they thawed.

– Duddy's funny, Sophie said suddenly. – He's a mesmerist, he told me.

– You really think he's funny?

– I think he's after me. Or is it my imagination?

– He has a big heart.

– That's what he says too.

– You've really seen those shares Max bought?

– He keeps them in his den.

Their knees touched and Blackie had to repress wanting to open his eyes to see if it had been accidental. He also wondered whether her eyes were open and if she was watching him. He wished Duddy wouldn't get back from the pool, wished for him to fall in.

– How are you feeling? Relaxed?

– I guess relaxed. Sure.

– How do you sleep most nights?

– For the shits.

– Don't open your eyes.

– I'm not. Are your eyes open?

– No.

Blackie did the breathing thing, silently counting Mississippis, trying not to move his lips while counting.

– Are you dating someone? she said.

– I'm curling. A lot. We're down to the 64s in the Manitoba Brier.

If they kept curling like they were, they'd make it down to the 32s for sure. And then five more wins and they'd be in the semis. Even curling away from home, they were doing swell. They'd beaten teams from the Grain Exchange, Rossmere and the club from Flin Flon.

– Why did you come here tonight?

– Duddy thinks you're lonely.

– That's sweet.

– He has a big heart.

– And why are you here?

He opened his eyes and found hers open, looking into his. She touched his knees with her palms.

– You're lonely? she said.

– That's how it is.

– Why be lonely?

Between two fingers she was now rubbing the fabric of his trousers, but no longer his knees.

He thought about touching her hand, but before he could work up his nerve Duddy was back and sitting down in yoga position, his elbow touching Sophie's.

The three of them shut their eyes and started doing serious yoga again until Duddy, with one eye open to see who had their eyes closed, said:

– Why don't we put on one of Max's videotapes?

– Don't talk, said Sophie.

– You have a VCR. I saw it.

– Don't talk.

– I relax when I talk.

Sophie got them breathing deep again until Blackie felt stapled to the floor and, finally, near oblivion.

– Okay, open your eyes and breathe normal, said Sophie.

– Can I see your video recorder? Duddy asked.

– First one on the block to have one, Sophie said, bitterly. – It's by the drinks cart.

Duddy sprang off the carpet and examined the machine. Blackie had never seen one before.

– We should play some of the adult movies Max sells.

– How do you know about those?

– I saw them behind the bar in the rec room. He's got stacks and stacks. Wrapped up for wholesale.

– They're so ludicrous, she said. – There's no plot.

– I'll be back in a sec, said Duddy.

– I'm not watching them, Sophie shouted as Duddy headed down the stairs.

Sophie and Blackie said nothing to each other. Blackie was still dazed by the yoga and what had or what had not happened while Duddy had been in the bathroom.

Duddy bounded back up the stairs and put a tape in the machine. Sophie poured out their dregs and mixed fresh drinks.

The first scene of the movie showed a scabby apartment building and a caption that said 'Bel Air, Beverly Hills,' but it could have been anywhere warm.

After two minutes a white guy in bell bottoms and a blond Afro

158

wrapped round tightly by a red ribbon came into a room and sat down and smoked a joint with a hippie woman in a mini skirt and high boots. He had just dropped by to see his friend, the girl's boyfriend. They talked about the girl's boyfriend who wasn't home yet because he was in San Francisco, the guy himself said. This was obviously phoney: Blackie wondered why the guy would drop by to see a friend that he knew was in San Francisco.

Sophie fell asleep just as the couple started heavy petting. She started snoring softly. The couple in the movie got almost bare naked, the guy with his socks still on. The woman unzipped her boots, and then they went over to a water bed. The camera zoomed in skin tight.

– That's the primary erogenous zone, said Duddy.

– That's a lot of hair, said Blackie. – That's really embarrassing.

– There's going to be a 69, said Duddy.

As Duddy predicted, the guy ended up upside down, almost standing on his head, his hair ribbon slipping but never actually falling off his forehead.

– Why's he wearing a ribbon?

– It's a headband, said Duddy. – If I do that, it takes me five minutes to get my bearings straight after.

So as the guy came around behind the girl, who was already crouching, it didn't feel right for Blackie to be watching this with Duddy, or any man. From behind the crouching girl, the guy squatted and lifted his chin and the camera zoomed in on his simper.

– It's like zoo baboons, said Duddy.

– Turn it off, Blackie said.

– I don't know how.

– Pull out the plug.

Sophie was out like a light.

– We can't let her sleep on the floor like this.

– What are you going to do with her?

Duddy picked Sophie up and lumbered her upstairs to the

master bedroom. Blackie pulled out the plug of the video recorder and followed Duddy to make sure he didn't touch Sophie once he put her down on the bed.

– I'll put her into pyjamas to make her comfortable, said Duddy.

– She might not sleep okay dressed. Max's isn't even talking to her. He doesn't even look her in the eyes, you heard her.

– She's in loungewear, said Blackie. – She's comfortable enough. She'll sleep okay in what she's wearing. Just take her shoes off.

– You take her shoes off.

Duddy went over to the *shaffa* and rummaged a bit in the top drawer while Blackie pulled off her shoes. She had the prettiest feet in the city.

– Don't take anything, Blackie said. – You shouldn't be doing that anyway.

– I'm not trespassing. I'm just looking for the shares. Look, Max's *tallis zekl*.

– They're in the den she said, Blackie said.

– That's what *she* said.

– Let's go, said Blackie.

Blackie took one last look at Sophie: she was flushed and sleeping soundlessly. As he flicked off the light and shut the door behind them, he felt pleased with himself that he hadn't let Duddy touch her

They went back to the front room, finished the ice cream, which had melted into a sugary vanilla soup. They left the greasy tub on the coffee table. Outside, the wind was baying.

– We're going to have to sleep on the chesterfields, said Blackie.

They cleared off the many petite, sequined, white and pink and silver cushions and bunked down on a chesterfield each. Duddy covered up with a rush-coloured throw rug and Blackie a blue afghan. Uncomfortable, Duddy picked up the pillows he'd thrown on the carpet and reclined on them, like a god on a cloud, humming.

160

Blackie turned off the lamp on the corner table and the vast room was illuminated solely by the boulevard street lamp whipped by flurries. They heard the wind shriek and bend the tips of Max's evergreens. Gusts sculpted drifts from powdery snow. Blackie and Duddy whispered in the dark to each other like kids at summer camp.

– We'll be better friends after tonight, said Duddy.

– We've been friends since you were born.

– You met Suddy first.

– When he was six months old.

– Friendship lasts if you keep up the payments.

– True is true.

– Life is a bitter pill, said Duddy, but friends make it go down easy.

– You're right.

– I'm almost everybody's friend. Many guys think *I'm* their best friend. There are guys who'd pay to be with me. Duddy shifted on his chesterfield, rearranging the pillows under his neck and trunk. He had at least half a dozen cushions under him. – I've told other people this so I might as well tell you.

– Alright.

– Do you believe in the Fires of Gehenna? – My father did. For me.

– There's no afterlife.

– What about the World of Love? After death I heard you go to the World of Love. Isn't that in the Torah?

– I think you go to the World of Truth, maybe. The *emes*. That's what they taught at the Little Talmud Torah. Or what I remember. The World of Love is something you made up.

– If the Torah is made up, then I can make things up too, said Duddy.

– That's just baloney what you're saying.

– Michael MacGiligary told me the Torah was made up.

– When did you see Michael?

– Sometimes, when I drop off mice to Davinsky, I go visit him and Tino at university. Look at the girls. I sit with the boys on the radiators sometimes and I look at the girls. You know, one day they took me to a common room for me to see the most beautiful Icelandic girl in the world. That's consideration. She was reading poems to herself without moving her lips in Icelandic. Tino said she studied ten hours a day.

– They're studying hard. You shouldn't bother them.

– They're talking hair styles. The permanent revolution this, the permanent revolution that. And about dead people. You'd think the dead were alive for those brats. And Viet Cong. And the Maoists want to kill Tino. It gets hot on the bum on those radiators. Mike says Tino's sticking to sciences and isn't going to be pre-med. If you ask me, from what I saw, the girls are prettier in arts.

Blackie hadn't heard anything about Tino not being pre-med anymore. He supposed Deirdre knew.

– Mike says the Torah was written by humans, with huge imaginations that were wild and violent. He told me God killed millions of people in the Torah, if you count them.

– I don't know about millions.

– In the Flood. How many drowned you think?

– How could I know that?

– Think about it. More than a million for sure. And in Jericho?

– Who knows how many people were alive then? said Blackie.

– But He said He was sorry, didn't He?

– I said that. I told Mike about the rainbow and being sorry. And he said 'yeah, the fire next time.' Then what kind of 'sorry' would follow that? That's why Gehenna has fires and not water.

The wind rattled the big picture window panes. Blackie tried to form a mental picture of the Fires of Gehenna, but instead he got a mental picture of the World of Love: he saw Sophie Foxman naked on pillows in front of luffing drapery.

– Is Deirdre coming back already?

162

– No.

– She might never. Brace for that. She still doing the laundry at least?

– Does a load, dries a load, folds a load. She comes to check in on me. She leaves me notes.

– You should leave her a note. I know what I'd say.

Saying that Deirdre checked in made Blackie feel warm. He recalled how much better he slept when he discovered traces of Deirdre's presence: the folded laundry, a clean fridge, and the notes.

– Who's she to leave the home? Duddy asked. – My policy is you have to know how to discard people when they disappoint you. Sluff them off.

– I've never lost a friend.

– I should have undressed her at least, said Duddy. Sophie, I mean. Max Foxman owes me that. At least seen her big ones. That's a sweetness that lasts forever. A victory. Listen exactly to what I'm going to say about that.

A long story began to purl from Duddy's brain. Blackie could have said he didn't want to listen exactly to what Duddy had to say but, out of fatigue, Blackie succumbed to the disorientation of the Duddysphere until Duddy woke him up.

– Are you asleep? Dumbest question.

– I was.

– He owes me that. Max owes me.

– He doesn't owe you anything.

– Oh yes he does. For closing the QV. And, and, and, and more.

– He hasn't closed it yet.

– Major Midgie sold out. And Max still owes us from when we played him skins.

Blackie had forgotten all about that. He could use that money.

– You think we have a chance to keep the club open? Duddy asked.

– As long as the guys stay solid. Not everything is money.

– Bloody Major Midgie.

– We don't know for sure. Max might just be playing with us. You said yourself.

– I saw the cashier's check.

– That's what you said.

– When's the AGM? Duddy said.

– After the Father and Son Banquet.

– That's pretty soon, but I can't go. It's restricted to fathers and sons.

– You could take Dee's kids, Blackie said.

– One's a girl.

– Take the boy.

– The guys might look at him funny.

– Since when did you care? You're a maverick.

– And he's not a status Indian.

– I don't think they'd care about that.

– What if I'm unfaithful to Dee? How could I take the kid then?

– So don't be.

– So how can I punish Max?

– Shoot him. You know where to get a gun. Two guns. But this thing with Sophie, as Oz says, it'll come back to bite you in the ass.

– But I'm starting to find Sophie tantalizing. She has a nice enough face.

– I thought she didn't appeal to you.

– I thought my appealing to her was enough for me. But she does have blue eyes, so I wouldn't feel demeaned — me going against my own criteria — laying her if I concentrate on those eyes. They were really beautiful tonight.

– They were.

– She's trying not to drink too much. I think that's your influence. And she knows stuff. That yoga was nice for BS. She could tell anyone she's been to India and they'd believe her. I felt something warm with her. I think I could get a bone on. What would

Max Foxman say to that? How'd he like that?

Blackie felt Duddy had more to say on the subject.

– I need to sleep, Duddy.

– So maybe I could find the appeal. Visually, I mean. But what if the soul is blind? Legally blind. I shouldn't need visual appeal. Does the soul have eyes?

Blackie had never thought about that and had no craving to start.

– It's not deaf, Duddy added. – You can talk to it, so it can't be deaf. But it could be blind. Except for a poet's. So maybe I could get off with her if she touched my soul deep inside with hers. Then once I've got a hard-on, I make her spin on it. Like a lazy Susan. I shouldn't have put the adult movie on. Bad move.

– It put her to sleep.

– They're mostly for men. Too hairy for you? I'd say they both had decent pelts. Did that disgust you?

– That and what poked out, said Blackie.

– You're too good, Blackie. That's your problem. Deirdre, too. You two always reminded me of Hansel and Gretel holding hands in the woods, then getting married happily ever after.

– Incest is innocent by you?

– It never dawned on me. Gretel was his sister. You know, I can see that video recorder thing catching on. I predict it. They'll say it's to watch movies with the family so you don't have to spend on popcorn and chocolate bars and soft drinks, but now I see why guys would buy it for when they're alone. He has a knack.

– Who?

– Max Foxman. For making money.

The wind howled in high pitches and the windows trembled.

– You know, said Duddy, the first night of the world could have been like this. Most people think it was nice weather because of the Garden of Eden.

– How would anyone know?

– How did the Indians survive living in this before we came?

165

– In tents. They were warm enough with a fire going. They had furs.

– They knew how to trap.

– There was lots to trap then.

– What if I go upstairs? Undress her? Duddy asked. – What would happen?

– Just let her sleep. Let me sleep.

– I wouldn't touch her. Just watch. I could whack off next to her.

– Just to set the mood?

– Lying down, she doesn't look like she has fat hanging from her *pupick*. I'd get into practice for when I have to do it. Psyche myself up.

– Heaven will punish you.

– I just might go up there.

Blackie wanted to keep an eye on Duddy so that he wouldn't go up to Sophie's bedroom, but he was falling asleep. His calf muscles were starting to ache from the trudge through the snow, his toes prickly as they thawed.

– I could get up those stairs in ten seconds. You could time me.

– That'd be wrong.

– People have demeaned me.

– But not Sophie.

– I'm hungry. I'd like to see their fridge from the inside.

– Go to sleep. In the morning we have to shovel out Suddy's cab. And then my car.

– Why do you always call it Suddy's cab? You and Chickie. We're partners him and me. That's what I mean about being demeaned. Like Alan Bates in *The Fixer*. They demeaned him. They dehumanized him.

– That was a good movie.

– People should be better friends, said Duddy. – I'm going to cut one. Oh-oh!

– How friendly.

– Sorry. Now look who's saying sorry. Always happens before

I fall asleep. A habit from the penitentiary. Talk about dehumanizing. But I met a guy there who could make it rain.

Duddy hummed the *shma yisroel* and that put Blackie to sleep.

TEN

B lackie sat alone, drunk on the smell of vanilla, percolating coffee, and simmering fatty roast beef. He had picked The Grill Room on Eaton's fifth floor for Sophie because it was a nice venue, and she had to know it well from meeting friends for lunches or teas, where they ate egg salad sandwiches and dainties. He had been worried that she wouldn't feel the same way about going with him, but when he had phoned, she'd been delighted.

Sophie was all smiles when she stepped carefully past the captain's lectern into the restaurant. Suddenly, she took a hop step, which thrilled Blackie, and then she was there. Her eyes lit up. Disturbed eyes. Very blue. She was wearing a low-cut dress under a red cashmere cardigan she'd left unbuttoned. Her skin glowed pink in the light of the overhead chandeliers. And her hair was rich and loose on her shoulders. Before sitting down she gave Blackie a long look. Her smile held only sympathy, the kind that comes from so far ago.

– Why did you want to see me?

– Sit. Sit, said Blackie.

She sat.

– I wanted to say sorry for the other night, the night of the blizzard, he said – We didn't even call to say we were coming over.

An elderly bow-legged waitress wearing nurse's shoes interrupted his apology. She set down a pot of tea and arranged the bowls and cups and saucers while Blackie looked out the window down to Portage Avenue, and sighed at the gentle snowfall. He was practically the only man in a huge room of broadloom, white linen, and fine china, all of it designed for the comfort of countless finely dressed women who came there to breathe and relax.

– Should I pour? Blackie asked.

– She'll come back and pour when it's steeped.

– And I'm sorry for putting that movie on, too. We didn't even watch the end.

– I had a good time, Blackie. At least you talk to me.

– We sort of invaded without calling. It was an intrusion. And Max wasn't home.

– Don't worry. He didn't find out.

– I didn't mean it that way.

– Are you sleeping better?

– From the yoga?

– Did it work?

– I haven't been trying hard at it.

– It makes me sleep like a log. I started it when I started sleeping badly. I didn't want to take pills. Drinking helps too but they say it doesn't.

– I don't want to take pills either.

– I don't sleep well alone. And Max is away a lot. Well, you know that. I'm repeating myself. Sometimes I have to ask people if I've told them what it is before I say what I'm about to say to them. Max came back the other night, you know. And he's still not talking to me. Going on maybe nine months now.

– You're still feeling neglected?

– What do you think?

I think you are, he wanted to say, but the waitress came and poured the tea and took their order for sandwiches. He wondered why he never came here with Deirdre.

– Max hasn't said a word to me in months and months. But you know that. Since the summer. Since I hurt his feelings at the cottage.

– Your low blow?

– Get out the violin. I just told you that. Do I repeat myself a lot?

– No.

– It's like being married to a corpse. What's he waiting for? He knows where the door is.

– Why don't you talk to Max about all this? Maybe he's feeling bad, too.

– Blackie, honestly. I told you he's not talking to me.

– That came out wrong.

– Max doesn't have a *nishoma*. It actually hurts to live with him now. Realizing it, that's a bitter pill. At first I started screaming at him. The neighbours thought we had an ambulance siren in the house.

– Did it work?

– Blackie!

– Sorry. Sorry.

– No. It didn't work. It just gave him another reason to stop talking to me because I was hysterical, and he said he wouldn't talk to a hysterical woman, on principle.

– You should write him a letter.

– I even stopped cooking for him to retaliate. But he can eat out. And then, there's the maid; she adores him. He helped bring her family over. Big shot. In her eyes.

The waitress brought the sandwiches, crusts removed, and they munched in silence. Blackie devoured his four triangles before Sophie could finish her first; he had been afraid he wouldn't get any food down, but he was always suddenly ravenous when food appeared in such small quantities.

When she finished, she undid the clasp of her purse, took out a compact and a brown paper bag with a fifth of gin. The purse emptied item by item: the compact and gin were followed by Kleenex, nail polish, gloves, lipsticks, bills and receipts, dice, a hairbrush, a pocket book, car keys, and, finally, her lighter and cigarette packet. She drew out a Craven A from the pack and lit it herself.

– What's that for? Blackie said, eyes on the gin.

– My medicine, she said as she stowed her articles back in her purse. – But I've gone without today.

She sat back, holding her cigarette to her lips, resting her elbow on her forearm, squashing the tops of her breasts up and over the neckline. She took a long drag and blew smoke out of the corner of her mouth up into the din, preparing to say something thoughtful, he thought.

– Maybe you're still hungry, she said.

– I'm okay, he said, liking the consideration a lot.

– You know I saw Deirdre the other day. Her clothes were amazing. What's going on with her?

– We're separated. Said she wanted to shine.

– I wish I had her guts.

– She doesn't have as much to lose as you.

– That kind of remark is more unfair to you than it is to me. You think I'm staying with Max for the carpeting?

– Maybe for the sake of the kids.

She scoffed at that and took a drag, and when she blew out the smoke, she scoffed again, making Blackie think that the kids teamed up with Max against her.

– Are you thinking what I'm thinking? Sophie said.

– What?

– That maybe Deirdre never loved you. Like Max never loved me. You can pick up on those things. Or supposed to be able to. Once it's too late.

– I wasn't thinking that at all.

– I was.

– I can't speak for Deirdre and certainly not for Max about you.

– You like poetry? I used to like it in school. I think about that. About lots of things. We used to neck like mad at the movies, you and me. Sometimes I'd miss the whole movie.

– That was a long time ago.

– But I knew you liked me. I never knew what Max was feeling.

You and me, we'd go to the matinee and stay till it closed, kissing. You never went farther, never tried to make a girl do what she wasn't supposed to want to do. I wanted to ask you to go farther. I wondered if you'd be disgusted by it or by me suggesting it. But I would have done it.

Blackie couldn't grasp any of that with his brain. His breath got laboured. His skin pulled tight across his cheekbones: they must've gotten red because they felt hot. Sophie mashed out her cigarette after a last sour puff.

— You want to go to the Fort Garry? she said.

— The hotel?

— No, the fort. Of course, the hotel.

The waitress came by and left the bill on a stainless steel tray. Blackie was in too much turmoil to get out his wallet. He watched Sophie lay a twenty down with a smile.

— You're married, he said.

— So are you.

— I'm separated.

— You know you should never reject a woman. It's very rude.

— It's a work day, he said.

Her eyes blurred.

— I'm not going to ask you another time. A girl has standards.

— And I don't want to break up a home. Those are standards too.

— I just want to feel close to someone.

— How come me?

— You have a clean heart.

— I have to get back to work. I only have an hour for lunch.

— What about after work?

— I have to be at the Fort Rouge Curling Club at 6:00 o'clock. We're down to the 32s. You can come and watch.

— That'd be a scandal. Me going to the Fort Rouge club to see you.

— More than the Fort Garry?

The ice at the Fort Rouge Club's was looking polished, looking fast. Blackie could tell right away by the ice that it was going to be their best game that season and that they'd still be in the Brier.

They were up against a stunning Fort Rouge team, playing at home and wearing one-piece plaid suits with matching tams, which Blackie's team thought were funny. But Blackie knew the game would get complicated. The Fort Rouge guys could make shots that weren't so funny.

They flipped. Blackie called it and got the hammer: it made his whole body happy and it was getting over how it had been buzzing and tingling over lunch with Sophie.

Blackie didn't know how it happened, but in the first end, by the time it was his last rock, Fort Rouge was lying three. They were going to steal three if he flubbed his shot, but the house was unguarded. He slid one snug to the opposing stone in the four-foot to score one and keep the hammer.

They banged each other's rocks out of the house until the fifth end when Blackie was sure they'd pull ahead. Fort Rouge were lying shot rock with a guard protecting it, but Blackie had two rocks to the back of it in the eight-foot and a tricky shot, but a shot after all, at Fort Rouge's shot rock. It was the kind of shot he was renowned for making, and he discussed it with Oz: get past the guard, get a piece of the Fort Rouge shot rock and pitch it out of the house while his own rolled to stick to his stones, earn a solid three points, and keep the hammer.

He slid out, his arm straight, and just before the hog line, he opened his fist and watched his rock catch the channel to float past the guard, knock out the Fort Rouge rock, lurch, spin, and careen to the eight-foot, and score three. It knocked the bloody soul out of the Fort Rouge team, who conceded with self-disgust in the tenth end.

They'd made it to the 32s.

och a mol, said Chickie to Blackie, hiking up his pants after his turn at the urinal. – I can't take these meetings.

– We have to have supper anyway before the game.

– But I can't concentrate on the food with all the talk. It's like eating and not remembering I ate.

– The guys are waiting, said Blackie.

– Let me wash up.

'How's Hazel?' he wanted to ask, but he'd put it off too long to mention it now. He hoped Chickie didn't realize he wasn't being as good a friend as he should be. That meant he'd have to figure Chickie to be pretty dim, which he wasn't. So he asked.

– How's Hazel and Linda?

– How'd you expect? It's a *shanda*. She's not going out of the house.

– I feel for the kid.

Chickie scoffed.

–Linda's out there living it up big as a house. It's Hazel who's the shut-in.

They got back to the table where the guys were sitting in the Nanking's fancy table-clothed salon. As always, Chickie had insisted on being seated on the carpeted side, with its red plaster dragon squirming from one end of the ceiling to the other, its maw quaffing a vent grill, and not the cheap linoleum and Formica side.

Oz had the floor.

– According to our lists we're having trouble not only with Sanders and the Saltzbergers, but I've heard Max Foxman has been probing Manny Vinsky, Sam Handelman, and Frenchie Litman. We're going down to the wire.

– Those three are on Blackie's list, said Chickie.

– They were sterling last week, said Blackie.

– I thought we were going to double canvass, said Michael.

– Easy for you, said Chickie.

– I'm doing exams and organizing an action to support the strike of support staff at the university. So if I have time to take on the doyen of the QV, then so do you.

– I'm busy too, said Chickie. – If we didn't have all these meetings, I'd have time to double canvass.

– We have to have supper anyway, said Suddy.

– Did you double canvass? Chickie asked him.

– I did. All my list are golden.

– Me and Blackie got the shit lists, said Chickie.

– I made them random, said Blackie.

– Eenie meenie miney moe, said Suddy. – I saw him.

– I'll call Frenchie tonight after the game, said Blackie. – He works days this month.

– How come Duddy's so glum? Chickie asked.

– Some of his mice are sick, said Suddy.

– Tom or Jerry? Chickie joked.

– I made a big investment, said Duddy to him. – What'll I do if they die?

– You'll sit *shiva*.

– Why are they sick? Tino asked.

– Neglect, said Chickie.

– We should get going, said Oz. – We're playing The Pas at Deer Lodge in half an hour.

– We know who and where we're playing? Duddy asked.

– They drove a long way, said Suddy.

Blackie had last rock in the fifth end and flung it with little concentration and less grace: not enough curl and not fast enough and he heard himself yelling his head off from the hog line for Suddy and Duddy to sweep. People must have thought he'd gone crazy. And when he saw the fruit of such a crap throw he was almost ready to cry. He shaved the skin of his own guard and tilted his rock into the boards. His chance to score three became a steal one for The Pas. Bugger but the 32s were tough. And after five ends it was three-three.

– Good try, Blackie, said Suddy.

– They practice all day in The Pas, said Duddy. – Nothing else to do there.

– My fault, said Blackie. – They got 1. And the hammer. Good for them. You pay your way.

Blackie took a good look at his adversaries. Maybe he had been figuring them wrong. The Pas were a modest team except for all the pins on their sweaters. When they had come in, like Blackie and his guys, they hadn't really known where they were at first, having played at so many clubs in such a short period of time. And, like Blackie's team, they also carried their boots and curling sweaters in paper bags. They were quiet and polite — real gentlemen — Blackie thought. Maybe aggression would work on them. But that was a soft maybe.

After missing the shot, while putting his glove back on, head bowed, Blackie looked up at the glass and saw Chickie give him a how'd-you-blow-that look. Tino was there too, looking down at the action, pushing his fingers through his curls and stretching them out in dismay. He looked like he had been electrocuted. Poor kid with that hair. Michael MacGiligary was also there, but he had maintained his calm. Blackie saw him huddle with Tino, the crowns of their heads touching.

Duddy saw Blackie looking up at Mike and Tino, and he slid over, scratched Blackie's elbow and pointed his chin up at the boys.

– The Little Socialists.

– You know it's Young Socialists, don't you?

– Yeah, I do.

– They're always talking, said Blackie.

– Maybe they're talking about me, said Duddy. – Is there anything they don't like about me?

– I don't know what they're talking about, said Blackie. – Politics, I guess.

– Maybe they've been hypnotized.

– By who?

– Not by Kripkin, said Duddy. – He's a professional. Did I tell you I'm having my portrait done?

– In oils?

– No. In Dunbar's Photo Studio. I'm getting all sizes. Even the wallet-sized ones. I'm going to give one to Sophie. You never know. I even got one in black and white for the wall at Kelekis's if we win the Brier.

– Kelekis's isn't going to put your picture on the wall for that, said Blackie.

– Did you have lunch with Sophie at The Georgian Room?

– The Grill Room. How did you know?

– I have my finger on a few pulses. Why didn't you call me to go? I always take you. What kind of friend are you?

– Not the time for this, said Blackie. – And I am a good friend.

Blackie's team did the simplest of hit and sticks for the next few ends, building tension in the twelve-foot and eight-foot.

In the ninth end, Blackie, after opting for a messier game, had two front rocks in the twelve-foot about forty inches apart, another in the eight-foot, which stupidly guarded The Pas's rock sitting smug on the bottom.

It was Blackie's hammer for a delicate 'go.' Oz was skeptical about what Blackie wanted to do: to go between his two rocks and take out the one on the button: a window of nothing. Oz marked the broom. Tino and Chickie, behind the glass, covered their eyes, making like they couldn't watch Blackie going for The Pas' shot rock. He'd have to wiggle at the speed of sound between his two guards in front of the house and then hit one of his rocks in the four-foot, stick, and make his stone ricochet against The Pas stone and push it off the button to stick himself. If it worked he'd pick up three and two if he didn't stick.

Blackie crouched in the hack, flipped the rock upside down against his thigh, and scrubbed it with his glove to remove straw blots and a gold shred of tobacco. Then he wiped the space in front of him clean till the ice glared. He squinted at Oz's broom at the other end of the lane where it marked his target. Oz could hold that broom pretty steady.

Like a goalie before a penalty kick, Blackie felt the anxiety ripple through his body. After a few seconds' concentration, he heaved the rock up behind his shoulder blade while pressing his right boot hard against the hack. He sprang in a rage out of it, eyes fierce with focus on Oz's broom, his nose right behind the wrist that connected it to the hand that squeezed the handle of the rock that seemed to be dragging him down the ice, till right before the stone approached the hog line, he opened his fist and the rock felt its deliverance.

The stone torpedoed down the channel without need of sweeping, and once it squeezed through the guards in the twelve-foot it smashed his own rock barely off dead centre to roll out of the house. Kinetic, his rock in the eight-foot lurched. The stone came alive: it bent hard and collided with The Pas's shot rock. Duddy pounced and swept it to the edge of the twelve-foot. Blackie picked up two to make it five to three, with Blackie keeping the hammer. Blackie had to look up to see if Tino saw it. The kid and Michael MacGiligary were bouncing off the walls like chimps.

Blackie feared that The Pas would make a comeback in the last end. After a hit and roll, he was lying one at the back of the house. The Pas had a rock in the twelve-foot, and so their skip faced a not-so tricky takeout to score two with his last shot. The skip marked his spot and his third held the broom right in front of Blackie's shot rock. The Pas' rock came blazing over the hog line and down the lane. Their skip was screaming 'hurry, hurry,

hurry' while his lead and second were sliding furiously to keep up with it, thwacking the ice with their brooms. He pounded Blackie's rock on the nose.

Then Blackie went for The Pas' stone and missed. The Pas tied up the game scoring two, and Blackie lost the hammer as the game went into an extra end.

When Blackie looked up at Tino and Mike and Chickie, he saw suffering and pain.

By skips' rocks in the final end, there were four rocks in the house, three The Pas stones, two lying shot possession in the eight-foot, and one QV stone in the twelve-foot. Oz suggested taking out the shot rock in the eight-foot, but Blackie relied more on his drawing skill for this end, a bit on tilt from missing his take out in the tenth end. He'd draw it into the four-foot and lie the closer to.

Gliding forward to the hog line on his slider, Blackie took one last squint at Oz's broom. He saw Duddy holding two fingers to his forehead like Kripkin, willing things to go right. That made Blackie think about doing that thing Duddy said by the Zoo on the yoga night, about putting himself into the thing like Dee's kids when they were at the Zoo. Sliding to the hog line, he tenderly opened his fist and released his stone. As it nobly cruised the channel, he inserted his mind into the rock and screamed 'don't sweep, don't sweep, don't sweep.' Suddy and Duddy slid along with and hovered over the rock, checking back with Blackie should he order them to sweep, looking down again at the rock, then checking back with Blackie. The stone had greatness as it drove into the eight-foot and then crossed centre. The Pas' skip started sweeping like a maniac so it would exit the rear, but the rock's momentum flagged and it stopped to bite the four-foot to sit shot.

Then, with rage, their skip went for Blackie's shot rock, and missed.

They'd made it to the 8s. One more win and they'd roll into the semis. Duddy came in off the ice roasting. His shirt was soaked in sweat.

– Maybe showers would be a good thing, he said.

The others, their faces hot and beaming with exertion and victory, ears red from being in the ice cold air, were met in the Fort Rouge cafeteria with congratulations from Tino and Michael MacGiligary. But Chickie spoiled their happiness.

– Jack Sanders sold his share. It's definitive, he said to Blackie.

– I didn't want to tell you before and ruin your concentration.

– He's the Malinche, said Suddy.

– Who told you? said Duddy – Max? He's manager of the Bullshit Department Store now.

– I got it straight from the horse's mouth.

– Jack Sanders told you personally?

– In person, personally.

– Major Midgie sold his too. Who knows who else?

– I know who else, said Chickie. – And you're not going to like it: Hy and Brian Saltzberger.

Each defection was like a stab to Blackie's heart.

– The vote's in two weeks, said Oz.

– Before or after the Father and Son Banquet? Duddy asked.

They all sat down: glum. Tino held Blackie's broom, while Blackie untied his greasy laces, removed his boots, and then banged the remaining ice off the soles. Blackie stepped in bit of slush on the cafeteria floor and got his curling sock wet.

In a jiffy they had had their civilian shoes on. Oz had a sporty new duffle bag for his boots, which he wiped down first. While everyone else slipped on half rubbers, Suddy wedged his Hush Puppies into big rubber galoshes. There was still a lot of snow on the ground even though winter was grinding slowly down; March skies still dumped a few inches of snow daily.

– You guys having nothing to protect your footwear, said Suddy to Tino and Mike.

– They're too cool, said Chickie.

– You might just get down to the semis, Michael said to Blackie.

– I'd like to see the look on Max Foxman's face if that happened, said Duddy.

– We're getting there, said Suddy. – One end at a time.

– We have to meet, said Michael.

– Let's go to the Sals for a nip. My treat, said Suddy.

– Not another meeting, said Chickie. – We just met at supper time.

– It's just a nip, said Suddy.

– But we're having a meeting now, said Chickie. – Isn't this a meeting?

– But what are we going to do about Jack Sanders? Michael asked. – And Hy and Brian Saltzberger. They were on your list, Chickie.

– Send them to Siberia, Chickie said to Michael.

– We're not Stalinists, Michael said.

– You're all Stalinists, he said. – Leftards. Baa, baa, baa. We the sheep!

– You know nothing of our positions, Michael said to Chickie. – We oppose Stalinism. Lenin's wife Krupskaya said in 1927 that if Lenin were still alive, he'd be in prison. We call for an end to the Stalinist bureaucracy that betrayed the revolution and for a political renovation of the workers' councils.

– A political revolution, said Tino. – Not a social one because the means of production have already been socialised.

– You guys and the means of production, said Chickie. – When have you ever produced anything?

– Are we going for nips or not? Suddy asked.

– Tino's right, said Michael. – Nevertheless, we defend the USSR against US imperialism in spite of the former's having renounced world revolution in favour of the doctrine of socialism in one country. To their disgrace. We disagree with the State Capitalist position that the USSR shouldn't be defended. So don't take us for Shachtmanites.

– Wouldn't dream of it, said Oz.

– You're all Stalinists, said Chickie. – On or off the ice.

– What's a leftard? asked Suddy.

– A cross between a leftie and a retard, said Chickie.

– Shouldn't it be Shachtman*ists*? Oz asked.

– What are we going to do about Jack Sanders? Blackie asked.

– You know, if you guys won the Brier, said Chickie, Max Foxman himself would vote against closing the QV.

– Thanks for the pressure, said Blackie.

– You'd bring the Brier trophy to the club, said Chickie. – If the QV is wound up, what'd Max do with the trophy?

– How much do you want to bet he won't vote against closing the QV if we win the Brier, said Suddy.

– We've been lucky to have made it this far, said Blackie.

– Don't forget, said Duddy, if the QV closes, I'm going to tell Max Foxman about me and Sophie Foxman. Out of spite. I'm almost wishing we lose just to see his face. It's an either/or win for me.

– You'll have to get in her pants first, said Chickie.

– With all my might, said Duddy.

– Not going to happen.

– You wait.

– Better make your move soon. No pussyfooting, said Chickie.

– I wouldn't do that. I don't have a foot fetish.

Duddy scratched Chickie's elbow before he could move it away and said:

– I wish you could be in the room when it happens. Then you'll see.

– I wouldn't do that, said Chickie. – I have manners.

– I thought you were going to use Sophie psychologically against Max *before* he liquidates the QV? Oz asked.

– I have two plans, and neither contradicts the other.

– Admit it. You're getting nowhere fast with her, said Chickie to Duddy.

– I've got her eating out of my hand. I did yoga with her. She wasn't wearing a bra either. Night of the blizzard.

– We should go, said Blackie. – I'm starving.

– Since when do you do yoga? Chickie asked Duddy.

– I'm for leaving now, said Blackie, standing up with his bag under his arm.

– You don't do yoga, said Chickie to Duddy.

– I do.

– Since when?

– Since the blizzard. I found out Max was in Vegas, so me and Blackie snuck over to Sophie's. She wasn't wearing a bra. We had to dig the cab out with a shovel the next morning and sleep at Sophie's.

– You went to Max's? Oz asked Blackie.

– He wasn't home, said Duddy.

– Right. That makes it okay? asked Chickie.

Blackie avoided Tino's eyes for as long as he could; it was like holding your breath under water. When he finally looked, Tino was biting his bottom lip, trying not to lose it.

– The cab got stuck and Sophie let us in to warm up, Blackie said.

– We watched an adult movie with her on Max's video machine, said Duddy. – Max has stacks of them. We . . . I . . . carried her up to her room. I went through Max's things looking for shares he might have bought up.

– That's B&E, said Chickie.

– We were invited in, said Duddy. – On humanitarian grounds. We would have died in the snow. Or had our toes amputated from frostbite. Believe you me, Sophie's not Max; she has a heart.

Recomposing himself, Michael said:

– Anyway, something's going wrong. And the vote's in two weeks.

– What should we do? Oz asked.

– We have to have a big meeting. Put the blocks to people. Beef them up. We have to make up with spirit what Max Foxman has in money. You're disingenuous if you think we don't have to mobilize people.

– This is a meeting, said Chickie.

– I mean of all the guys who are with us. Hold the line.

– You mean toe the line.

– I'm not a Stalinist, said Michael.

– Who's going to organize the meeting?

– We'll have to meet to discuss that, said Michael.

– That's two more meetings, said Chickie. – And if we meet at the Sals tonight, that's three. And this is four.

– So?

– You're meeting us to death, said Chickie. – That's your problem. That's why you'll never achieve socialism. No one wants to go to meetings. And with the games left in the Brier, when do we get a chance to rest?

– It's the QV on the line, said Michael. – We need a mass meeting.

– I doubt there's time before the Father and Son Banquet to call a meeting of all the guys, said Oz.

– We'll look ridiculous, said Chickie. – Organizing a 'mass meeting.'

– Are you ashamed? Michael asked Chickie.

– It's embarrassing. Is that shame by you?

– Max is chipping away at us.

– There's just no time, said Oz. – I'm not saying it's a bad idea.

– Blackie? said Michael.

– Oz is right.

– Oz is calling it, said Suddy. – We're not ashamed of anything.

– I'm a maverick, said Duddy.

Michael shook his head vigorously. He and Tino walked away dejected, not liking to lose.

– They can buy their own nips, said Chickie.

TWELVE

Blackie heard the dryer going from the landing. Deirdre was in the basement, and that made him feel pretty good because it was the first time they'd run into each other at home. She couldn't have come over too soon as far as he was concerned; he was buying underwear and socks at Kresge's every other day because he had run out of clean clothes.

He went down to say thanks. He stood watching her: she was separating clothes into piles. Sophie was right about Deirdre dressing better; women know these things about each other. It seemed like every time he saw her, she'd had another shattering change. Today, her hair looked fabulous: rich and clean, like years ago, before that permanent fad.

Without looking up from the clothes piles, she said something that surprised him:

— What's this about you and Sophie Foxman? Tino said you were doing yoga at her house. That she wasn't wearing a bra.

Blackie's face burned hot. He looked at the floor.

— Was she? Deirdre asked.

— She wasn't, I think.

— You think? I think it's filthy what Duddy wants to get from her. Tino told me everything. Stag movies on videotape? Really, Blackie?

— I'm trying to stop Duddy, actually. That's why I was with him.

— There's no controlling Duddy. How often do I have to tell you that?

— Till you break the record?

185

– None of it is my business.

– I never held a torch for Sophie Foxman. She never got in the way of my feelings for you.

– When did I ever say she did?

– I was a good husband. Even in my imagination.

– I'm not here to talk about Sophie Foxman. She's a lush. I came to say I'm not coming over to wash your clothes anymore or to vacuum. You'll have to learn how to use the machines. You can watch me. It's not difficult.

– Is there someone else in your life?

– To wash clothes for? She was so annoyed she didn't even bother to look at him.

Blackie didn't feel so good anymore about her being over at the house. It was just another disappointment. He was getting sick of them.

– It's hard to . . . Sorry. You're right. You're right. But . . .

– But what?

– It's hard living without you.

– Still lonely?

– What do you think?

– What do I think? Like I said to you before, you'll be shacked up with someone before you know it.

He didn't like the term shacked up. He'd have never said that to Deirdre if the shoe was on the other foot.

– I'll write down the dial settings before I go. Remember not to mix whites and colours.

– What about the blacks? Do you wash blacks separately?

– Blacks are colours.

– Doesn't seem right that black is a colour.

– It's not a white.

– I was just saying.

– You know Tino wants to drop out of sciences altogether, she said.

– You mean pre-med?

186

– I mean out of sciences altogether. It's that Michael MacGiligary.

Blackie's mouth dried up.

– I didn't know that, he said.

Deirdre stuffed whites into the machine.

– He's afraid to tell you. You know, if you hadn't taken him curling, he'd never have met Michael.

– Me? Just a while back you said I never taught him how to curl properly.

– That's what happens.

She dropped the lid and got on tip toes to press it with her palm till it made a connecting pop. Blackie could hear water rushing into the machine. He hadn't realized that was the way it worked. Now it made perfect sense for it to fill first. Who thought of this stuff?

– Confront him.

– Me?

– There we go.

– I'll have a talk with him.

– When?

– After the Father and Son Banquet. We're down to the eights.

– I don't care if you're down on all fours. Do it. I told him he can't quit. I confronted him. I hope you'll back me up, for once. And get him to trim his hair. I'm not saying cut, just layered.

The washing machine motor came on and the clothes started to swish.

–You know he wants to be a poet now.

Blackie's stomach started to rotate like the blades of the washing machine.

– Poet? Is that a job?

– Get him to finish the year. Can you do that? He'll change his mind.

– Can you make a living from that?

– Blackie!

– What kind of poet?

– How should I know? A nature poet? Who knows? He said it as if telling me it was nothing special. You know what he said when I told him he was ruining his future? He said: 'I never asked to be born, but now that I'm here I have full autonomy.' He probably got that from Michael MacGiligary. I'd hate it if Tino was a follower. I didn't raise a follower.

Blackie thought there weren't any poets anymore, at least the ones he had to read at high school had to be dead by now. He remembered a show he'd seen years ago on CBC. Two poets were talking to Pierre Berton, but they were Quebeckers. Maybe they didn't have poets on TV anymore.

– Are you okay at Edith's? Blackie said.

– I'm getting my own place.

Blackie got out a cigarette and lit up.

– You shouldn't smoke in here. If they finish the year they'll make the dean's list. Both of them. Michael MacGiligary's dropping out of sciences. Their professors are puzzled. Yes, I went to see them. I saw the Dean, too. Tino was embarrassed as hell when he saw me there. Good for him.

Blackie felt like he was going to be sick.

– Tino says Michael's moving to Toronto. To where their secretariat or something is.

– What do his parents say to that?

– You think a kid like that has parents like me and you?

– Are you okay at Edith's?

– I'm getting my own place.

uess who I saw getting out of Max Foxman's car in the Shanghai Restaurant parking lot? Oz asked.

It was a supper meeting at the Nanking to plan for the AGM. They wouldn't have time for a long supper because they had a game at 6:30.

– Come on, Oz said to Chickie. – Guess who I saw?

– There's no point in guessing, said Chickie. – No point in asking someone to guess either. I'm quoting you.

– Morley Permut, said Oz.

They were all glum about that.

– He was one of us, said Blackie. He had arrived at 5 o'clock p.m. with butterflies in his stomach because they were playing the hottest team from Winnipeg's oldest curling club, the Granite, and on their home ice. But once he smelled Chinese food, his appetite had roared back.

– I said we should have had a big meeting, said Michael. – Beef up the ranks.

– *Noch a mol*, said Chickie.

– It was way too late, Mike, said Oz. – Wouldn't have been enough time to book a venue.

– We could have booked the Little Talmud Torah basement, Blackie said. – How busy could it be there?

– Now it's up to 'Him,' said Chickie, pointing up in the direction of the plaster dragon on the ceiling.

– And 'He's' been so just in the past, said Tino.

– He does okay. He's a fair guy.

– Polio in kids? Think that's the work of a fair guy?

It took a platter of breaded shrimp, plunked down by a Chinese waiter in a white busboy coat with so much starch in the sleeves and cuffs that his arms seemed to be held up by strings for them to cheer up.

– Are you guys getting any? Duddy said to Michael and Tino.

– Pass the shrimp, Duddy, said Chickie.

– Are you? Duddy asked.

Duddy took a few shrimps with his fingers and was reprimanded by Chickie.

– Use your chopsticks.

– I eat with my appetite, said Duddy.

– You can use a fork, Suddy said to Michael.

The waiter served relentlessly until there wasn't a single patch of empty space on the lazy Susan, laden as it was with dishes of steaming breaded shrimp, chop suey, fried wontons, chicken fried rice with peas, breaded veal, breaded ribs, white rice, egg rolls, and chicken chow mein. Chickie made everybody spin the lazy Susan even if something was right in front of you.

With his Hush Puppies off under the table, Suddy sipped Orange Crush out of a straw between bites, enjoying himself.

– Give the kids some shrimp, said Duddy. – You like shrimp? Dip them in the sauce, Mike, like this, that's what it's for.

Duddy illustrated how to dip shrimp in sauce. After the shrimp, he polished off a narrow platter of cold barbecue pork, dipping the strips one by one on both sides, in mustard sauce. After that, he had a roll, followed by two generous scoops of egg fried rice and six fried wontons.

Michael and Tino ate some more shrimp before Duddy could finish them. Michael ordered some consommé with green onions.

– Another soup *mensch*, said Suddy.

– Where did you say you saw Max Foxman and Morley Permut? Chickie asked Oz.

– Right in the Shanghai parking lot.

– What were you doing there? Blackie asked. – You know you can't eat there.

– Parking the car. Ruthie wants to move to the South End, so I was just seeing how it would feel if I had to park at the Shanghai.

– No way you're moving south, said Duddy. – I predict it.

– The Oracle! said Chickie.

– Why can't you eat there? Michael said to Oz.

– Mike, North End Jews don't go to the Shanghai, Chickie patiently explained to Michael.

– Only South Enders, said Duddy, as if Michael couldn't draw a conclusion.

– The South End Jews like their Chinese food wet; we like it dry, explained Chickie.

– It's pretty phoney Chinese food over there, agreed Duddy.

– You wouldn't catch me dead in the Shanghai, said Chickie.

– This is like Ulster, said Michael.

– Could I get some shrimp over here? said Suddy.

– I guess your family goes to the Shanghai, Mike? said Oz.

– We've never eaten Chinese food, Michael said. – My parents think it's pretty vulgar.

Chickie set the lazy Susan gyrating with his heavy thumb.

– Stop the spinning! The shrimp will get dizzy, said Duddy.

– It's right in front of him. Why spin it? Oz said.

– So you saw Morley and Max? Blackie said to Oz. – Does that mean Morley sold his share too?

– They looked pretty buddy buddy. Morley's not in Max's clique.

– Where's that other order of shrimp we ordered? Suddy said.

– I want them hot. They know that here.

Blackie looked around the table. – You guys know the game starts in less than 45 minutes? You're not going to have time for more shrimp.

– Blackie, the Granite's just 20 minutes from here. Fifteen if you know how to get there, said Duddy. – So I think there's time for more shrimp.

– I know where the Granite is, said Blackie. – But the roads are icy. It's still March. You guys drive carefully, Mike.

– Whose car are you driving tonight? Chickie asked Michael.

– Same as always. My father's.

– You know it came from the sweat of the workers?

– What we should discuss is how to stop the proliferation of Morley Permuts and Jack Sanderses and Hy and Brian Saltzbergers, said Tino. – We're hemorrhaging votes.

Blackie noticed Tino had a Michael MacGiligary timbre to his voice now.

– You guys win tonight, people will swing back, said Chickie.

– If you can hack the pressure.

– That's a good word. Proliferation, said Duddy. – Do you think it's fair Granite gets to play us at home?

– Luck of the draw, said Blackie.

– By my way of thinking, according to my tally, we still have more shares than them, said Oz. – But something's going on.

– Max is trying to set up a sensation of inevitability, said Michael.

– It's *noch nila*, said Suddy.

– Good night, Irene, said Duddy. – Ever notice how one traitor can do more harm than forty good people. – Not fair.

– La Malinche, said Tino.

– Why do you think Morely sold?

– Like Jack Sanders, he needed the money, I suppose, said Oz.

– And the Saltzbergers' upholstery shop might be in receivership.

– Half the North End needs money, said Chickie. – We should have concentrated on the guys with money problems.

– We can't start suspecting people just because they need money, said Michael. – That's class bias.

– We have to suspect the greedy too, said Tino.

– As victims of class bias yourselves, you should be wary, said Michael.

192

– We're all going to have to call the guys on our list again, said
Tino.

– Not again, said Chickie. – I refuse.

– Do you want the QV to go down?

– Think of it this way, Tino. At least we got down to the 8s.
– And worst comes to worse, if the club goes, Israel will get
something out of it.

– That's a good cause, said Suddy.

Michael MacGilligary drank off his soup from the bowl and
said to him:

– Israel's a colonial settler state, Suddy.

– I don't know from that.

– It was built on land stolen from the indigenous population.
– Like Canada or the United States.

– It's socialist, said Oz. – I thought you were socialists.

– Giving to Israel is like giving to other Jews, said Suddy.

– Israelis aren't Jews, said Tino. – They gave up the right to
be Jews when they became Israelis. Like Americans, they gave
up the right to be English when they became Americans. Or the
Boers, who gave up the right to be Dutch when they became
South Africans. Et cetera.

– That's some real BS, said Chickie. – Israelis are Jewish.

– What about Arab Israelis? Are they Jewish?

– They're not real Israelis.

– Israelis have nothing in common with us, said Tino. – They
don't speak Yiddish or English. They speak Hebrew.

– I know Hebrew, said Duddy. – We went to the Little Talmud
Torah. Not one of those fake *shules*.

– With your Hebrew you couldn't find a toilet in a restaurant,
said Blackie.

– Your kid should go back to Russia, said Chickie.

– That's not even stupid, said Tino to him.

– We're running late, said Blackie. – We'll forfeit the toss if we
don't get moving.

– Get the bill, said Oz. – We're not getting into this.

Blackie's butterflies were back because so much depended on this game.

There was a good crowd at the Granite Curling Club to watch the 8s, mostly local Granite members and a couple of sports reporters from *The Winnipeg Tribune.*

Chickie and Michael and Tino were there, and so was Hazel with Linda, who was looking round and jolly, and Sammy Ostrove and a bunch of QV loyalists, including Minnow Pasner.

The Granite team was on the ice waiting patiently for them to do the toss. Blackie could pick out the skip right away. He had a knack for it. It was tails and Blackie had said 'heads', so Granite took the hammer and Blackie played the blue stones.

– Who'd they *shmear* to get to play at home? Duddy said to Blackie.

– Luck of the draw, Duddy.

– Did you see how they tossed the coin?

– Fair is fair.

It was a tight affair from the first end. Blackie was tense; the eights were serious, and he needed to think of it as the most important game he'd ever played. He had to concentrate to concentrate, with so many concerns noodling his brain, but he was the first to get on the board by stealing one in the second end after Granite blanked the first. Blackie's idea was then to hang on to the hammer no matter what and blank the fourth and fifth end to show he meant business. He posted a double in the fifth end and for the first time he looked up at the spectators behind the windows.

Granite were good but they must have been biding their time, hiding their best shots, because they punched back with three exceptional points in the seventh end to take the hammer. But then Blackie stole two in the eighth and got the hammer back.

Going into the ninth end 5–3 he allowed Granite to make the house a jumble, but with an unguarded channel, all Blackie had to do was put last his rock on the lid. He even had a Granite shot stone to cozy up against.

Where was his head when he squatted in the hacks? He struggled for concentration and was sure people thought he was taking too much time. Making the shot would be sweet. He started counting his chickens: a point here would put them up two and give them last rock in the tenth and things would fall into place. Deirdre would come home. Tino would find a girlfriend and go to med school.

It was such an easy draw down the channel. Maybe the last thing he saw was the cracked dazzle of the ice and not Oz's broom marking the spot.

Right before the hog line, when he let the handle go, he was off the broom. He didn't even bother screaming to sweep, and when he caught up to his rock, which was veering into a guard, he gave it a good shove with an infuriated foot into the boards and conceded the point. The game was 5–4. He had handed Granite the hammer in the final end. He was trying to look down at his curling boots, but he looked up at the spectators.

What? Tino gave him a big shrug, palms up, eyes bulging at him. Chickie shook his chins.

They fought back, led by impeccable shooting by Suddy, Duddy, and Oz. But Granite were sterling and making hotter shots, and although they had a chance to tie the game and go into the extra end with last rock, the Granite skip stood in the four-foot, looked down on Blackie's first and second shot rocks, his own third shot rock, and whispered to his third, who gave him a head shake, then a nod. Blackie figured they were talking about how to swing past the garbage in front of the house and hit Blackie's shot and stick to score one. What he didn't want to acknowledge was that the guy was going to go for the tougher shot, to hit both of Blackie's stones, and score two to win.

He watched the Granite skip slide to the other end of the rink and get down on wide haunches in the hack to clean his stone. He could see the guy wasn't scared, that he trusted himself. He polished the bottom of that stone like a diamond.

Blackie jumped when the Granite skip took his shot; he knew as soon as the guy let go of his stone at the hog line that it was a shot you couldn't argue with.

He could hear cheering from the Granite fans behind the glass. They were entitled, Blackie thought. It was his fault; he'd miffed some shots. But that wasn't why the other team won. They won because they played better, because they were better. Blackie's team were just interfering in the Brier; they had met their match and got knocked out. It hurt all over. They didn't deserve to go to the semis.

FOURTEEN

There was a tremendous thaw underway on the day of the AGM. Blackie came out of the house through the winter kitchen sniffing the sunny morning air. The mild beginning of April had started the melt. Everything was melting: you could hear it in a crackling of crusts on snowbanks that were hollowing out and in punctures in transparent ice that were opening over sewer drains. You could see it in sheets of snow sliding off shingles and in the smutty icicles dripping everywhere. Dissolving snow exposed patches of urine Blackie hoped were mostly from dogs. It felt unusually good to him for a Sunday morning; it was an excellent day for a showdown.

Blackie had never seen such a big turnout. Almost a hundred and fifty guys were there: pushed up against the snack counter, leaning against walls and the windows giving onto the ice, or sitting in formation in bridge chairs in the middle of the room. There were lots of juniors, even some lady curlers. Mike and Tino had to be behind that. Except for Duddy, Blackie's friends were milling at one end of the crowded lunch counter.

The first person Blackie noticed was Max Foxman, because he stood out next to his two strapping sons, mingling with his clique, looking self-important.

– Budge over, Blackie said, and the guys made room for him.

– I ordered you a hot dog, said Oz. – There's a wait.

Blackie spotted Michael MacGiligary talking to a kid who looked like he'd just been liberated from Auschwitz, shaved head and all, by the Red Army. He and the new kid walked up to the guys.

– What'd you do to your hair? Blackie said to Tino. It looked like someone had taken an electric razor to it. It wasn't barbered, but shorn.

– I layered it.

– Down to nothing.

– Don't make a face. I wasn't scalped. It was too much of a hassle anyways. And long hair is just repressive de-sublimation now. Even reactionaries are wearing their hair long.

Suddy thought the QV AGM was a formal affair and was in a suit that was too big for him. Eddie Zachs, getting his hot dog, came up to him and said:

– Suddy, you look like you shrunk.

Nobody laughed except Eddie who looked twice at Tino but didn't say anything and left with his hot dog in his fist.

Duddy was sulking at the other end of the lunch counter, squinting, looking edgy and introspective, as if he'd hypnotised himself into earnestness. He wasn't rotating his dickie or fidgeting with his mole.

– Max's looking pleased, Oz said to Blackie, nodding toward Max Foxman.

– Don't say that, said Blackie.

– What's with Duddy? said Oz.

– He's despondent, said Suddy. – Dee told him to shit or get off the pot.

Blackie saw Rita was standing behind the counter, arms crossed over her bosom, a cigarette in her right hand. She nodded hello at Blackie, who nodded back. Blackie wondered whether the wieners and patties on the griddle would burn. Rita was looking worried because if Max had the shares he needed, then she'd be out of a job. Werner stood next to Rita, looking pale and frightened. Fumes of fried grease lifted off the griddle behind them. Somebody's getting a burnt cheeseburger this morning, thought Blackie just as Rita stubbed out her cigarette on the floor with her toe and turned back to the griddle.

Blackie sipped coke from a bottle to pacify the butterflies. He still wasn't sure if they could win the vote in spite of all their canvassing and mobilizing and motivating and patient explaining. After all the meetings, he wondered how many other Morley Permuts and Jack Sanders and Saltzbergers were out there and had been keeping secret their true intentions.

Blackie peeled his bottle of coke from his lip and said:

– Somebody go get Duddy.

Suddy fetched Duddy and brought him into the circle.

– How's it looking? Oz said to Duddy.

Oz's deference swung Duddy's mood and he beamed himself out of his funk.

– I tell you. It's ours to lose. – We're hacked up.

– You were looking pretty serious over there just now.

– Dee's acting up. Told me to shit or get off the pot. Nothing to do with the vote: that's in the bag. I wish I had a camera to take a picture of Max Foxman's face when he goes down. I'm telling you I might stand for President next year and leverage this thing.

– Him and his pals are looking pretty confident, said Blackie.

– We've got them where we want them, said Duddy. – We'll purge the Foxmanites today. Morning of the long knives.

Duddy had been telling all sorts of guys he was thinking of defenestrating the whole Executive and running for President, which he would make a remunerated post to avoid *shmearing*.

– It's a smack down. It's going to be a smack down, said Duddy.

Blackie saw Duddy raise half a lip to sneer at Max.

The place kept filling with people and smoke. Blackie saw Tino light his cigarette and then hold the flame to Michael's cigarette. Blackie couldn't look at Tino with that short hair. He had a cigarette of his own now between two fingers of the hand wrapped around his coke bottle. In half an hour people'd need oxygen.

There was a great crowd now: lots of curlers without shares who came to watch and lots of shareholders who came to vote.

Too many South Enders were there for Blackie's taste; he could tell them apart: they had on their cashmere Sunday cardigans, bottom buttons unbuttoned, sleeves rolled up, necks open, that Dean Martin look. But still, as things looked, there were tons of guys who wanted to keep the QV.

Rita called Blackie's name and he got his hot dog.

– Two of those and you'll be farting all day, said Duddy.

Guys kept pouring in and people were starting to get pressed shoulder to shoulder, beginning to sweat while Max was biding his time.

– Where's Chickie? Blackie asked Oz.

– I thought he was coming with you?

The pressure was building when Max Foxman and his entourage waltzed toward the dais, swaggering in that proprietorial way they had. Max was working the crowd, looking big and handsome as usual, acting especially disengaged, underlining his power.

– *Mishlockt yiddin*, Duddy said, watching Max's clique hop on the dais. – I'd like to see if he shaved his legs for the meeting.

– Guys! Guys! Let's get this over with, Max said.

He sat down presidentially behind the table. He pulled on his nose and took out the shareholder registry and told everyone to first bring their shares up and check them against their names on the register. He'd do the same thing with his proxies, then Oz could do it with his proxies. Then they'd vote.

– We have to call the meeting to order first, someone said.

– We're not starting yet. This is just checking bona fides. Oz?

– What?

– Do you want to check the registry? It's been notarized.

– I'm good.

The guys formed a line and showed their shares one by one to Leo Wasserman, who swiveled his head and read out their names in a low voice to Max, who checked them off. Some guys had their certificates in folders, others had them folded in the back pockets of their pants.

Oz and Blackie and Michael went up to the dais and scruti-neered Max Foxman checking the shares against the registry to ensure everything was on the up and up. Mike's idea.

They had 115 shares present and 23 proxies accounted for, for a total of 138 voting shares, requiring a vote of 69+1 of the shareholders for a majority. But there were way more guys there than 115. Blackie figured. Way more.

– Is that good for us? Blackie asked, looking worried and defen-sive.

– It's more or less what I calculated, said Oz.

– I can't hack it, said Suddy.

– We can proceed to the vote, Max said. – We'll count the proxies first.

Max dealt out his and Oz's proxies.

– I've got 15 in favour of liquidation and 8 against.

Blackie, alarmed, looked at Oz.

– Did you hand in Mona's proxy?

– Top of the pile.

– Did you figure 15 to 8?

– That's what I figured.

– I was figuring the other way around, said Blackie. – We're *bakukt*.

– Nothing's *bakukt*. They always had most of the guys who quit curling years ago. And they always had the dead guys whose shares went to the wives. Subdued, Oz, who had his tally sheet rolled up in his fist like a racing form, unfurled it for Blackie and the guys. Look! he said. He and Mike were side by side now, with their lists of guys who'd said that Max could fuck himself, looking at their tallies like they were comparing picks for the daily double.

– The dead guys' proxies went to Max, said Michael. – We called it.

– He *shmeared* everybody, said Duddy.

– The dead guys, too? Tino asked Duddy.

– They need 55 votes in person to win, Oz nodded. – 55 plus 15 proxies would give them 70, the number they needed. We have more than that.

Then Max said they would proceed to the vote of the shareholders present by calling the roll.

– So they need 55? Blackie wanted to be sure.

– I think we got them beat, said Oz.

– I'm going to call the roll, said Max. – If you're in favour of liquidation say 'aye,' against, say 'nay.'

– I'm going to be sick, said Blackie.

– No way they have 55 votes of the guys here, said Duddy.

– How do you know?

– I have my finger on a few pulses. People confide in me.

– You didn't even canvass the guys on your list, said Blackie.

– Mike had to do your guys.

– That's what he says. It won't be easy to vote against me if I'm here. I'm a big factor. The human factor.

From Adelman to Gurvitch, they did pretty good. They had some disappointments from Handelman to Litman, and the Ms to Ps were pretty depressing.

– I didn't figure Frenchie Litman, said Oz, making a mark on his notes. – That's a heartbreaker.

Blackie didn't like the anguish Oz showed when he compared his list to Michael's again. He liked it better before the voting, when Oz had been mellow. It was neck and neck for longer than it should have been.

– We'll pull ahead in the Rs, Oz told Blackie.

– I can't hack it, said Suddy.

Oz was right. They swept the Rs from Ratner to Rosenberg and the 'nays' pulled ahead.

– We're way ahead, Duddy told him. – As I predicted. They've blown up.

– But they have more proxies. They only need 55.

– How many till they have 55?

– 8, said Oz. – But we'll do good in the Ts.

– That's what I figure too, said Michael.

The presidium was getting bothered by all the noise.

– Could we have some quiet? We can't hear the names.

The Ts didn't go so hot, and the Foxmanites were only 3 short by the time it came to Ed Vinsky.

– Vinsky! I didn't figure he would go for Max, Oz said, looking at Michael's list. – You had him for Max.

– He doesn't like our politics.

– A real reactionary, said Tino. – He told us to our faces. And he's got cousins in Israel.

Max already had 54 'ayes' when it got to the Zs.

– We're still ahead, said Duddy. We've got over 60.

– But they have more proxies, said Oz.

– How does that work again?

– They just need one more, said Suddy. – I can't take it.

The crescendo was back: lot of buzzing confusion from the masses. Max struggled to make himself heard from the dais.

– Lawrence Zabler? Max barked. – Lawrence Zabler?

Nobody answered.

– Lawrence Zabler? How say you?

There was a squeak from someone crushed by the crowd at the windows that gave onto the ice.

– Aye.

That made 55 for Max.

For Blackie, time stood still.

– Who's Lawrence Zabler? Michael asked. – He's not on my list.

– I can't talk, said Blackie.

– How could he be? said Oz, sarcastic and crestfallen.

– What do you mean? Michael said.

– He's not on mine either, said Oz. – For the same reason none of us are on our lists.

– I don't understand you.

– Lawrence Zabler is Chickie. Chickie Zabler.

Max spoke merrily:

– Well, we've got 55. Plus the 15 proxies. Gives us 70. And over the top.

Max looked and only saw the hard, blank faces of the guys who wanted to keep the club, who were the majority in attendance, but the losers nonetheless. They scared him enough to make his voice go quiet.

– So that's the vote. The QV is wound up by order of its shareholders.

The response to Max's delicate proclamation was mute but hostile and Max sensed the chill again.

In the silence, Blackie felt that if there was any cheering, he would kick someone's testes the hard way.

Fearing a riot, and with his voice even more hushed, Max stumbled painfully through the rest of the legalese that came with the winding up.

No cheers went up from Max Foxman's side. You could hear a pin drop when he finished. There was some polite applause, quickly followed by harsh 'boos.' The losers started getting agitated. They wagged fingers, which annoyed the Foxmanites, who suddenly no longer felt they had to muffle their satisfaction, not if they were going to be treated like that.

– I'm not apologizing, said Jack Sanders. – So bugger off. I hate a poor sport.

A squashed voice, and more poignant for it, was heard: Suddy trying to suppress his tears.

– It's *noch nila* for the club, he said to Oz and Blackie.

Oz blew his cool at Suddy. – This is *nila*! It's after *nila*!

– Suddy, said Oz, feeling crappy and regretting what he'd said. – We're cooked.

– Cooked and eaten, said Suddy. His eyes had tears. They'd be streaming soon.

– Suddy. Don't. Come on. Don't. Suddy!

Hearing his name come from Oz's mouth made Suddy sob and choke, giving off a wheeze of disappointment and farewell.

– Duddy was sure we would win, he said.

Except for Duddy, his eyes looking as if they'd been soaked in hot spices, squinting at Max, they were all looking about for Lawrence Zabler, who was standing by the glass, hanging his head.

Chickie's eyes looked as if they'd been pecked out by birds. He hiked up his pants and ran his chocolate ring through his hair.

Only Michael MacGiligary could speak.

– We the Sheep?

– Fuck's sake, Chickie! Blackie said.

– I don't even curl anymore, Chickie said.

– What are you saying?

– And some other things, said Chickie.

– Why didn't you at least tell us how you were going to vote? Oz asked him. – You humiliated us. Me.

– I felt guilty, Oz.

– You should have said something to me.

– I felt guilty, Oz.

– You, you, you. You're the Malinche! said Suddy to Chickie.

Suddy's face was flushed with righteous fury. By the way Suddy hunched his shoulders, which made his suit look even bigger on him, Blackie saw that Suddy wanted to kick Chickie with one of his Hush Puppies. Or cry again.

– I needed the money, said Chickie. – You guys don't know what it's like.

Duddy was unfazed by what had transpired, oblivious to the confrontation with Chickie. He had already stepped onto the dais and had his eyes on Max Foxman. Indignant, incensed, he shouted:

– Point of privilege!

– The meeting's over, said Max.

– When was the motion?

– The QV's wound up. No need.

– It hurts, doesn't it, Duddy? said Leo Wasserman, poking Duddy, sinking two fingers into his chest.

Duddy slapped Leo's knuckles down hard and said:

– Asshole piece of shit.

Duddy stretched his dickie out from his neck, enough to pat his mole from below and then do a 180 with the dickie. He glowered at Max Foxman.

– Who's laughing now, Duddy? said Max. – I told you I'd make you swallow that laugh.

Leo Wasserman and Harry Finn pushed Duddy off the dais, then jumped off themselves, and shoved Duddy into his friends, who had Chickie cornered.

– It hurts, doesn't it, Duddy? said Leo.

The meeting was breaking into clusters of people arguing with, some screaming at, each other.

– Dominion *shmeared* him! Duddy shouted. – *Mishlockt yiddin*!

The whole place was roaring now, voices foaming and churning.

His kids behind him, his clique on each side, the Max Foxman phalanx bore down on Duddy through a bit of daylight that had opened up, Max thrusting his face within a foot of Duddy's face, then being forced back. In his anger Max's upper lip slid high up his gums. Out between his teeth came these words:

– Why don't you fuck yourself, Duddy?

Duddy couldn't make out what Max said.

– What?

Max pushed his face up closer, tried to make his voice carry above the arms and shoulders that were separating him from Duddy.

– Why don't you fuck yourself, Duddy?

In the din, Duddy couldn't hear Max, and Max couldn't hear anything that Duddy was saying back to him, so he just kept shoving to get closer. Duddy was boiling. He ripped off his dickie and stuffed it in his pocket. His mole was red and agitated.

– What? said Duddy.

– What I just said, Max said.

– I don't want this to get ugly, Blackie said to Tino. – Let's get Duddy out of here.

– If this were Paris, May '68, we'd be burning things down, Tino said. – Making barricades.

They formed a scrimmage in front of Duddy.

Seeing Duddy's face so flushed and his mole sizzling, Michael MacGiligary merged into the anti-Duddy cluster from the side to help Tino and Blackie protect Duddy from himself and others. And then came Oz into the fray, pushing people out of his way with his knuckles.

A bouquet of bodies, pro- and anti-Duddy, had formed in the Duddysphere, with Duddy in the nucleus, radiating heat and pain. Thank God the cluster was so tight nobody could throw a punch.

– It hurts, doesn't it Duddy? said Leo Wasserman.

Duddy tried to get off a punch at Max Foxman.

– Why are you mad at me anyway? shouted Max. – It was Chickie who cracked. Chickie voted against you. Duddy heard that.

– Chickie wouldn't vote against us, Duddy said.

– Goodbye, Duddy!

Duddy tried to get an arm up above his shoulders and take a slug at Harry Finn, but ended up looking like he was trying to pirouette.

– Hey, slugger! said Leo.

– Goodbye, Duddy! Harry said.

– Look, he's *broigas*, Leo said to Harry. – *Broigas*.

– I'm not *broigas*, said Duddy.

– You're *broigas*, said Leo.

Blackie now found himself crushed up against the small kiln that was Duddy's body, with Max Foxman behind him, pressing into his ribs. He recognized the Foxman family odour.

Through the crowd Blackie guided Duddy towards the front doors.

– Okay, said Blackie. – Let's get some fresh air.

They got down the stairs and left the building. Duddy turned to go back inside, but Blackie grabbed him by the elbow.

– But I'm just so mad.

– Get a grip, Duddy.

– Let go of my elbow!

– That's rich, said Blackie, who gripped Duddy's elbow tighter.

It was fresh and cool outside; the air was free of the smell of grease fumes and grilling wieners: alas, the last wieners to be served. Rita'd end up on UIC. Werner too.

– You can let go of me now, said Duddy.

Blackie released Duddy's elbow.

Like a drunk playing maracas, Duddy waddled and tramped in circles in the melting stained snow and slush. He almost stepped in a dog poo that had been frozen under the snow for months.

– The world is spinning, said Duddy.

Most of the guys were pouring outside now, milling and mingling in calm.

– The guys'll probably go for pancakes, Tino said to Blackie after he'd come out. – Suddy has a craving.

– I could go for pancakes, too, said Duddy.

– I feel bad for us, Suddy said to Blackie.

– Right now I feel bad for Rita, Blackie said. – And Werner.

– Not a lot of demand for ice-makers in summer.

– He can make hockey ice.

– Not the same.

– Other clubs are falling by the wayside, said Suddy. – Maybe curling will die out.

– It'll survive in Scandinavia, said Duddy. – Seen my dickie?

– No, said Tino.

There was a pause to look at Chickie. He was standing alone, cuff deep in melting snow on the boulevard about twenty yards away.

– Should we ask Chickie to come? said Blackie.

– Did someone take the Malinche out for pancakes after she did what she did? said Oz.

They turned their heads away from Chickie. For good reason. Nobody except Blackie wanted to see him or talk to him. He could go for pancakes with Max Foxman as far as Oz was concerned.

They agreed on the Pancake Place on Main. They'd feel a lot better with a stack of buttermilk pancakes in them. They made the bacon properly crispy there. And they whipped the butter.

– I can't stay long, said Suddy. – Mona's home alone. It's Morris's *yahrzeit*.

– I never had Chickie down to be the Malinche, said Michael.

– He had an animus against you, said Oz to him. – It wasn't personal. It was political.

– The dif?

– You'll see, said Oz. – You can't fight human nature, Mike. And I'm surprised you don't know that.

– I don't want to fight human nature, Oz. I want human nature to be realized. Human nature is by definition empathetic. Justice is in our genes. The true natural nature of Man is noble.

– Man is a wolf to Man, said Oz. – I can quote too.

– It is the State and private property that has perverted Man's nature.

– *Mutatis mutandis*, said Duddy, bitter and dejected.

From across the street Max Foxman stretched out an arm, cupped his hand as if he had a yo-yo in it, pointed it at Blackie and swished his fingers back and forth. It took Blackie a moment to catch on that Max was summoning him.

Blackie crossed the slushy street, side-stepping light blue runnels of water running between grooves in snow and sand. Oz followed him.

Max seemed bigger and handsomer with his victory under his

belt. Blackie felt jittery. He wouldn't mind it if Max gloated or laid a hand on him so he could punch him hard.

– What? said Blackie.

– A new roof would have been really expensive, said Max, attempting to justify himself.

– Look where your weaselry has brought us, said Oz to Max.

– Oz. Come on.

– It's the end of the Jewish community up here, said Oz. – You'll see.

Max looked sick. – The cost of the roof would have killed us off, Max said.

– It's a terrible blow to the North End, said Oz. – And we could have raised more capital.

– From who? Nobody wants to curl anymore. The kids are leaving Winnipeg. Curling's dead.

Oz, with a disgusted wave, left Blackie alone with Max.

– It wasn't personal with you, Blackie, Max said. Then ruined it by giving Blackie his cold smile.

– Is that a real smile?

– I'm telling you. It wasn't personal with you.

– You guys killed the QV, Max. You took something away from us.

– The QV will live on in the Negev.

– You called me over to say that?

Blackie was about to walk away, already had his head turned, shoulders tilted, pointing at his friends.

– But it got personal for you, said Max.

Blackie's head snapped back.

– I know you're sniffing around Sophie. She's this close to being dumped on the street, you know. The kids are grown up now. You think I don't know you slept over at my house alone.

– I'm not sniffing around after Sophie.

– I never had you down for a homewrecker. My kids are here; we're going to Vegas so I'm not going to do anything in front of

210

them, you should know that, when I get back, people are going to get hurt. Out on the street with nothing. Gournisht.

The snarl of confusion affected Blackie's walk back to his circle. He and Oz lit up and the cigarettes calmed them down.

– No matter what Max says, curling will never die, said Oz to Blackie.

Duddy had gone awfully quiet again.

– Coming for pancakes? Blackie said to him.

– Did Tino cut his hair or something?

– Coming or not?

– Sure. But I can't find my dickie.

Duddy shanghaied Tino back inside to look for his dickie.

– Why do they hate me? Duddy asked him.

– Because you're a threat to their mediocrity, said Tino.

That was all it took to make Duddy feel better.

– I don't see your dickie, Tino said.

– It's gotta be here. They ripped it off me.

– That had to be difficult.

– They're capable. *Mishlockt yiddin.* I'm ashamed of my own people. People of the Book, my ass. I'm people of the flames. The flames of Gehenna. Why are Jews the way they are, Tino? You read books.

– It's from eating chopped liver, said Tino. – I don't see it, Duddy.

– You go back. I'm going to look around a bit more, said Duddy.

– It's my best one.

Back out in the street, Blackie said to Tino:

– You coming for pancakes or what?

– What about Chickie? Tino asked, tilting his head Chickie's way.

– Some Bolshevik you are, said Oz to Tino.

Blackie looked at Chickie still standing alone on the boulevard. Why hadn't he gone home already? he wondered. And is there anything more alone than someone who's just lost his friends?

Is that the Fires of Gehenna? He wanted to go tell Chickie to come along. He wanted to say it, but his mouth felt like it was filled with worms.

Suddy was ready to relent, too, maybe because he was the hungriest.

– Grab Chickie and let's go. We'll have lots of time to be mad at him.

– *Et tu?* said Oz to Suddy.

– We can't leave him there alone, Blackie said to Oz.

– He betrayed us. – You're too much, you guys.

– So what can we do about it now? said Blackie. – A good friend gets one betrayal free.

– We're all going to get our money, said Suddy. – At least.

– Ours is going to Israel, said Oz. – He's keeping his.

– Speak for yourself, said Duddy. – Mona's not giving hers away.

– Go ask him if he wants to come with us, Blackie said to Tino.

– Me? Why me?

– You're the socialist.

Tino didn't budge.

– We can't stay mad at him forever. – He's been crying.

– Blackie thinks like a friend, said Suddy.

– *Mit an eige ois vishen*, said Oz.

– He doesn't even curl anymore, said Blackie. – Go ask him, Tino.

– You go, said Oz to Blackie. – Why should Tino go?

– Okay. Bugger.

From close up now, Blackie saw Chickie's eyes were red. His heart went out to Chickie, and in no time at all his own eyes were smarting. Go figure yourself for what you'll do in certain situations: the urge to forgive was irresistible.

– We're going to the Pancake Place on Main. You coming?

– I can't, said Chickie. – Prior engagements.

That galled Blackie; he was going out of his way and feeling for the guy.

212

– You could say sorry, Blackie said.

Chickie clenched his right fist. Then his left fist. Blackie stepped back. Then Chickie pounded the bottom of his right fist into the top of his left fist, then vice versa, a vicious one-potato, two-potato thing.

–Hazel's picking me up to go to the hospital. See the baby.

Geez. Yeah. Had it been nine months since Chickie grabbed that kid in the lane? Blackie counted names of months in his head. Deirdre would have kept track. She would have known when the baby was due, and born. Blackie didn't know whether to apologize or say congratulations to Chickie on his grandchild. But then Chickie squeaked:

– They didn't even announce the birth over the P.A.

– Boy or girl?

– Boy. It's a relief. – Girls have a harder life.

– Mazel tov! He was mad at Chickie but the guy deserved a *mazel tov* and a *siman tov* but he only gave him a *mazel tov*.

– Thanks, said Chickie.

– Ever catch that kid? – The one in the back lane who did it?

– No.

– You call me if you catch him. We'll give him the paddy whacks.

Hazel drove up. With the car door half-open, Chickie turned around:

– Bye, Blackie. I'll call you for the *briss*.

Blackie watched Hazel drive off spinning sand and slush, and when Blackie turned around, the guys had left for pancakes.

Heading alone to the parking lot, he stopped for a second beneath the sputtering blue neon sign that fell under the red maples and thought about going inside for a last goodbye. But he didn't. The QV no longer appealed to him. That's probably how Deirdre had felt about him when she left, and now he finally got it.

FIFTEEN

They sat in an upholstered booth. Duddy still hadn't arrived so they discussed ordering without him while the waitress poured the coffee and the busboy poured the ice water.

– We should wait, said Michael.

– He said he was coming, said Blackie.

– I'm hungry, said Oz. – Who knows with that guy. He could be another half an hour.

– He was looking for his dickie, said Tino. – He said that he lost it in all the pushing and shoving. That they ripped it off him.

– I'm ordering without him, said Blackie.

They ate their pancakes and slurped coffee. They were feeling better by the time they started the post-mortem.

– We lost because of the North End guys like Chickie and Jack Sanders, said Oz.

– I truly hate losing, said Michael.

– Get used to it, said Oz. – If you want to be what you are.

– But it's better to fight and lose than lose and lose.

– A Trotskyite would have to say that. Just you get used to it.

– Trotsky*ist*.

– *Kumen vet nokh undzer oysgebenkte sho*, sang Tino, wondering if Oz got the reference.

He did. – Where'd you learn that?

– Not in Hebrew school.

– It's coming. – And so is Christmas, said Oz.

– That's why we're not Stalinists or Social Democrats, said Michael.

214

Oz turned his head to look at him.

– They both folded without a fight against the Nazis.

– The Nazis finally got theirs.

– Way too late: after 50 million dead. Six million of your co-religionists.

– That's on the Nazis, said Oz.

– It's also on the Social Dems and the appeasers during Hitler's rise to power in the 30s. On Churchill, who admired Mussolini. On Chamberlain, who made a pact with Hitler against Russia until 1939, when they gave Hitler a chunk of Czechoslovakia. On the Americans and Swiss, who financed Hitler in the 20s and 30s. On the US and Britain, who embargoed Republican Spain while allowing Hitler and Mussolini to bomb Barcelona and Guernica, the testing grounds of the second world war. It's on them. On the Stalinists who liquidated the Red Army high command on the brink of war, and who assassinated Leon Trotsky so no one would be able to stage a coup and replace Stalin with the only man who could unify the soviets, the man who founded the Red Army. I could go on.

– You will.

– I forgot to mention the Stalin-Hitler pact.

– You're an angry young man, said Oz.

– Shouldn't we be angry?

– What's this got to do with curling? Suddy asked.

Tino looked at him with a wry smile and said:

– It's all politics, Suddy.

– You've got some birthday money coming your way, Suddy said to Tino, beaming with impending generosity.

– I'm okay for money.

Suddy took a white envelope out of his inside suit jacket pocket and gave it to Tino. Inside was a birthday card and two crisp tens. – You should bank that.

– Thanks, Suddy.

Blackie looked in disbelief at the envelope. He'd forgotten it was Tino's birthday.

– Duddy chipped in too. I thought he'd be here to give it to you together.

Oz pulled out a wad, peeled off a ten and gave it to Tino.

– I'll settle with you later, Blackie told Tino.

It was Michael MacGiligary who looked the most embarrassed about Tino getting the cash. But then they relaxed and lit up cigarettes. Blackie watched carefully just how Michael lit Tino's cigarette.

– See, said Oz. – Duddy didn't make it.

– We were right to order without him, said Blackie.

– Why does that make it right? Suddy asked. – Just because he didn't show. You're not in the right, Blackie.

– We should ask for the bill. People are waiting for tables.

– Where do you think he went? said Oz. – Duddy never says 'no' to a pancake.

– I told you, said Tino. – He stayed to look for his dickie.

– All this time? Blackie asked. – Doesn't add up.

– I'm waiting for him, said Suddy. – Get the lady to get us more coffee.

– Maybe he went to Dee's, Blackie?

Blackie was as mum as a fish, his body tingling with all the sugar and butter and starch.

– Blackie? Blackie? We're talking to you, said Oz.

Oz honestly thought Blackie was having a stroke until Blackie gave his face a raw scrub.

– I have somewhere to go. – Can I get the check?

– Your money's no good here, said Oz.

– Duddy. Duddy. Duddy, Blackie kept saying. He drove like a maniac. Sand and salt sprayed out from under his tires, flinging the crap against the odd car in the next lane or as far as the grimy snowbanks.

The South End wasn't that far away on a Sunday, especially if you were motivated. The tire rubber hummed crossing the steel

216

grills of the Midtown Bridge, and he got vertigo when he looked down through the grid for a second at the ice cracking on the Assiniboine. Quite a drop.

Blackie just knew Duddy had to be at Max Foxman's house exacting his revenge by getting cute with Sophie. Putting his Plan B in Sophie's pants.

He parked a good couple of blocks away because people talk. Once out of the car, he saw the road was veined by rivulets of run-off coursing through grey and silver slush. In his haste, he stepped into a puddle up to his shoelaces.

He realized he had left his half rubbers under the table at the Pancake House. His shoes were drinking in the icy slush as he trod onto the gravel and pavement underneath it; it felt as if he was walking on two cold sponges. There were some dry spots on the road and he hopped onto them whenever they appeared.

He hesitated just before he got to the house. If Sophie and Duddy were getting cute he thought his presence would embarrass her, so he ran around the side of the house and looked into the front-room from the side. He didn't want to be looking in from the front yard because the neighbours could mistake his good intentions for burglary. He rounded the corner and stepped onto the stonework of the flower beds and had a good view of what was going on in the front room: nothing. Maybe Duddy and Sophie were in the basement. He got off the flower bed and squatted low to look through the rec room window. No one was down there either. So he ran to the front door and banged violently on the door with two fists until Sophie opened up.

She couldn't hide her delight.

– Blackie! What are you doing here?

She was blushing so hard her face had to hurt. She was very excited, and he could make out her breasts through her blouse.

He went in the house. His shoes dripped slush on the marble tiles, making a real mess.

– Is Duddy here?

– No.

– Whose flowers are those?

Blackie was pointing to a tall bouquet of zinnias on the coffee table in the front room. He knew they hadn't come from Max Foxman.

– I did get those from Duddy. He said you said he should send me flowers. To apologize.

– Send them back!

– How can I send them back?

His voice turned dark and stiff:

– Throw them out.

Sophie went from the tiled vestibule to the carpeted front room, gathered up the flowers out of the vase, opened her arms and dropped the bouquet on the floor. Some stems landed on her little feet, which were wrapped in black satin, her seamed stockings, with tiny ribbing showing on the big toes. Maybe they were on inside out, he thought.

– I thought he might be here, he said, calming down.

– You didn't come to see me?

Sophie sat on the sofa.

– Come here and sit, she said, patting an invisible circle on the upholstery next to her.

– I . . . he was supposed to meet us for pancakes. I should find him. He was upset after we lost the vote. I can't sit. But he was already starting to lower his bum onto the spot she was patting. He couldn't look at her because he was feeling ashamed.

– What vote?

– To liquidate the curling club.

– Oh. I didn't know that was today. When Max and the boys left this morning I thought they were going straight to the airport. To go to Vegas. Her pout made her look like a girl. One he remembered well. It made him ready to be engulfed.

– I thought Duddy might be here. He was upset. I thought he might want to demean you.

– Why would he want to demean me?

– To get back at Max.

– So you *didn't* come to see me?

Sophie folded her legs and drew her stockinged feet under her bum and thigh. She rubbed the fabric of his trousers between her thumb and forefinger. He almost touched her cheek. He could tell she was waiting for it.

– What is it with you? she said impatiently.

– Are you going to say you're sorry to me or not? Blackie asked.

– Sorry for what?

She had to know what he meant.

– I'm regretting things, she said. – But I'm not sorry.

– You should have waited for me.

– You should have asked me to wait for you.

– It was understood.

– Not by me. And I'm not getting off to a start by saying sorry to anybody.

Were there only defiant women in this world? he wondered.

Her point made him forget his point, and he finally touched her cheek. When he did, she let go of the fabric of his trousers and grasped his whole knee.

Blackie, Blackie, Blackie. Deirdre was right. He'd found some-one else in six months.

He was going to succumb. There was going to and had to be kissing, but his curiosity held him back from what he hungered for.

– What did you say to Max that day at the cottage?

– What do you mean?

– What you said? In front of everybody at the cottage? That thing you said that ended the argument you were having. Why he stopped talking to you?

– My low blow?

– That.

Her eyes lit up.

– What I said in front of everybody?
– Out with it.
– I said 'I should have waited for Blackie Timmerman.'

ACKNOWLEDGMENTS

This book would not have been possible without Rolf Maurer and that damn axe of his, nor Melva MacLean and that trick she does with a scalpel. Health and thanks to Paul Peters, who has made the literary life less lonely all these years; to Pawel Eisner, already on the top rung of the ladder of poetry; to Catherine Lejtenyi and her snow and sparrow poems; to Ben Rowden, who showed me what funny was. And to Virginia, bright star.